Memorial for Death

A Mortician Murder Mystery-Book 3

A. E. Howe

Books in the
Mortician Murder Mystery Series
(in order):

Return to Death
Gambling on Death
Memorial for Death
Search for Death

ISBN-13: 978-1-7346541-7-2

CHAPTER ONE

"We're in no better shape now than when I came back home." Kay Lamberton was sitting behind the desk in the office of her family's funeral home on a Thursday morning in February, staring glumly at the accounting books spread out in front of her.

"Brad Garland has made it his life's goal to force us out of business," said her brother, Lee, as he paced around the room. "I know for a fact that he's done four funerals in the county for *below* costs."

"The business can't survive like this." Kay tapped a ledger with her finger.

"There has to be something we can do."

"We can't compete with him. His family has three funeral homes in the surrounding counties. If he wants to run us into the ground by doing services for prices that we can't match, then he has the capital behind him to do it. At least for a while. I imagine even he would get tired of losing money eventually… or at least his dad would."

"The Garlands have deep pockets," Lee said darkly. Scott Garland was the head of the company, but his son Brad was the heir apparent and called a lot of the shots these days. He was also, in Lee's estimation, an obnoxious little snot.

"I did manage to get us one piece of business today," Kay said, watching her brother.

"Really?" Lee asked with a grin.

"Don't get too excited. It's just a memorial service. A hundred and fifty dollars. The body has already been cremated."

"Cremated." Lee's face fell. While he accepted the fact that some people preferred cremation, he was an artist when it came to embalming, and showing off his art was part of the pleasure he got from running the business. "A hundred and fifty dollars." He repeated the sum with an air of defeat.

"I know. But every dollar counts," Kay said, trying for a positive spin.

When she'd come home to the small Florida town of Lang after their father's death in 1981, Kay had been determined to sell the business and divide any proceeds with her brother. While their father had been both a good mortician and a competent businessman, her brother had proven to be an excellent mortician and a very poor businessman. Against her will, Kay had let Lee talk her into taking over the business side of the funeral home with the belief that together they could turn it into a growing concern. Since that time there had been brief moments of success, but they'd been few and far between and Kay was starting to lose hope.

"Who's the deceased?" Lee asked.

"A man named Danny Reynolds. He passed away in Indiana with no family, so some of his old Korean War buddies that live down here are taking care of the arrangements. One of them, Art Butler, is expecting the ashes to arrive tomorrow and he'll bring them over when he gets them."

"Work is work," Lee grumbled, then walked out of the office.

The next day Lee was in the carport, polishing the new Cadillac hearse for the tenth time in a week. *I should call it the new, NEW hearse,* he thought ruefully. Their previous new hearse, which his father had purchased less than a year before his death, had been destroyed by a madman with a fire engine. Luckily, insurance had covered most of the cost of replacing it as their other hearse, an ancient Lincoln affectionately known as Bertha, was too unreliable to be depended on for much.

A six-year-old Impala station wagon pulled into the driveway behind him and, for a moment, Lee had hopes that it meant a new piece of business. But when he saw the ramrod-straight bearing of the man who got out of the car, along with the box he carried, Lee knew that it was Art Butler with his buddy's ashes.

"Mr. Butler?" he said, extending his hand.

"That's right."

"I'm Lee Lamberton. My sister said you'd be coming by."

Art shook with the firm grip of a man who used handshakes to determine the grit of other men. Lee kept his grip steady, but not challenging.

"I've got Danny's ashes," Art said, holding the box out to Lee.

"Let's go into my office and discuss the service."

As they walked into the funeral home, Lee noticed that Art Butler was almost a foot taller than he was, with broad shoulders that were slightly hunched with age. His grey hair was cropped in military fashion.

"I want this done right. Danny deserves a great sendoff. He was the best lieutenant I ever had."

"We'll do our best," Lee said, adding in his head: *for the money.* How far did the guy think a hundred and fifty dollars was going to go?

Once in the office, Lee directed him to a seat in front of the desk and placed the late lieutenant's remains on a side table.

"What are you thinking would be appropriate?" Lee asked as he sat down at the desk.

"I just want a nice graveside service. There's only half a dozen of us down here. Figure with some family members, we'll have maybe thirty people at the service. The guys from the VFW over in Gainesville are going to give a salute. You can clear that with the sheriff?"

Lee made notes and nodded. "We have a deputy that works with us. He'll have to inspect their weapons and ammunition ahead of time."

Art nodded.

"You said graveside. Do you have a plot to bury the ashes?" Lee asked.

"Yeah, sure, at the city cemetery. Brendan Rhodes is donating one of his family plots."

"I'll just need to clear everything with the sexton. I'll need the exact location of the plot."

"I'll ask Brendan to give you a call."

They settled on the date and time for the service, then shook hands again.

"Give me a day or two to get all the arrangements finalized," Lee said as he walked Art to the door.

"Thanks a million. This means a lot to us guys."

"The service will be next Saturday," Lee told Kay that evening. One of the benefits of cremation was that it eliminated any concerns about waiting for out-of-town mourners to arrive.

"I'm not much better at quoting a price for business than

you are," Kay said, looking at the sheet Lee had handed her that detailed the expenses for the service. "After paying Jerome and all the other costs, I figure we're going to make about fifteen dollars."

Lee shook his head. "It's okay. I've never felt right about the way our veterans were treated after Vietnam." He held up his hand. "I know that these are Korean War vets, but still, it's a start at righting some wrongs if we can help them out."

Kay thought about her own return from Vietnam where she'd served as an Army nurse. "When my flight landed in California, there were protestors at the airport spitting and throwing things at us."

"I never told you, but I was proud of you. I even bragged to the other kids at school."

Surprised at the emotion she felt, Kay quickly shifted the conversation to their father. "Dad was lucky that he never saw battle."

"Yet he still griped about having to do guard duty in Germany."

"Everybody gripes about guard duty," Kay said.

Saturday morning was cold as they loaded equipment for the memorial service into the Cadillac. The frosty night had left a layer of white across the lawn of the funeral home.

"Man, it's freezing out here," Lester Andrews, Lee's assistant, complained as he hefted folding chairs into the back of the hearse.

"I don't want to hear you complaining. A drunk ran off the road out at Turner's Creek last night. I was stuck out there until two in the morning," Jerome Carter said, handing him two more chairs. Jerome had a full-time job as a deputy with the Melon County Sheriff's Office, but he worked for the funeral home as a driver and, occasionally, as security. "What about the tent?"

"We set it up yesterday," Lee told him. "I'm going to put the urn up front."

He had hesitated to use the new hearse, considering how little they were being paid. But when he'd thought of the small group of veterans trying to give their comrade a good sendoff, he'd relented, arguing with himself that the new hearse needed to be driven occasionally anyway.

"When are we going to get some real funerals?" Lester asked.

"How many funerals did Garland steal in the last two months?" Jerome asked at the same time.

"I'm working on it, guys. What can I tell you?" Lee grumbled. "The Garlands undercut me on every funeral."

As they finished loading up, Kay came outside wearing her old Army dress uniform. All three men let their mouths fall open.

"You've got medals," Lester said in awe. He moved in closer to look at them.

"They're service medals, good conduct, nothing special," Kay said with modesty, not pointing out the Purple Heart that was also pinned discreetly to her chest. "I'm heading over to the cemetery. I told Mr. Butler I'd be there at nine-thirty."

"I'll meet y'all there in a few minutes," Jerome said, hurrying to his motorcycle.

Before Lee could ask Jerome where he was heading off to, Ruby Bowen came outside carrying several thermoses. "I made up some coffee." Ruby was the funeral home's resident cook and housekeeper, living above the carport with her two fat tabby cats. "Nice and hot. Keep those guys from freezing."

"Thanks. I'll take them in my car," Kay told her.

Less than thirty minutes later they were all at the cemetery, joined by Art Butler and four men from the VFW post who would be firing the salute.

"We'll fire three volleys," the sergeant told Kay, "and place three spent casings inside the folded flag that we present to the next of kin."

"Duty, honor and sacrifice." From the dozens of military funerals she'd attended, Kay knew well what the three shells represented.

"Where are the ashes going to be placed?" Art asked her.

Kay looked for Lee, but he was over by the hearse taking a flower arrangement out of the back.

"I'll show you," she said and walked over to a spot under the green funeral tent that was marked by a temporary metal stake with a card that read: *Lieutenant Daniel Reynolds*.

"See this plate?" Kay knelt down awkwardly in her skirt. "Lift the lid and the cannister with the ashes is dropped down the tube." She stood back up. "It's better than having the urn above ground where the maintenance crew might hit it with a mower or someone can kick it over."

"I appreciate all the thought you've put into this," Art said. "I've never had to handle... something like this. I buried my parents, but that was all preplanned."

Kay had taken a liking to Art Butler. There was a sincerity to him that was endearing. He also seemed to be under some sort of emotional strain. At first, she'd thought it was just the responsibility of planning a service for his friend, but now she thought there was something else causing the concern in his eyes.

He invited her to follow him to where a small group of mourners was gathering.

"This is Chaz Dixon. He was the guy that kept us fed over there," Art said, putting his arm around a stout, bald man with a lopsided grin.

"It weren't easy keeping you fed," Chaz said, poking Art in the belly. "This guy could eat a side of beef by himself."

"I damn near did that day we came upon a field of cows that had been shelled. Chaz butchered one of them right there in the field with his bayonet. We ate like kings. Where's Vickie?"

"She's here somewhere," Chaz told Art, then turned to Kay and with a smile said, "Vickie's my wife. She can't walk through a group of people without talking to everyone. So where's Betty?"

"She's with her sister out at Cedar Key. They planned the trip before I knew when the memorial service would be," Art explained.

After Chaz, Art introduced Kay to Brendan Rhodes.

"He kept a hundred Chinese with pitchforks off our tails with his Thompson." Art clapped the man on the shoulder.

"We worked as a squad," the lanky, grey-haired man with a more-than-passing resemblance to Gary Cooper demurred. "Frank and Lyle were loading magazines and handing them to me almost as fast as I was running through them. There's Lyle and his wife now," Brendan told her as a man and woman walked up.

The woman gave Brendan an extended hug that seemed to surprise him. The husband and wife both looked like they were trying to be twenty years younger than they were. Kay had to admit that the wife was doing an amazing job of maintaining her looks.

"I'm Lyle Grant and this is my wife, Kelly," he said to Kay. "Frank Hayes was helping me load those magazines he mentioned. He'll be along in a minute."

He pointed over his shoulder to a man who looked frailer than the others. Walking with him was a younger woman who bore a striking resemblance to Frank, but who was oddly dressed for a funeral in jeans and flipflops.

"That's his daughter. Frank's had some health issues," Lyle said, wearing a sad expression that was mirrored by his wife as they watched Frank walk unsteadily toward the group.

The last member of the group was introduced to Kay as Benny Hampton. He had an everyman appearance and wore a neutral expression that caused Kay to feel like the man was working hard at not being noticed. When he walked, he had an unusual gait. Kay wondered if he had been injured in the war.

Jerome showed up in his own dress uniform and Kay realized why he'd left them so quickly. She watched as he spoke with the squad from the VFW and inspected their rifles and ammunition. None of the men looked annoyed to be questioned by Jerome.

"After seeing you, I thought I should step up my game," Jerome said when he walked over to Kay.

"You look sharp," she said, admiring the cut of the dark green uniform against his chocolate brown skin.

"Look who's talking. Man, you must have had those soldiers standing at attention," he said with a chuckle that caused Kay to blush.

"I once slapped one of those soldiers into next week for a comment like that," she said in a tone that made it clear she wasn't kidding.

"I bet you did." From past experience, Jerome knew that Kay wouldn't hesitate to use appropriate force when she thought it was necessary.

CHAPTER TWO

Lee stood back from the group and watched the friends of Danny Reynolds talk and mingle. Out of the corner of his eye, he noticed a tall older woman with a camera stalking through the tombstones behind the tent. She would stop occasionally to put the camera up to her eye before lowering it and slowly walking forward again.

Curious, he moved toward her to see what she was trying to photograph, then shook his head when he saw a portly tabby cat swishing its tail among the grave markers. Ruby's cats made a strange habit of walking the few blocks from the funeral home to haunt the cemetery. Lee was about to go over and tell the woman who her subject was, but then he heard the sound of a car approaching the gravesite.

Everyone turned to watch the ratty old Plymouth New Yorker as it drove a little too fast through the cemetery, then screeched to a halt behind a pickup truck. A middle-aged man wearing a black frock and white collar climbed out of the car and hustled toward them, half waving the Bible he was carrying.

"Reverend Eccleson," Lee said with a slight shake of his head.

"That man's a menace," Jerome muttered under his breath.

"He was the only local preacher available today. I'm sure the service will be fine," Lee said, hoping he was right. Eccleson had a way of being present whenever things went sideways. Though he couldn't always point to a direct cause and effect leading back to the good reverend, Lee couldn't keep the word *jinx* from popping into his head whenever he saw the man presiding over a service that went wrong.

"I saw him perform a wedding only to have the bride demand a divorce before they were even out of the church," Jerome said darkly.

Lee was on the verge replying, "What could go wrong here?" but he bit his tongue before the words were out of his mouth.

"Sorry I'm late. My car." Eccleson waved toward the New Yorker, now surrounded by a light cloud of smoke.

"Nothing to worry about." Kay came forward and took the minister over to introduce him to Art.

"How much of that hundred and fifty dollars are y'all gonna have left?" Jerome frowned and walked toward the tent, shaking his head.

Lee looked at the mourners and thought about the fact that the youngest appeared to be in their early sixties. *Maybe this will generate some future business*, he thought while trying not to wish anyone an untimely demise.

The set-up for the service was simple. Thirty chairs had been placed under the green tent, facing the metal stake marking where the ashes would be buried. There was a lectern for the reverend to rest his Bible, and the urn with the ashes sat on a small table beside it. Art had already ordered a headstone and the stonecutter had guaranteed that it would be done in a month. Lee would meet with the man once it was delivered to make sure all the text was correct and that it was properly installed.

They had set up a small table a short distance from the tent with the thermoses of coffee, a stack of paper cups and an assortment of sugar packets and creamers. With the cold wind blowing through the tombstones, almost everyone was helping themselves to the hot coffee.

As soon as Reverend Eccleson got himself oriented and ready, Lee stepped in front of the group of twenty people and asked that they be seated.

The reverend opened with a heartfelt message. For all of his bumbling, Lee had never witnessed Eccleson phoning it in, unlike other ministers who essentially gave the same speech at every funeral, changing only the names of the deceased and switching out a story or two. Eccleson spoke of coming together to say goodbye to a man who'd touched many lives and served his country bravely.

Then Eccleson turned the service over to Art, who gave the first of the eulogies. This was the toughest part of the service for Lee. He'd heard hundreds of eulogies, and while they were all sincere, most were not engaging if you didn't have a personal relationship with the deceased, and he would frequently find his mind wandering. Today was different. The eulogies from Danny Reynolds's comrades-in-arms in the Korean War kept him riveted.

"Most of the men in our platoon will tell you that they are alive today because of the actions of Danny Reynolds," Art began. "He saved my life on numerous occasions due to his decisions in the deadly fields and mountains of Korea. To make the right decisions took brains, common sense and experience. But more than that, this man had courage. It was that courage that caused him to stop and come back for me when I took a bullet in the leg.

"We'd been left exposed in the middle of a field when a platoon on our right fell back without warning, causing the Chinese troops to surge forward. I was the first to be hit. The rest of our boys were pushed back toward the tree line. All except for Danny, who ran up and dragged me back toward cover, firing his carbine at the approaching enemy all the while. His courage under fire inspired other men to come to our aid. I can still remember the sound of submachine guns rattling out .45 rounds as he carried me to safety. Sweet music. I guess that's why the old-time gangsters kept them in violin cases."

Art paused, seemingly lost in his memories. Wiping at his eyes, he finally said, "Of course, there was more to Danny than courage. He had heart. I think Chaz is the best one of us to talk about how much Danny cared."

Chaz made his way up to the lectern, giving Art a quick hug and pat on the back before turning toward the mourners and clearing his throat.

"Hard for me to talk about Danny now without getting choked up. He'd hate all this fuss. Anyway, I guess what I'm most grateful for was the day that I got a letter from my wife at the time. This was '52, winter, cold as a witch's... toes outside. When I read the letter, it hit me like a dump truck. Stupid now, looking back on it. That who... woman wasn't worth two minutes of my time. But then, sitting in a tent freezing my ass off and already scared witless by the crazy crap going on every day, I was wore down and that note pushed me right off the edge.

"I remember a couple of other guys sitting around the tent. No one noticed the look on my face, I guess, or saw me shaking as I stood up. When you live with guys packed in like that day after day, you kinda learn how to ignore each other as a way to get some privacy. Anyway, I stood up and picked up my Garand. We were sleeping with our rifles. No one said a word as I left the tent." Chaz stopped and wiped at his eyes.

"I'd gotten beyond the last tent when I saw Danny coming back from the latrine ditch. I kept my eyes down and sped up, trying to make it to a small rocky outcropping where I planned on blowing my brains out. Sounds odd saying it out loud, but that's what I was saying over and over in my head. *I want to blow my brains out.* I heard Danny coming up behind me and cursed under my breath. I didn't want anything to stop me from getting to those rocks.

"'Where you going?' he asked me. I gave him the typical GI answer: 'Nowhere.' But he grabbed my rifle. Just like that, he knew something was messed up with me. 'We're going to talk about this,' was all he said, and he yanked the rifle away from me. Five hours we talked. He just wore me down. Then he gave me the last of his bourbon and sat with me until I fell asleep." Chaz began to cry and Art guided him back to his chair.

There were more tales of courage and heartbreak before Eccleson stepped up again and asked everyone to bow their heads in prayer. After the prayer, the honor guard fired three volleys and a folded flag was presented to Art. He invited everyone to come forward, touch the urn and say their goodbyes to Danny Reynolds.

By the time the service was over, the wind had picked up and the tent bucked against its tiedowns. Kay leaned over and, nodding toward a small car that had just pulled into the cemetery, told Lee, "As odd as she is, she's worth everything we pay her."

Ruby walked toward them carrying six more thermoses filled with piping hot beverages.

"The two blue ones have hot Lipton tea," she said as she

set them down on the table.

Art, Chaz and Reverend Eccleson gathered around the table and poured drinks for themselves and others. Everyone seemed to want a paper cup, if for no other reason than to warm their hands.

"Is he okay?" Kay asked Lee, pointing toward Frank Hayes. He'd joined the group at the coffee table, but now his daughter was helping him to sit back down in one of the folding chairs.

"I'll check," Lee said, feeling a knot grow in his stomach. In the last ten years he'd seen four mourners have heart attacks at funerals.

"Can I get you something?" Lee asked Frank, looking hard at the man to see if he needed medical attention.

Frank shook his head. "I'll be fine. This is my daughter, Jenny. She's fussing over me enough."

"He stayed up the last two nights talking to his old Army buddies," Jenny said with a stern tone of disapproval. The full-bodied woman had to keep pushing strands of blonde hair back into place as the wind whipped it around her head.

"I don't need you nagging me," Frank told her in a way that suggested it was normal banter between the two of them, and he winked at Lee.

Lee decided the man was being honest and just needed a breather. "Sit here as long as you like," he said.

Frank nodded and returned his gaze to the urn containing his friend's ashes.

Lee glanced around at the dozen or so people still talking and decided to wait another half hour before encouraging Art to move everyone to his house, where he'd arranged for a small wake.

"Thanks again for doing this," Kay said, walking up and putting a hand on Lee's shoulder.

"It's nothing."

"You could have given me a harder time about the deal I cut with Art."

Lee shrugged. "You put up with my bad business practices. I guess I can't give you a hard time for the one instance where you let your heart lead you."

A scream pierced the air. Lee's first reaction was to look over to where Frank was sitting, but the man and his daughter looked as startled as everyone else.

"Help!" With everyone already on alert, the second cry enabled them to focus on where it was coming from. A woman had risen up from behind a large family tombstone ten yards behind the coffee station.

Jerome and Kay ran toward her and Lee followed them. Jerome stepped past the woman and bent down behind the stone monument. Kay took the woman and eased her gently away.

When Lee got to the monument, he saw that Jerome was kneeling beside Brendan Rhodes, who was stretched out on the ground and twitching violently. There was vomit on the ground near him.

Kay quickly knelt down beside him. "Give me your belt," she ordered Lee, who took it off as fast as he could and handed it to Kay. She folded it over and forced Brendan's clenched mouth open. "Does he have a history of epilepsy?" she asked the people gathered around them, forcing the belt between his teeth as another seizure convulsed his body.

"No," several people responded.

"I'll radio for an ambulance." Jerome stood up and pushed through the mourners, who'd formed a circle with Kay and the convulsing Brendan in the center.

Lee watched Jerome trot down to his car, then turned his attention back to Kay's efforts. Several men were trying to help keep Brendan from hurting himself as the periodic seizures continued. Figuring he would just be in the way, Lee walked over to the woman who had screamed. She was visibly shaking. Lee recognized her as the same woman who'd been taking pictures earlier.

"Are you all right?" Lee asked her.

"No." She wiped tears from her eyes.

"I'm sorry. Of course you're not. I meant do you need to sit down or need some coffee?"

"I just want the ambulance to arrive. Why aren't they here yet?"

"We're a rural county. If there isn't an ambulance in the area, then they might have to send one from as far away as Gainesville. It could take a little while. Are you related to Brendan?"

The woman half-smiled through her tears. "I'm his ex-wife. Which isn't as bad as it sounds. We're still good friends."

"I'm Lee."

"I'm Lora Rhodes." She seemed calmer now and her hands were shaking less.

"Does Brendan have any medical conditions?"

"High blood pressure. I know he takes medication for it. But nothing… nothing like… this."

"Many things can cause convulsions. The doctors will be better able to gauge how serious it is."

"If they ever get him to a hospital," Lora fretted.

Lee was glad to hear the sounds of an approaching siren a few minutes later. Everyone watched in silence as Brendan was carried away on a stretcher while Lora walked alongside.

Funerals, especially services where the deceased had led a full life, often left participants feeling uplifted and satisfied that they'd given their friend or family member a proper goodbye. However, with a mourner being rushed to the hospital, Lee and Kay knew that this particular service wouldn't be leaving anyone with good feelings.

"Will you let us know how he's doing?" Kay asked Art as the ambulance drove away.

Art nodded, looking befuddled by his friend's collapse. "I don't understand it. Brendan was always the toughest member of our unit. The man plays golf for eight hours a day sometimes."

He shook his head and Kay watched as he walked away, his head hung low.

CHAPTER THREE

"Let's tear it all down and pack it up," Lee said when the guests were gone.

"I'll take the Cadillac up to the house and bring back Bertha. I want to change anyway," Kay said. She felt drained, the adrenaline rush she'd experienced while trying to help Brendan now long gone.

"We'll stack everything up and be ready by the time you get back," Lee said with a nod. He preferred to use Bertha to transport items to and from a funeral site when he could, especially the tent.

Lee, Lester and Jerome made quick work of dismantling the tent, placing it and several stacks of chairs by the curb.

"I think one of the thermoses is missing," Jerome said as they were taking down the coffee table.

"I don't remember how many there were." Lee was surprised that Jerome had noticed.

"There were two blue ones with tea," Jerome said.

"You don't drink tea," Lester pointed out.

"Exactly, Sherlock. I paid attention to the ones I didn't want to touch."

They looked around the area where the tent had been.

"I don't see it," Lee said.

"Maybe someone took it." Lester shrugged.

Jerome looked unconvinced and started walking in bigger circles, looking behind the gravestones and monuments nearby. Lee watched him and noticed something moving between the stones. He recognized it as one of Ruby's two cats and assumed that it was the same one Brendan's ex-wife had been taking pictures of earlier. He was getting ready to point out the cat when Jerome had his eureka moment.

"Ha!" Jerome cried from about twenty feet away. He stood up from behind a large family stone, holding the missing thermos in one hand and its lid in the other. "I told you there was another blue one." He screwed the lid back on as he walked toward them.

"Never said there wasn't," Lee said. "Come on, Kay's coming back with Bertha." He recognized the guttural sound of the old hearse as it turned into the cemetery.

"Funny it being all the way over there," Jerome mused. "Why would someone carry it off and drop it behind those tombstones? And why leave it lying there with the lid off? Wasn't like there were a bunch of kids here."

"Maybe they were drinking from it over there and, when that woman screamed, they dropped it. She damn near made me piss *my* pants," Lester said.

"Grab the flowers," Lee said, ignoring Jerome's obsession with the lost thermos.

As Kay opened the back of the hearse, Lee said, "We'll need to put some of this in the trunk of the family car." He saw that Jerome was still holding the thermos and looking at it with a puzzled expression on his face. "And you can start with *that.*"

Jerome shook his head. "It's just weird." He picked up some of the other items from the coffee table and took them to the family car.

"What's his fascination with the thermos?" Kay asked Lee.

"It was lost but now it's found, hallelujah." Lee shrugged. "Don't ask me."

Once they'd unpacked the vehicles at the funeral home, Jerome drove off on his motorcycle while Lester headed for the kitchen to see what goodies he could get from Ruby.

Lee and Kay went inside through the embalming room where the phone was ringing. Lee got to it first.

"Not good news?" Kay asked, seeing Lee's face as he hung up the phone.

"That was Derrick, the long-haired EMT driving the ambulance," Lee explained. Lee and Derrick had known each other for years. In a small town, ambulance drivers and morticians often ended up in the same place at the same time. "He said that Brendan died. He was alive when they arrived at the hospital but died before they could figure out what was wrong with him."

"Did they have any idea?"

"Derrick said there would be an autopsy."

Kay looked thoughtful. "You know, the way he presented, it could have been poisoning."

Lee's eyes grew wide. "What? How could he have been poisoned?"

"I've seen several poisonings. The vomiting and seizures… that's not uncommon. Most of the ones I saw were accidental or self-inflicted, though I did have a patient in Saigon who was poisoned by someone in a brothel." Kay shrugged.

"Oh no!" Lee ran from the embalming room to the kitchen with Kay following close behind him.

"What's wrong?" she yelled.

Lee burst into the kitchen, startling Ruby, who was standing at the sink with a dish towel in her hands.

"The thermos, one of the blue ones, *both* blue ones…" Lee was stuttering as he tried to get the words out. "You didn't wash them!" He looked from the sink to Ruby.

"If you're looking for the blue thermos that Jerome asked me not to wash, it's up in that cabinet," Ruby said calmly, pointing behind Lee.

"He asked you not to wash it?"

"Don't y'all ever talk to each other?" she chastised him gently. "Jerome said that a man got sick at the funeral, and he told me not to touch the thermos until we find out what happened."

"Could *you* have accidently put something in the tea?" Lee asked, his voice rising to falsetto range.

"If I ever poison someone, it won't be an accident," Ruby said in a way that made Lee feel a little nervous about her cooking. *Remember to stay on her good side*, he told himself.

"Other people drank out of that thermos," Kay said, and they both turned to look at her. "I poured tea out of one of the blue thermoses while someone else was using the other one. Only Brendan got sick, so if it was something in the tea then someone other than Ruby put it there."

Lee looked a little frantic. "If he was poisoned then we need to find out who did it. Otherwise we're going to be blamed for it, as if we don't have enough trouble with Garland poaching our funerals."

"Poison is a tricky way to kill someone," Ruby mused. "Awful chance you'll get the wrong person… or be seen doing it."

"Or give the victim too little or too much," Kay said.

"Too much?" Lee asked.

"Too much and they might taste it and not drink it, or

they might throw it up before it has a chance to be lethal. Whatever they used, it wasn't cyanide or strychnine. They both leave too many telltale signs."

"That's right. Cyanide has the smell of almonds," Ruby said. "I've been catching up on my Agatha Christie by reading to Yin and Yang before bedtime."

"Speaking of those two rascals, I saw one of them in the cemetery today," Lee told her.

"Did they give you any clues?" Ruby asked with a mischievous smile. She couldn't help herself from occasionally reminding Lee how the cats had once provided unlikely assistance in solving a murder.

"As much as I hate to admit it, he wasn't far from where the thermos was found," Lee muttered.

"We don't know that it was murder… yet." Kay tried to sound optimistic. "Brendan wasn't young. He might have accidentally poisoned himself. More people kill themselves by screwing up their medications than you'd think."

"Then why was the thermos emptied?" Lee asked.

"There is that," Kay said reluctantly. "Maybe he dropped it when he collapsed."

"Could someone have poisoned the thermos while we were all standing there?"

"I wasn't watching the table that closely."

"If they wanted to make sure that Brendan got the poison, they would have had to hand it directly to him," Lee said.

"They might not have cared who was poisoned," Kay responded.

"That's a scary thought. If that was the case, then why not leave the thermos on the table? They could have gotten a two-for-one deal."

"We're just speculating. Until we know what they find during the autopsy, we're just wasting time."

Lee nodded, then thanked Ruby for keeping the thermos safe. He left the kitchen and wandered morosely into the office.

"No matter what the outcome of the autopsy is, we're in trouble," he said when Kay joined him.

"We just need to up our game."

"How does that help if the Garlands keep undercutting our prices?"

"People pay more for some items all the time because they see value in one product or business over another. You are the best mortician in a hundred miles. We give a personal touch that we'd both agree the Garland funeral homes don't."

"Maybe," Lee mused.

"We need to make sure that everyone in the county can see the difference between us and the Garlands. If we can do that then maybe not everyone, but certainly *some* people, will chose us, even if we cost a little more." Kay knew she sounded like a motivational speaker.

"After today we'll also need to convince people that they won't die if they attend one of our funerals." Lee was having a hard time seeing the sunny side of the situation.

"Dad had people die at funerals," Kay reminded him.

"True. At least three that I remember. Old people, lots of stress. It happens. We'll get by okay this time if it doesn't turn out that we served Brendan Rhodes poisoned tea."

"We didn't do it."

Lee sighed. "I'll call my buddy at the morgue in Gainesville tomorrow and see when they've scheduled the autopsy." He paused. "I shouldn't bring this up, but is there any chance we'll get his funeral?"

"I won't push it. I'm going to call Mr. Butler. If he brings it up..." Kay shrugged.

"Long shot. I wouldn't blame them if they choose

another funeral home. He might have made arrangements already. You can tell Butler that I'll try and learn when the body will be released."

"I may as well go ahead and call him," Kay said, reaching for the phone even though she felt cringy at the thought of talking to Art so soon after the loss of another friend.

Lee reached out and stopped her hand. "Best not to mention the poison. Nothing is official yet."

"Understood." Kay nodded and Lee took his hand away.

She took a deep breath and picked up the phone, dialing slowly and almost wishing the man wouldn't answer.

"Hello?" Art Butler sounded worn out.

"Mr. Butler, this is Kay Lamberton. We just heard that Brendan passed away at the hospital. I'm so sorry."

There was a long silence from the other end of the phoneline. Kay prepared herself for whatever accusations might be flung at them.

"He survived things that no one should be able to survive and then he dies at our lieutenant's funeral. It's crazy." Art spoke as though he were talking to himself.

"Lee will contact the morgue tomorrow and find out when the autopsy is going to be performed and when his family can expect the body to be released."

"Yeah, an autopsy. I wondered about that. I guess they've got to do one. Wasn't like he was sick or anything."

"Or under the direct care of a physician. We'll do what we can to help," Kay said.

"I appreciate it. Who would have thought…" His voice trailed off into mournful silence.

"I'll call you as soon as Lee finds out something from the morgue," Kay said and hung up, grateful to get off the line.

Despite the unhappy events of the day, Lee had pleasant

plans for the night. He had rekindled a relationship with Alison Dobbs, a middle-school crush, after her father had been murdered a year ago. Alison had moved back to Lang to reopen and update her father's appliance and electronics store, and a lowkey romance had been simmering between her and Lee ever since.

"Lester told me about the guy who died at the memorial service," Alison said as Lee inspected the VHS and Betamax machines she'd just put up on the shelves.

"How can anyone afford these?" Lee glowered at the six-hundred-dollar price tag on the Phillips VCR.

"The Sony is even more. Which is part of the reason they don't sell as well. The worst part is I have to stock both VHS *and* Betamax movies."

"You've explained it to me, but I still don't understand the difference between the two types of video recorders."

"Really it's just Sony and JVC getting in a fight to control the market, and all it does is create a dilemma for the rest of us. My money is on VHS, but I still have to stock the Sony machines 'cause a lot of people want them."

"How many have you sold?"

"Two VHS machines and a Betamax. Then those same people signed up to rent movies from me. The real coup was the recorder and cameras I sold to Walt Lawson. Right now, I'm still making more off of TVs and stereos."

"Walt, the guy that owns the Fast Marts?"

"The very same. He wants me to set up the cameras for his stores. Remember last month when that guy robbed the Fast Mart out by the interstate and beat up the clerk? They still haven't caught him. I convinced Walt that a camera and recorder might prevent it from happening again."

"Or help the sheriff's office catch the guy next time."

"Exactly," Alison said.

"You're pretty good at this." Lee couldn't help but

admire her entrepreneurial skills.

Alison turned from the shelf she was organizing and looked at him. "I like the shop. My biggest regret is that I didn't come down and help Dad run it when he was alive."

Lee walked over to her and put his hand on her arm. "How could you have known that your father was going to be murdered?"

She took his hand. "You know, I used to think I was too much of a nerd to deal with people. What I've figured out is that a lot of the people who come in here are as big a nerd as I am."

"Including Lester?" Lester had been fascinated with the store since Alison had taken it over and she'd hired him on as a part-time assistant.

"He's a nice guy. A little crazy and smokes too much weed, but he's been a big help."

"As much business as the funeral home is getting, *I* could have been here helping you. I'm kinda glad you've been able to give Lester some work."

At eight, Alison locked up the store. "What do you want to watch?"

She walked over to the shelves where about a hundred video tapes were displayed. Lee joined her and scanned the shelves. Half a dozen of the tapes had been rented out, leaving a mix of newer films, classics and some schlock horror titles.

"*Friday the 13th*?" Lee suggested.

"Sure, if it's not too scary for you," Alison said.

"I'm a mortician," he scoffed.

"You jumped when we watched *Alien*."

"I couldn't sleep for a week after I saw that in the theatre. That thing was… terrifying. But I think I can handle a summer camp with a stabby maniac."

"Did you see it when it came out?" Alison asked, picking

up the tape.

"Nope. I didn't have anyone to hold my hand back then," he said with a smile.

"You can be kinda sweet when you try. I walked to work this morning, so we can ride over to my place together." Alison held up an envelope. "We just need to swing by the bank so I can deposit this."

After making the deposit, they talked about Brendan Rhodes's death as Lee drove Alison home.

"Do you think it was murder?" she asked.

"Kay thinks he was poisoned. We'll know for sure when they do the toxicology." Lee looked thoughtful. "Something you were talking about earlier…"

"What?"

"When you were talking about the video recorders…" He took his right hand off the steering wheel and snapped his fingers. "Cameras. You were talking about the cameras at the Fast Marts helping to solve crimes. Brendan's ex-wife was taking pictures at the memorial service. I first noticed her when she was stalking Yin or Yang, one of those two darn cats. Maybe she caught something on film. I mean, if this *was* murder then she could have some valuable evidence."

"Assuming she isn't the killer. I mean, you know, the ex-wife," Alison said pointedly. "She sounds like a prime suspect."

"Yeah. Usually. But they seemed to be getting along just fine. Not everyone hates their ex."

"What if there's money involved or child custody?"

"They're both in their sixties, so child custody probably isn't an issue. Money? Maybe." Lee slowed the car to pull into the driveway.

The old craftsman-style house was dark except for a porch light that Alison had running on a timer. While the house where her father had lived had burned down after his death, he'd owned several other properties in the county and Alison had been able to move into this house when she'd reopened the store.

She unlocked the front door and Lee followed her into a hallway that smelled of old books and oiled wood.

"I need to clean Dad's stuff out, but I haven't found the heart to do it," Alison said.

"If you want, I can help," Lee offered, not for the first time.

"Someday," she said wistfully.

They spent the rest of the evening watching the movie and then engaging in other, more adult pursuits.

CHAPTER FOUR

"You look happy," Kay said when Lee walked through the kitchen door Sunday morning.

"I know." He took the plate that Ruby held out to him. "Even though I don't have any right to be happy with the business in the crapper."

"Love is worth smiling about. Get yourself some of those pancakes," Ruby said.

Before he could sit down, the phone rang.

"Funeral?" Kay looked up hopefully as Lee answered the phone that hung on the wall.

Lee's end of the conversation started with: "I know who this is," and ended with: "I'll be there."

"Who was that?" Kay asked, puzzled.

"Brad Garland. They caught the funeral for the family that was killed when their station wagon overturned on I-75 Thursday night. Five dead. The family wants one funeral for all of them, so Garland needs another hearse."

"And he had the gall to call us?" Kay felt her face grow

warm.

"A thousand dollars for five hours' work," Lee said, trying not to choke on his words.

"Damn it!" Kay pushed her plate away and leaned back in her chair.

"We need the money."

"That's my line," Kay grumbled. "You're right, but I hate it."

"Not as much as I do."

"When is the funeral?"

"Tuesday in Gainesville. I'll take Lester."

"Watch everything the Garlands do. If we're going to beat them, or at least push them out of our territory, we need to know how they work and how they think," Kay instructed. "I'll debrief you when you get back." She had a tendency to slip into military-speak when facing the enemy.

"That's the spirit," Ruby said before dropping another pancake onto Lee's plate. "Of course, there's also a murder to solve."

"We aren't sure it was murder," Lee said and received a stern look from Ruby.

"If it was, they used my tea to kill that man." Ruby shook her spatula at him.

"We can still hope he died from natural causes," Lee argued.

"Ruby's right. The more I think about what happened, the more convinced I am that it was a poisoning," Kay said. "I'm going over to talk with Mr. Butler and see what I can learn about the other people at the memorial service."

"I'll go with you. Brendan's ex-wife was taking pictures. We need to make sure that they get developed properly. There could be a clue to what happened on them."

"That's right, she was the one who found the body. We'll go after lunch. Give Art a chance to get home from church."

As they were leaving the house at one o'clock, Jerome roared up on his motorcycle.

"Where are you two headed?" he asked, sitting astride his Kawasaki.

They explained their mission.

"I got some bad news about the investigation. Sutton is going to be the lead on it if the coroner decides Rhodes was poisoned. The other not so great news is that the sheriff said that I was to be included in the investigation since I was on scene at the time. Sutton wasn't happy."

Kay and Lee shared a look. Deputy Wade Sutton was one of the least competent detectives working for the Melon County Sheriff's Office, but he was also the sheriff's brother-in-law.

"Last time I saw him, he told me to stay out of the investigation business," Lee said.

"He's still pissed that we were three steps ahead of him on the last murder we were involved in. And it should be pointed out that we didn't go looking for this one. It came to us," Kay stated.

Lee told Jerome about the photos Lora Rhodes had taken.

"Guess I better follow you and see about collecting the film for evidence. Second thought, I'll meet you there. I'll go by the office and pick up a car and evidence bags."

Jerome spun his motorcycle around in the driveway, pivoting on his inside foot and leaving a black half circle on the pavement before taking off down the street toward the sheriff's office.

Kay and Lee took Kay's Chevy Nova which, unlike Lee's car, didn't scream "funeral home."

"Is there any chance that Art Butler is involved in the murder?" Lee asked, knowing that Kay liked the old soldier.

"How can I rule him out?" She shrugged. "You know the

drill: means, motive and opportunity. Right now, everyone who was at the service had opportunity."

"Means would be who could get their hands on the type of poison used. Assuming it *was* poison. And it's too early to know who has a motive. That will have to wait until we find out who benefits from Brendan's death."

"Maybe it was poison, but Brendan wasn't the specific victim. The thing with poison is, it's tough to target one person out of a group."

"That's a happy thought," Lee said.

"The poisoner could have been after someone else or… anyone," Kay said, turning onto the street where Art Butler lived.

They were in one of the oldest subdivisions in the county. All the homes had been built using the same postwar cinderblock construction. Most were starter homes with a few fancier places sprinkled here and there. Art's house was at the end of a cul-de-sac of carefully maintained homes and neatly manicured yards. There were not a lot of bicycles or kids' toys in the yards, suggesting that the homeowners were more likely to be middle-aged or older.

They pulled into the driveway of a pastel-colored house with a closed-in garage and an impressive hedge of azaleas. Kay had called ahead to ask if they could come by, and Art was already coming out of the house to greet them.

"Have you heard anything about Brendan's cause of death?" Art asked, holding out his hand to Lee.

"No. It will be a while before they make a determination. Even after the autopsy, the coroner will have to wait for the toxicology results to come back," Lee said, shaking Art's hand.

Kay gave Art a hug. "We can't tell you how sorry we are," she told him.

"Everyone is pretty broken up over Brendan's death. I

have to say, I can't believe that it was murder."

"Have you all talked much since the service?" Kay asked.

"Some. Most of us live here." He waved his hand at the houses around him.

"The other guys live here too?" Lee said, surprised.

"Yeah, we all bought lots when they were laying out the subdivision. That's Chaz's house across the street. Brendan lived in the house at the end of the street. He moved to Gainesville after the divorce, but Lora still lives there and Brendan would come and stay sometimes when we were having a get-together."

"Must have been an amicable divorce," Kay observed.

"The divorce had more to do with Brendan's appreciation of the female form than any animosity between him and Lora."

They heard a car coming down the street and Lee turned his head to see Jerome approaching in a marked unit.

"Is Lora home?" Kay asked.

"I think so. That's her car in the driveway." He pointed out the blue Oldsmobile parked in front of the house.

Jerome pulled up behind Kay's car and got out.

"Lora was taking pictures yesterday and Jerome thought he better collect them for evidence, just in case Brendan was poisoned," Kay explained.

"Guess that makes sense," Art admitted as Jerome walked toward them. They shook hands.

"We explained to Art that you're here to pick up the film from Lora Rhodes's camera," Kay said. "I'll go over there with you. Maybe Lee and Art can stay here so it doesn't look like a delegation."

"That sounds best. I guess you all met her yesterday," Art said to Kay and Jerome. "She's still pretty upset."

"Naturally. We'll go easy," Kay said. The truth was, she wanted to have a chance to talk with the ex-wife without Art present.

"I just want to pick up the film so we can have it professionally developed," Jerome assured Art.

"You said that more of your friends live here?" Lee prompted Art as Kay and Jerome walked away.

"Yep. Lyle and his wife Kelly live next door to me. She was the looker at the funeral yesterday." Art turned around and pointed to a white house a little bigger than most on the street. "That's Frank's place. He's divorced, but his daughter lives with him. She was the one walking around at the memorial with jeans and sandals on. Nice enough girl, but a couple of years at the University of Miami and she came back a little… spacey." He touched his head.

"Could I get a glass of water?" Lee wasn't sure why, but he wanted to see the inside of Art's house.

"Come on, I'll get you one."

"Does Benny live here too?" Lee asked, remembering the last veteran as he followed Art into the house.

"Sure. Benny's place is on the other side of Frank's. Frank helps him out when he needs it."

Lee thought that was a little odd. He remembered that Benny had a limp, but it wasn't like he was paralyzed. Still, Lee figured it might make some chores difficult. "Is there something wrong with his leg?" he asked, unable to think of a more polite way of asking.

"He was hit by a jeep in Seoul and his leg was crushed. The surgeons did the best they could." Art shook his head.

The inside of Art's place looked like the layout from a 1960's issue of *Better Homes and Gardens*. There was even a white shag rug in front of the white brick fireplace, along with furniture that screamed "space age"… in 1959.

Lee followed Art into an avocado-colored kitchen that stood in stark contrast to the white of the living room.

"My wife had the kitchen redone five years ago," Art

said, as if he could read Lee's mind. He pulled a clear amber tumbler from a cabinet and reached for the freezer door.

"I don't need any ice," Lee said and Art shrugged, taking a pitcher of water out of the refrigerator and filling the glass before handing it to Lee.

"Whose house is at the end of the street?" Lee asked. It was the only house that Art hadn't pointed out.

"Don't even get me started." Art swatted his hand in front of his face in irritation. For a moment Lee didn't think he was going to explain, but then Art sighed and went on, "That's Arthur Clegg's place. The house sits on three lots. He bought them out from under us. The man's an asshole."

Art's hands clenched and unclenched as he talked. "We'd made a deal with the developer that we would buy the plot where Clegg's house stands now within a year. After that time, if we didn't have the money, then the developer could sell it to someone else. We were going to make it into a little park for our kids. This was when we'd just started building our homes and the whole bunch of us were full of piss and vinegar. Going to conquer the world and be friends forever. Not that we didn't have our problems. Still, we thought we'd always come out on top. But when we went to buy the lot, Mac—that's the developer—he'd gotten an offer from Clegg that was twice the price per lot than what we'd paid for ours."

"But he'd promised to sell it to you if you had the money," Lee said, feeling betrayed on Art's behalf.

"That's right, but we hadn't agreed to a price. We didn't think someone would come along and cause the price to go up like that. We were… upset. Went to Mac and he told us he needed to get what he could out of the property. Business, that's all. Said when Clegg came to him, he'd told him the lots were promised if we could come up with the money."

"And the money you had to come up with was three times what you'd expected to pay," Lee finished for him.

"Exactly."

"That couldn't have made for good neighbors."

Art waved his hand. "We could have gotten over it. But it wasn't just the money. The guy is a real jerk. Always the one to complain about a party or someone's cat in his yard. Still, you got to live. Most of us just pretend he isn't there."

"Most of you?"

"Yeah. Lyle gets worked up about once a year and wants us to harass Clegg until he moves or sue him or some such. Not that any of it's going to work. Lyle's plans would be brilliant for a twelve-year-old. So we just ignore him and he settles down after a couple of weeks."

"What sets him off?"

"Usually?" Art asked.

Lee nodded.

"Lyle loves to throw barbeques. He's the one that draws most of the noise complaints from Clegg. There's the parking thing too."

"Parking?"

"For the parties. Last month Clegg had a car towed that was parked in front of his house. He said it was blocking his driveway, but… well… it really wasn't blocking it. Maybe he'd have had to drive across a little bit of his grass, but it wouldn't have been a big deal for anyone else. Clegg made it a big deal. The car he had towed belonged to a woman-friend of Lyle and Brendan."

"Both of them?"

"I mean friend, not… you know, that kind of friend. She works at a pool hall in Gainesville that they go…" He stopped himself when he realized that Brendan wouldn't be going anywhere anymore. "…went to a few times a month."

"Was Brendan upset about their friend having her car

towed?"

Art tilted his head and squinted his eyes while he thought about the question.

"I remember I was actually surprised at how upset he was. Lora even asked me if I thought he had a thing for her. Of course, Brendan had a thing for any woman. He always fancied himself as a playboy."

"What did Brendan do about it?"

"Nothin' really. He was just feeding Lyle's rants about Clegg. Which was the opposite of his normal position. He typically was the one to try and talk Lyle down from the cliff. That's why they made a good pair. We never worried when they went somewhere together 'cause Brendan would level Lyle out if he got worked up to do something crazy."

"But not this time?"

"I don't know. We all thought it was just Lyle's usual blowing off steam; at least I did. Kelly, Lyle's wife, told me later that Lyle and Brendan paid to get the woman's car out of the impound lot."

"Did they confront Clegg?" Lee asked.

"Lyle didn't. I don't know about Brendan. Knowing Brendan, I can't imagine he did."

"How can you be so sure about Lyle?"

Art chuckled. "Two years ago, Clegg got a restraining order against Lyle. If he steps foot on Clegg's property, he'll be spending a night in the county jail… maybe more than a night."

"Other than Arthur Clegg, did everyone else on the street get along?"

"We have our share of drama. Nothing on the *Peyton Place* scale, you understand, just petty crap."

"Like?"

"Hey, what's with all the questions? Do you really think Brendan was poisoned?" Art asked.

"You met Kay; you know her history. Do you think she makes many mistakes?"

"No. And she thinks this was murder?" Art frowned.

"I could give you some wishy-washy answer, but the truth is, yeah, she does."

"Damn."

"Can you think of anyone who was at the service that might have wanted to hurt Brendan?"

"Yesterday I would have thought you were joking. Brendan was just... unoffensive. You know how on those TV mystery shows you always know who's going to get killed 'cause they're pissing everyone off in the first five minutes? Brendan wasn't like that. He even got along with his ex-wife. Who does that?"

Lee almost started to ask about Lora, but then he remembered that Jerome and Kay were talking with her. No sense digging in that hole until he knew what they'd found out.

"Can you think of any old grudges?"

Art just shrugged and shook his head.

Lee began to wonder if the wrong person might have gotten the poison.

"Did you see when Brendan got his cup of tea?"

Art shook his head. "I was too busy talking to everyone."

"If Brendan wasn't the target, do you have any idea who *might* have been?"

"What, like the wrong person got the poison?" Art seemed genuinely surprised at the suggestion.

"Just one of the possibilities," Lee said.

"Look, we've all lived full lives. Made friends and enemies. But we're also getting up in age where you take a long-range view of life. Not like when you're a hot headed kid."

"There have been plenty of senior citizens who were

murderers… and even more who were victims," Lee pointed out.

"You got a point there." Art looked thoughtful. "I don't want to be airing other people's dirty laundry."

"What about you? Anyone who might have a grudge?"

"I spent my career as a salesman. My job wasn't to piss people off. When I was still in high school, I got a job selling appliances in a little town in Ohio. First day the boss told me, 'Make the customers happy. Whether you sell them something or not, make sure that when they leave the store, they feel better than when they came in. If you do that, then they'll come back. And if they come back, you get another chance to get them to buy what you're selling.' When I became a salesman after the Army, I remembered his advice and followed it. So not many enemies." Art wasn't bragging, just stating a fact.

Lee figured he'd gotten as much as he was going to out of Art Butler. Besides, Kay and Jerome should have been getting back pretty soon.

"If you think of anything else, let me know." Lee let Art walk him back to the front door. "And I'll call as soon as I find out anything about the autopsy and when Brendan's body will be released."

CHAPTER FIVE

Kay followed Jerome over to Lora's house. "I'll let you take the lead," she told him.

"First we get the film and then, if you can get her talking, I'd like to get a look around the house."

Lora's house was smaller than Art's, with a baby-blue stucco finish and jalousie windows. Jerome did a triple tap on the door.

"Coming!" a woman's voice shouted from inside.

When Lora opened the door, she was wearing a flower-print house dress and tennis shoes. Her hair was mussed and her eyes were red and puffy. She stared at them for a minute before speaking.

"Can I help you?"

"Yes, ma'am. I'm Deputy Jerome Carter. We met at the memorial service yesterday."

She nodded. "Of course. I'm sorry. Seeing the uniform at my door threw me off." She looked past Jerome at Kay, who had hung back several feet. "And you're one of the funeral…

directors or something, I guess. I don't understand..." Lora looked confused.

"You were taking pictures at the service yesterday," Jerome explained. "I'd like to collect the film so that the sheriff's office can process it."

"I still don't understand. Why do you want the film?"

"With an unexpected death like your ex-husband's, the coroner has to look into all possible causes. One way to do that is to examine everything that was going on at the time of death."

"You were there. Can't you tell him what happened?" she said, then quickly added, "I mean, sure you can have the film. I just... It just seems odd." Lora stood back and made way for them to enter the house.

The door opened into a small foyer that led to the living room, which wasn't as neat as Kay had expected.

"Sit anywhere." Lora waved her hand toward the powder-blue chairs and couch. Jerome and Kay had to shift some books and magazines to make room on the couch. "I'll go get the camera."

"Don't take the film out," Jerome told her. "If you don't mind, we'd like to take the camera and have our guy remove and develop the film." Jerome didn't want to risk the film becoming accidentally exposed.

Lora came back with a cheap Kodak Instamatic. Kay recognized it as the one she'd been using at the memorial service.

"We'll get the camera and pictures back to you as soon as we can," Jerome assured Lora as she handed him the camera and sat down across from them.

"We'd like to ask you a few questions." Jerome tried to make it sound casual.

"Art mentioned something about Brendan being poisoned. Could that really be possible?" Lora beat Jerome to the first question.

"At this point we don't know anything for sure. With luck, the autopsy will give us some answers. If he *was* poisoned, do you have any idea who might have done it?" Jerome asked, trying to regain control of the conversation.

"Brendan was a nice guy. I mean, really nice. We got a divorce because… he was too friendly with other women, not because we didn't get along."

"If he was having affairs and you found out, didn't y'all fight about them?" Kay asked.

Lora shook her head. "Brendan just liked to live large. I got mad, but he was like a big kid. I know he never meant to hurt me. He just… got caught up in the moment. I'd yell at him and he'd look like a puppy who'd chewed up your shoes, then apologize and swear it wouldn't happen again. I knew he was sincere, but after the first couple of times I also knew he wouldn't be able to stop himself."

Jerome and Kay nodded encouragingly.

"What about the women he… saw? Did they ever get mad at him? Or their husbands?" Jerome asked.

"I don't think he fooled around much with married women. As for the women themselves, I think most of them were like me. They thought he was a lot of fun, but realized he wasn't steady boyfriend material."

"Did he get mad at any of *them*?" Jerome asked.

Lora shook her head. "I know every devil who dies becomes an angel, but it's not like that. Brendan occasionally got frustrated with people, but not angry."

"Where did Brendan work?" Kay asked.

"He was a truck driver and retired a couple of years ago"

"You know most of the people who were at the memorial service. Was there anyone there that Brendan had a problem with?" Jerome said.

"No. That gang got along too well most of the time."

"Too well?" Kay asked.

Lora waved her arms toward the window that looked out on the neighborhood. "Oh, yes, they went everywhere and did everything together. That was another small bone of contention in our marriage. After a few years they bored me to tears. There was always the newest get-rich-quick scheme or the newest fad that we all had to participate in. Gag me."

"What kind of get-rich-quick schemes?" Jerome wanted to know.

"Oh, the usual. One year it was Amway, another year it was raising minks. Of course, it never amounted to anything. Just another pit to throw money into. Lyle, it almost always started with Lyle. He'd come over all excited about some nonsense or other. I'd tell Brendan that it was a waste of money, and the next day he'd be taking money out of our savings and handing it over to Lyle to invest. Invest my ass." Her fingers were tapping out an irritated beat on the arms of her chair.

"Sounds like it really pissed you off," Kay sympathized.

"Oh yeah." Lora shook her head. "Not at Brendan, though. He couldn't help himself once Lyle started talking."

"Where has Brendan been living?" Jerome asked.

"He has an apartment in Gainesville. Gatorwood, that's the name of the complex."

"I know it." Jerome had friends who'd lived there. The majority of its residents were college students, with most of the apartments designed to be shared by multiple people.

"I could use a glass of water," Kay said, garnering an appreciative glance from Jerome.

"Sure, I'll get it." Lora stood up.

"I'll come with you," Kay said and followed her into the kitchen, which wasn't much neater than the living room. Finally given the chance, Jerome stood up and started looking around the living room for anything of interest.

"How long have you and Brendan been divorced?" Kay asked as Lora took a glass down from a cabinet.

"Two years. I don't know why we waited that long. I guess we'd just gotten comfortable."

"Was there a straw that broke the camel's back?"

"No. Just another affair. Maybe it was both of us going through a mid-life, or I guess a late-life, crisis." Lora shrugged. "I was relieved when he suggested that we separate."

"Relieved?"

"We were…" She paused. "…friends. I never wanted to talk about a divorce 'cause I thought it would hurt him too much." Lora pulled a tray of ice cubes out of the freezer and cracked the cubes loose.

"But he suggested it?" Kay pressed.

"Like I said, maybe he needed a change."

After dropping the ice into the glass, she filled it from the tap and handed the glass to Kay. There was a smear of something—grease or maybe lipstick—on the rim of the glass. Kay didn't want to drink the water now but felt obliged. She took a quick sip from the clean side.

"Did you still see much of each other?" she asked.

"You can't get away from Art and the gang," Lora said with a small laugh. "There are always neighborhood get-togethers, so we'd see each other then. Maybe twice a week."

Lora made a move to go back into the living room, but Kay stood in her way. She took another tentative drink from the glass.

"I'm surprised that you continued to go to the gatherings. You don't sound that keen on his friends."

"After all these years, they're still my friends too." Lora waved away the question and headed for the living room.

Kay fell in behind her and was relieved to see Jerome sitting on the couch when they came back into the room.

"We should probably be going," he said, standing up with the camera in his hand. "I'll get this back to you as soon as I can."

"No hurry, though the pictures of Brendan are very important to me. If I'd known it was the last time I was going to see him..." Lora's voice trailed off. "I'll walk out with you."

Kay and Jerome felt Lora's eyes on them as they walked back to Art's house.

"What'd you think?" Kay asked.

"I got a chance to look around the house a little while you were in the kitchen. She's no housekeeper, and there was some of Brendan's stuff still lying around."

"They've been separated a couple of years. Seems a little odd, but if there wasn't any animosity, who knows."

Lee was waiting for them in front of Art's house. Before they had a chance to get in their cars and leave, a Pinto station wagon pulled into the driveway, blocking them in.

"Hello!" a woman in her late sixties called to them as she climbed out of the Pinto. Her hair was blonde from a bottle and her clothes were two sizes too small. "Are you here to see Art?" Then she did a double-take at the patrol car. "The sheriff?"

"I'm Deputy Jerome Carter, ma'am," Jerome said with a brief nod.

"This must be about poor Brendan. I... I..." she stammered. "I'm really at a loss for words. You're supposed to get used to your friends and family dying as you get older, but that's just not the case. Every time you lose someone, it's a stab to the heart. Do you want me to go get Art?"

Before the words were out of her mouth, the front door opened and Art came down the driveway.

"Betty, I've already spoken with them. You'll need to let them out of the driveway," he told her.

Instead of getting back into her car, she walked up to Lee, Kay and Jerome.

"I'm just devastated about Brendan. I was with my sister out at Cedar Key and couldn't make the memorial service. I never imagined that it would end with… a death." Her words were pouring out in a rush now. "I'm sorry, I haven't introduced myself. I'm Betty Butler. The alliteration is awful, but what're you gonna do? I fell in love with Artie the first time I saw him."

"Mrs. Butler, I'm Lee Lamberton and this is my sister, Kay. We own the Lamberton Funeral Home."

"Of course you do. Artie told me all about you." She turned to Kay. "He was especially impressed with you being a nurse in the Army and all. He's very proud of his service. That's why we're here. The men bonded in the Army and a lifetime of friendship was born," Betty gushed.

Art came up and took her gently by the arm.

"They need to leave now, Betty. Do you want me to move the car?"

"Oh! I'm so sorry. I'll do it right away." With that, she turned and hustled over to her car.

Lee and Kay breathed a sigh of relief when they were on their way back to the funeral home.

"That woman talks faster than anyone I've ever met," Kay said. "And that's some stiff competition."

"Maybe she was nervous," Lee suggested, giving a slight wave to Jerome as he turned off the road in front of them and headed for the sheriff's office.

"She wasn't at the service, so she can't be directly involved in Brendan's death," Kay pointed out.

"True." Lee went on to tell Kay what Art had said, then Kay filled him in on her conversation with Lora.

"It's certainly an interesting neighborhood," Kay said. "I want to talk to Lyle and his wife. From what Lora said, Lyle and Brendan were close."

Lee nodded as he drove. "I might go on over to the morgue this evening."

"Why? I thought you were just going to call."

"Glen's a lot more helpful if I show up with a bottle of whiskey."

"Want me to ride along? We could go by the Gatorwood apartments and check out Brendan's place."

"We won't be able to get in."

"Maybe, maybe not," Kay said cryptically.

"If we're going to get involved in some skullduggery then we better give Jerome a heads-up."

"We can go back to the funeral home first. I'm hungry and Ruby was making lasagna."

Yin and Yang were lying by the kitchen door when Kay and Lee got home. After gently nudging one of the cats out of the way with her foot, Kay's nose was assaulted by the smell of garlic, butter, hamburger and tomato sauce as they entered the kitchen.

"I knew y'all wouldn't be late for lasagna." Ruby smiled.

"Your two Garfields are waiting patiently outside for their share," Kay told her.

"I gave them some of the ground meat after she fried it up," Lester said from the counter where he was slathering butter on a slice of bread before shaking a vampire's nightmare worth of garlic salt on top.

Ruby dished out the food in hearty portions and had just sat down to her own plate when Jerome came in.

"I could smell the lasagna a block away," he said, breathing deeply as he walked in the door.

"Did you get the camera to the techs?" Kay asked.

"No one is in the office on Sunday. I put it in an evidence bag and stashed it in my locker," he said, taking a plate from Ruby. "I left the thermos there too."

"There wasn't anything wrong with that tea when it left here," Ruby said, sitting down again. "Y'all need to eat up now."

"We know the tea you served was fine. The question is, was it fine when Brendan drank it?" Kay said.

"Is there another way that he could have been poisoned?" Lester asked.

"Depends on the poison," Ruby said, causing everyone to turn to her. "What?"

"What do you know about poisons?" Lee asked suspiciously, remembering her earlier comments. He was still learning about the many hidden talents Ruby had acquired during her mysterious past.

"I learned a bit from my grandmother who… dabbled in herbs. And some during my time with a certain organization that one is better off not talking about. What do you all want for dinner tomorrow?" She also had an irritating habit of switching subjects in the middle of a conversation.

"What organization?" Kay asked. She'd taken it upon herself to occasionally challenge Ruby's claims as she couldn't stand a braggart. On the other hand, Ruby was amusing and her knowledge of the arcane was extensive.

"I told you I was in Cuba before the revolution. Some not-very-nice folks in the government got it into their heads that a good-looking woman who knew her way around might come in handy." Ruby looked at Kay and mimed zipping her lips shut and throwing away the key.

Kay thought about pressing the point but didn't want to start an argument.

"So what do you know about poisons?" Lester asked, stuffing a forkful of lasagna into his mouth.

"Poisoning is an art. In ancient Rome there were professional poisoners like Locusta. Later there was Lucretia Borgia… Edward Squire in Elizabethan England. Back then, women often murdered with poisons. Probably because of their access to the kitchen and their knowledge of herbs and flowers. Can I get you more lasagna?" She gave Lester a crooked grin.

"Uh." He looked at his empty plate.

"I'm not going to poison you or anyone else. Not that I couldn't." She took his plate. "I wouldn't even poison Castro." She got up and cut another square of lasagna for Lester, who hesitated only a moment before digging in.

"We're going to Gainesville to talk with Lee's friend at the morgue," Kay said, looking at Jerome.

"Let me know what he has to say."

"We also thought we'd take a look at Brendan's apartment."

Jerome stopped eating and looked back and forth between Lee and Kay.

"Why don't you just say you're going to go to Gainesville and get into trouble? 'Cause that's what's going to happen."

"We just want to look around," Kay said innocently.

"You can't fool me. You're going to try and get into that apartment. You won't be able to help yourself."

"I might see if the manager will let us in," Kay admitted. Lee was sitting back, watching the exchange.

"I'm coming along," Jerome said.

"You're following us around like you don't trust us," Kay said.

"The way things stand with the sheriff right now, if you cause trouble then I get a nasty note in my file. I might want to move up someday and having a four-inch-thick personnel file isn't going to help," Jerome grumbled.

"Fine. We can drop Lee off at the morgue while you and I go look at Brendan's apartment."

"Hey, I want to see the apartment too," Lee said, drawing looks from everyone at the table. "What?"

Kay rolled her eyes. "We'll all go to the morgue and then to the apartment. Happy?" she asked.

"Yep."

"What about me?" Lester asked.

"No," the others responded in unison.

"Someone needs to stay here and answer the phone," Kay said, catching Ruby's eye and shaking her head before Ruby could offer to take any calls that came in.

"Whatever," Lester pouted.

CHAPTER SIX

An hour later, with the sun still above the trees, they were headed for Gainesville.

"The ice man creeps me out," Jerome said.

Two months earlier he'd been the primary on a fatal car accident. It was a single-car crash with clear skid marks where the driver had tried to slow down before taking one of the more treacherous curves in the county. Since it had appeared cut-and-dry, Jerome's supervisor had allowed him to do all the follow-up rather than assign it to an investigator.

"You're the one who wanted to look at the victim of that car accident," Lee reminded Jerome now. When the deputy'd had some questions about the autopsy, Lee had taken him to meet Glen Doyle.

"He stood there eating ice the whole time we were looking at the body. Who does that, man?"

"You drink beer in the embalming room," Lee pointed out.

"That's different," Jerome said defensively.

"You can wait in the car," Kay suggested.

Jerome shook his head. "You know that's not going to work."

Lee pulled around to the back of the hospital, where the entrance to the morgue was discreetly tucked into a corner. The only evidence of its location, other than the small sign above the buzzer, were several parking spots marked off for funeral home vehicles. The morgue was usually quiet on Sundays and today was no exception. Lee was able to park in the spot closest to the door.

"You didn't say it was a party," Glen Doyle said as he answered the door and stood aside to let them in. "Jerome, right? And I guess you're Lee's sister." He gave Kay a smile. "He says nice things about you."

"He's certainly said some things about *you*," Kay said, returning the smile.

Glen put his hand over his heart. "Ouch. I like you."

Kay was able to size people up quickly and the older man struck her as a kind, if mischievous, soul.

"Payment." Lee pulled a bottle of Johnny Walker Black out of a liquor store bag.

"Bless you." Glen took the bottle and pushed it back into the bag. "But not in front of the others." He winked at Jerome and Kay, set the bottle on the floor beside his desk and nodded toward the hall. "On the phone I told you there isn't much to see, but let's go on back to the lockers."

They followed Glen down a hallway and into a room where one wall was lined with steel drawers with pull-out shelves for bodies. About a third of the lockers had cards labeled with case numbers and last names. Glen opened the door bearing Brendan's name and slid out the drawer, revealing a body bag with an inch-thick file folder on top.

"They haven't assigned him to any of the pathologists

yet," Glen said, picking up the file and handing it to Lee. "But I read through it after you called." He'd been a pathologist up in New Jersey until his license had been revoked for an incident he'd never revealed to Lee. He was now content to work at the morgue as a glorified caretaker, but he wasn't above providing Lee with unofficial examinations when the need arose.

He unzipped the bag, revealing a disturbingly discolored body. "Poisoning is almost certain, both from the symptoms he presented and the condition of the body. Whether it was accidental, which most poisonings are, or intentional will be for others to decide. Of course, if it was intentional then there's the possibility that it might have been self-inflected."

Kay, Lee and Jerome exchanged glances.

"Not likely under the circumstances," Jerome said for the group.

"Knowing what the poison is would help," Kay said, stepping forward and looking closely at Brendan's face.

"You must have been a good nurse," Glen said, admiring the way she studied the body. "Like a doctor, a nurse needs to be curious by nature. The dull ones never notice anything."

Kay ignored him. "Can I have a pair of gloves?"

Glen pulled a pair of latex gloves out of his pocket. "He's still in full rigor mortis, so you won't be able to open his mouth."

"Please." Kay shook her head. "I did grow up in a funeral home. I knew about rigor mortis before I was out of elementary school." She put on the gloves, then parted the lips and studied the gums. Next, she pulled up the eyelids.

"There are three groups of poisons," Glen said, taking on the role of lecturer. "Industrial and agricultural is one group, which is made up of things like insecticides, fungicides and all the different types of industrial chemicals, including heavy metals like mercury. The second group are the drug and healthcare products. These are the ones that suicides turn to. Barbiturates are a favorite. Heroin and recreational drugs are part of this group too. Last you have the poisons that are biological in origin—biotoxins. Things like mushrooms and poisons produced by animals."

"And your best guess in this case?" Jerome asked.

"A biotoxin because of his neurological symptoms. That's only a guess and not a very well-informed one at that. The good news is that the physicians attending him when he was admitted to the hospital ordered testing immediately. So samples were taken while he was still alive. Since it was a matter of life and death, they sent them off marked urgent. I would imagine the ones that could be completed quickly have been. And those results would be available if a doctor called and asked for them."

The others looked at him.

"Wait now." Glen held up his hand. "Johnny Walker's a solid Scotch, but I'm not sure it's good enough to get me to impersonate a doctor."

"You *are* a doctor," Lee said.

"I have a *doctorate*. They couldn't take that away. What I don't have is a license to practice medicine. That's what physicians who call up for lab results have." Glen shook his head and, with a sigh, took the folder back and flipped through it. "I know one of the ER doctors pretty well. He might do me a favor. *Might*."

"Is he working today?" Kay pushed

Glen shrugged. "I'll call upstairs and find out. Let's go out to the front desk."

Fifteen minutes later, a tall black-haired doctor wearing a bored expression came walking down the hall from the service elevator.

"I'm glad most of my patients don't end up down here,"

he said, grinning at Doyle and handing him a manila envelope. "It's your lucky day. This was in my mailbox."

"Nice." Glen took the envelope.

"I didn't know you have parties down here on the weekend," the doctor said, noticing the others.

"Introduce yourselves," Glen instructed, too preoccupied with the lab report to look up.

Lee obliged for the others.

"Dr. Alan Eckhart." He nodded to Lee and Jerome before looking directly at Kay. "You can call me Alan."

"Thank you, Dr. Eckhart. You can call me Ms. Lamberton," Kay said sweetly, and he gave a sharp laugh in return.

"Nicotine," Glen said, looking up from the report. "That's your poison."

"Where did it come from? Did he smoke too many cigarettes?" Lee inquired.

"This wasn't from smoking," Eckhart said. "It only takes sixty milligrams of nicotine to kill an adult, but you have to ingest it, not inhale it. About five cigarettes is enough. There have been cases where people who were deranged, or simply stupid, died from eating tobacco. About ten years ago, a young boy died because his friend dared him to eat cigarettes. In another case, a young girl ate them to keep her parents from finding out she was smoking."

"But that's not where nicotine poisoning normally comes from," Glen pointed out.

"And certainly not in this case. I think someone at the service would have noticed if Brendan had been eating cigarettes," Jerome said.

"There's nicotine in some insecticides. That's the most common source of nicotine poisoning, to the point that banning it has been discussed," Eckhart told them.

"Could it have been an accident?" Lee asked.

"It's not impossible. The first question would be: Does the cemetery use any insecticides or other products that contain nicotine?" Glen said.

"An accident would be better than having a killer on the loose," Kay said, then frowned as a thought occurred to her. "We should check and make sure that Ruby doesn't have any insecticides in the kitchen."

"I guess it's possible. Maybe it just got in the one thermos… Or since other people took tea from that thermos, maybe it was in his cup." Lee said a silent prayer that this wasn't the answer. Morbidly, he knew it would be better for the funeral home to have a murderer running around town than for them to have accidentally poisoned a mourner.

"Poisoners are hard to catch," Glen said. "My first job in a morgue, up in Connecticut, we had a series of deaths. Old men. Our office missed the first two. The police didn't notice something strange was going on until the third old guy passed away. They still might not have picked up on it, except that one of the officers had attended two of the deaths and noticed an odd flyer for a charity sitting on the nightstand at two of the homes. The Sisterhood of Man Foundation. Funny that I remember the name. The officer volunteered with his church doing a lot of work with the homeless and those in need, and he'd never heard of the organization. When he went to the address, it was just a small house in a residential neighborhood."

"Let me guess, an old lady ran the organization?" Eckhart said.

"She ran it and was the only member of it," Glen answered. "Turned out she'd swindled the old fellows and, when they got upset enough to threaten her, she'd poisoned them with their own medications. She'd left a string of half a dozen more across the country. She was right out of that movie with what's his name, Cary Grant."

"*Arsenic and Old Lace*," Lee said.

Glen snapped his fingers. "That's it. Only she was doing it for the money."

"So we look for cigarettes or insecticides," Jerome said thoughtfully.

"We'll know more after the autopsy. It should be able to tell what he ate and drank prior to his death… and if there are any other substances present," Glen promised them.

The trio gave their thanks and headed to for the exit.

"Did you give him your phone number?" Jerome asked Kay once they were back in the car and on the road. He'd seen Dr. Eckhart pull her aside as they were walking out the door.

"Maybe," Kay said demurely. "Okay, I gave him the number because he said he might remember more about Brendan's case."

Jerome and Lee both rolled their eyes.

"Aren't you dating someone?" Lee said.

"Zach? Sure, we go out. But we're friends… At least that's what he is to me."

"She strings him along for dinner and movies," Lee said, causing Kay to punch him in the arm. Though she had to admit that he had a point. Her relationship with her old high school friend, Zach Terrill, was a source of some confusion for her.

"Oooooh, I hate women like you. I've spent a lot of my hard-earned cash feeding and entertaining women who just tease me unmercifully," Jerome told her, ducking as Kay reached into the back seat to give him a punch of his own.

"It's not a woman's fault if she wants a nice night out. There's no law that says I have to be in love with a guy to have a date with him."

"If it ain't romantic then it should be Dutch treat! That's

my motto," Jerome said.

"Amen, brother," Lee agreed.

"So what about you and Alison?" Kay asked, glad that she had been able to divert the conversation away from the somewhat obnoxious, albeit interesting, Dr. Alan Eckhart.

"I wish Lester didn't hang out at her shop all the time," Lee grumbled.

"Surely you don't think Lester is moving in on you?" Jerome sounded like he wanted to burst out laughing.

"No!" Lee shouted back at him. "It's just that having him around cramps my style."

"You've got a style?" Jerome shot back.

"You're a big talker. Where's your girlfriend?" Lee asked.

"I got a lineup of girls."

"Okay, boys, that's enough," Kay said, putting an end to the conversation before it devolved into locker-room talk.

"There's Gatorwood," Jerome said, leaning forward over the seat and pointing to the apartment complex on the left side of the road.

Lee pulled in and parked next to the office. The hours listed on the door stated that it was closed on Sunday. An after-hours number for the manager was printed at the bottom of the sign.

"I'll call," Lee said, getting out of the car and heading for the bank of three payphones at the end of the small building. Off to the right was the large swimming pool, but with the cloud cover and steady north wind, the pool deck was empty.

The first phone wouldn't take his quarter. The second one worked.

"What?" asked a gruff voice on the other end of the line.

"I need to get into one of your apartments."

"Who are you? Which apartment?"

"One of your renters has died," Lee explained. "I'm a

funeral director and I'm here with a deputy. We need to get inside the deceased's apartment. His name was Brendan Rhodes."

"What's the apartment number?"

"I don't know."

"Crapola," said the grumpy voice. "Where are you?"

"At the phones by the office."

"Give me ten minutes."

Lee went back to the car where he filled the others in on the conversation.

"Apartment managers can be the worst," Jerome said, getting out of the car.

Fifteen minutes later, the manager came walking across the parking lot. Lee was surprised at how young he looked. Lee had assumed from the curmudgeonly attitude on the phone that the man must have been well over sixty. Instead, he looked to be in his late forties and had the bearing of retired military or law enforcement.

"I'll need to see some ID," the manager said, looking at the three of them.

Jerome pulled out his bifold and showed the man his badge. "And you are?" he asked, trying to take the initiative.

"Pete Walker. Come on in. I'll see if I can figure out which apartment he's in. Are there roommates?"

"We don't know."

"We've got three hundred people living here. Most of them students." Walker nodded toward the dozen or more individual apartment buildings, each of which were identified by a four-foot-high orange letter. He unlocked the office door and held it open while they filed inside. "Why do you need to get into the apartment?"

"Just being thorough," Jerome said in a tone that implied he wouldn't be offering any more explanation.

"You said Rhodes?" Walker was thumbing through a

metal filing cabinet. "It's easier to do it the other way. I've got a master list of the apartments by their building and number." He closed the drawer and opened the one below it. A minute later, he said, "Here it is. Brendan Rhodes. Funny, I don't remember him at all. Must not be a complainer. Older guy too. And there isn't anyone else on the lease. You'd think I'd remember that. Eighty percent of our tenants are students. Building G, apartment six."

He went over to a safe, turned the dial back and forth a few times, then opened it. "We keep the master keys in here when we aren't using them," Walker said as he pulled out a ring of keys.

They all walked across the parking lot to the building with an orange G on the side facing the center of the complex. Kay looked around at the people going about their business, unaware that one of their neighbors had died. Student housing was transient by nature and not a lifestyle that led to neighbors becoming close friends.

Why was an older man like Brendan Rhodes living here? Kay wondered. She remembered that both Art and Brendan's ex-wife had said that he was a skirt-chaser, which might explain his choice of living accommodations.

"He's got one of our smaller units, a two-bedroom," Walker said as they walked up to the second floor of the building. "Most of them are four-bedrooms leased by students who all share the rent."

Once they found apartment six, Jerome stepped in front of the manager and knocked on the door. Three raps, answered by silence. He knocked a little harder. After another ten beats, Jerome stepped back and nodded to Walker, who opened the door.

"Don't touch anything," Jerome reminded everyone as he slipped on a pair of latex gloves.

The air inside was stale and cool. Lee walked over and

looked at the thermostat. "Sixty degrees seems a little low," he commented.

"Spartan," Kay said, looking around. There was furniture, but no personal touches. The walls were bare without pictures or prints. There wasn't even any mail on the counter or dishes in the sink.

"I've seen this with divorced guys," Jerome said. "Like they left everything that was personal or special behind them when they moved out of their house."

"My ex-wife didn't let me take anything," the manager huffed.

Kay and Lee followed Jerome as he checked out the rest of the apartment. The smaller of the two bedrooms was completely empty. Jerome checked the closet anyway, just in case.

Lee led the way to the master bedroom, where at least they found furniture. There was a utilitarian bed without a headboard or footboard, made up with sheets, a light coverlet and pillows without cases. The nightstand held a digital clock, a lamp and nothing else. Inside the dresser were a few pairs of socks and underwear.

When Jerome pulled open the closet, they saw half a dozen shirts and pairs of pants, along with tennis shoes and one pair of Hushpuppies.

"Where's the phone?" Kay asked. "How many guys wouldn't have an extension next to the bed?"

They walked back to the kitchen and found a slimline phone with an answering machine, a red number nine blinking to indicate the waiting messages.

"Aren't you going to listen to them?" Kay asked when Jerome started to leave the kitchen.

"No. I don't want to screw up and accidently erase them." He'd read about that happening in a missing persons case up in Springfield, Missouri. A family member had played a message on the answering machine, which then automatically erased it. "If this turns into a murder case, we'll let the crime-scene folks handle it."

Kay didn't like it, but she knew he was right. They were already on thin ice being in the apartment at all.

Jerome opened the refrigerator. It held a bottle of Pepsi, some condiments and a half-eaten, moldy-looking Publix sandwich.

"Man didn't eat much," Lee said.

"Don't let anyone else in," Jerome told the manager as they were leaving.

"What if someone else has a key?" Kay asked.

"I can have the locks changed. We do it all the time," Walker offered.

"Do it," Jerome told him.

CHAPTER SEVEN

As they headed back to Melon County, the radio station was playing "A Horse with No Name." Jerome had called shotgun, so Kay was in the back seat.

"He's got another place," Kay said, reaching over the seat to turn the radio down.

"I was listening to that!" Lee complained, but then asked, "What makes you think that?"

"The way he was dressed at the memorial," Kay said. "He had on a nice shirt with cufflinks, a black tie, quality slacks, patent leather shoes. Does that sound like the kind of guy who would live like he'd taken a vow of poverty?"

"He still got along with his ex-wife. Maybe he kept some stuff over there," Lee offered.

"That wasn't the feeling I got. He hung around a lot, but didn't live out of the house," Kay said.

"I got a look in all the bedrooms at the Rhodes house. Only Lora's room looked used. I found a few men's shorts and T-shirts, but not much else," Jerome seconded. "The apartment was the address on his driver's license."

"I'll ask Zach to look into it. He can use his connections working for the county to request a property records search."

"You badmouth him, then use him. Typical woman." Jerome shook his head.

"I didn't say anything bad about him. I'm just not sure if we… click."

"Typical woman," Lee and Jerome said in unison. Kay kicked the back of the front seat.

It was fully dark by the time they pulled into the funeral home's driveway.

"I got to work tonight," Jerome told Ruby regretfully when she asked him in for a piece of freshly baked red velvet cake.

"You two *are* going to eat some of this cake," Ruby informed Kay and Lee.

"No argument from me." Lee smiled.

"What's a diet?" Kay followed them into the kitchen where Lester was reading the paper, a plate in front of him holding just a few red crumbs.

"Did you all have fun?" Lester groused from behind the paper.

"We went to the morgue and Brendan's apartment. Not really very exciting," Kay reported.

"I'm sure it was boring, running around playing detective," Lester replied.

"Anything happen while we were gone?" Lee asked, trying to get past Lester's hurt feelings.

"Nothing very much. I got us a funeral, that's all."

"You're kidding?" Kay said as she sat down at the table with an oversized slice of the blood-red cake.

"Nope," Lester said, still playing coy.

"Okay, I know you're bent out of shape 'cause you

couldn't go with us," Lee said. "I'm sorry. But you see, someone *did* need to stay here and answer the phone."

"They came by in person," Lester corrected him.

"Even more important that there be a knowledgeable person standing by to talk to them. Now that's as much butter as I can put on it. Tell me who the funeral is for," Lee begged.

"Brendan Rhodes." Lester lowered the paper and smiled at them. "That ex-wife of his came by and said that she wanted us to handle the funeral. Whenever they release the body."

"That'll be a couple of days. Though I'm a little surprised that she wants us to do it, seeing as he was poisoned at one of our services," Lee mused.

"We'll take it," Kay said decisively.

"Absolutely, I'm just surprised. I guess you and Jerome made a good impression." Lee smiled.

"What exactly did she say?" Kay asked Lester.

"She said she'd talked to everyone concerned, and they all felt like we should handle it."

"Did you ask about the whole 'he died at our service' thing?" Lee asked.

"I kinda did, yeah. She said they didn't hold it against us."

"Yang found an old firecracker," Ruby said, and they all turned to look at her. She was holding out a weathered Black Cat firecracker in her hand.

"Probably picked it up in the cemetery. I found a couple of bottle rockets out there after New Year's. Kids, I'd imagine. I remember going to the cemetery with Larry, a kid from school, to set off fireworks a few times when I was growing up." Lee looked thoughtful.

"I wouldn't be messing around in a cemetery like that." Lester was shaking his head.

"If Yang brought it home, it must mean something,"

Ruby said.

"That cat doesn't solve murders," Kay said.

"Just sayin'." Ruby didn't like her cats' abilities questioned. "More cake?" She started cutting more pieces before anyone could answer her.

"No." Kay grabbed up her plate, stopping Ruby from putting another piece of cake onto it. Then she left the kitchen while everyone else stayed for a second helping.

Kay wanted to call Zach about doing a records search on Brendan Rhodes. In the office, she sat down and picked up the phone. Oddly, she found herself thinking about Dr. Alan Eckhart. *Why would I think about that jerk when I'm getting ready to call Zach?* she asked herself.

Shaking it off, she dialed Zach's number.

"I was hoping you wanted to go out for a drink," Zach Terrill said after she explained what she wanted. By his tone, she could tell he wasn't joking. "But instead you want me to research some guy for you." He paused briefly, then figured it out. "Oh, the guy that died at the funeral."

"It wasn't exactly a funeral, but, yeah, that guy."

"And why do you want to know about him?"

Kay inwardly sighed before explaining the situation.

"I see." Zach sounded thoughtful. "I'll call around and pull in some favors. Give me a couple of days."

"That would be great."

"And…"

"We'll have dinner."

"I'll take what I can get."

"You're such a nice guy." Kay meant it.

"Ouch. I'm not sure that's the image I want to have."

"It's not the worst." Kay smiled to herself, then Eckhart's face popped into her head. *Is he nice? Do I care? Let it go*, she told herself.

"I'll call you when I have something," Zach said and

hung up.

After breakfast on Monday, Lee left Lester in the kitchen talking with Ruby and headed for the embalming room to get a head start on a long list of mundane chores. He immediately noticed an envelope on the floor by the back door. Someone had apparently shoved it through the old letter drop slot in the door that hadn't been used since before he was born. The envelope had his name neatly printed in thick black ink.

Lee picked up the envelope and turned it this way and that. Puzzled, he tore it open and took out the neatly folded piece of paper. The note read: *If you would like to save up to 50% on the cost of embalming fluid and other items, possibly including caskets, I can arrange it. Call this number anytime and leave a message.* The number was not local.

Is this a joke? Lee thought. Something about the note and the way it had been delivered made him think it wasn't. The very factors that made him believe the note was sincere also made him think that it represented something very shady.

How desperate am I? he thought. Very carefully, he folded the note and tucked it into his pocket. Moments later, Lester came in and they got started on Lee's list of chores.

Jerome's motorcycle pulled into the back driveway as Lee and Lester finished polishing the new hearse.

"Looks good," Jerome said, admiring how the spotless black vehicle seemed to glow under the winter sun.

"We have a big funeral in Gainesville tomorrow," Lee grumbled.

"I forgot that you're helping out the Garlands."

"We're not helping them. We've been hired to work their funeral."

"That accident was horrible. No matter how awful the

Garlands are, helping out the family is a good thing," Jerome said.

"That's what I have to remember," Lee said testily.

"What time do we have to be there?" Lester asked.

"Funeral's at eleven, graveside is at noon. So we need to get to the funeral home by ten," Lee told him.

"They'll have the full court press going. Father *and* son," Jerome observed.

"I don't like that little shit," Lester said in an unusual display of irritation that caused both Jerome and Lee to look at him.

"What'd Brad do to you? Not that you're wrong," Jerome said.

"Last couple of times I've seen him, he's been calling me Igor," Lester complained.

"Are we talking original *Frankenstein* or *Young Frankenstein*?" Jerome asked, causing Lee to stifle a laugh.

Lester stood up straight. "You take that back."

Jerome and Lee glanced at each other.

"Sorry. Just a joke," Jerome said, raising his hands in apology and feeling a twinge of regret. Lester normally took their joshing for the good-natured fun it was intended to be.

"Sure," Lester said, but Lee saw him bite down on his lower lip as he tried to keep his emotions under control.

"I agree that the son is worse than the father. At least Scott Garland pretends to be nice," Jerome said.

"Brad was a senior when I was a freshman in high school. There was a group of kids who tolerated him hanging with them because his father would let them use his limousines for dances or donate money for their field trips. I couldn't ever decide whether Brad really thought they liked him or if he knew they were just enjoying the fringe benefits," Lee said.

"He's a jerk," Lester said, gathering up the buckets and

containers of car polish.

"I told my supervisor that I went to Rhodes's apartment and about the toxicology report. He's going to push the sheriff to open it as a homicide."

"What about the thermos?" Lee asked.

"He had the crime-scene guys send it to FDLE." The county sent any forensic work off to the Florida Department of Law Enforcement for analysis. The department's primary mission was to assist local law enforcement agencies.

"The big question at this point is where did the nicotine come from?" Lee said.

"My two cents is on insecticides," Jerome said.

"We need to talk to the caretaker at the cemetery."

"You know him. Why don't we ride over there now?" Jerome offered.

Lester cleared his throat.

"Do you want to come along?" Jerome was still feeling bad about the joke he'd made earlier.

"Sure." Lester smiled.

"We'll take the Lincoln," Lee said, heading for the rack in the embalming room where the keys to the family cars were hung.

It was only a short drive to the cemetery where they found Sid Fuller's rusty Chevy truck parked beside the maintenance shed. The door of the shed was open and, when Lee rolled down the window, they could hear a lawnmower in the distance.

Fuller was the perfect image of a cemetery caretaker. Tall with a leathery face, his age appeared to be somewhere between fifty-five and a hundred-and-five, and he worked in the cemetery even when there wasn't any real work to do. On this bright winter's day, they found him mowing the dead leaves along the northern border of the graveyard.

Fuller turned off the lawnmower as soon as he saw the

three men walking toward him. Lee waved to him and Fuller smiled and waved in recognition as he climbed off the machine.

"Hey, Sid," Lee said as the old man removed the glove from his right hand so they could shake.

"That was a hellava thing the other day," Sid said.

"Sure was."

"We've had a few people die at funerals. Right after I started working here, I found an old woman slumped over by her husband's grave. Sad thing."

"We wanted to ask you a few questions," Jerome said, stepping forward.

"Ask away." Then Fuller's eyes narrowed. "But if it's about the dead guy, I don't know what you think I can tell you."

"Do you use any insecticides around here?" Jerome asked and Fuller's eyes looked wary.

"Yeah, especially on the wasps and things that build their nests around the monuments."

Lee realized that he didn't know what types of insecticides had nicotine in them. He'd envisioned powder, but could it have been a liquid like a wasp spray?

"Any other type?" Jerome pressed.

"I put stuff on the ant beds. What's this about?"

"We're just trying to eliminate some possibilities," Jerome assured him.

Fuller didn't look convinced. "How'd that man die?"

"We won't know until they do the autopsy." Jerome told the partial lie with conviction.

"So why're you asking about insecticides?" Fuller's eyes were narrow slits.

"From the way he died, the doctors believe that he might have been poisoned." Lee came to Jerome's defense.

"I didn't poison no one." Fuller's voice was suddenly

pitched higher. He looked left and right as though he was going to make a run for it.

"We aren't saying you did. We just want to eliminate the possibility that he might have been accidentally poisoned," Jerome told him.

"That's all," Lee chimed in.

"You with this lynch mob?" Fuller pointed to Lester, who'd been hanging back.

Lester was surprised to be singled out. "Mr. Fuller, I don't think—"

"You're all out to get me!" Fuller backed up and bumped into the mower. "Go look in the damn shed if you want!" He climbed onto the mower and, with hands that were visibly shaking, he started the engine and turned the mower around, almost running over Lee's feet in his haste to escape.

"What the hell was that all about?" Lee asked.

"That's a nervous man." Jerome shook his head. "Y'all ever seen him like that before?"

"Never. He's always been nice to me. Until now I'd have said that he's one of the most laidback old men I know."

"He's never been crazy like that," Lester agreed. "I've talked to him a couple of times about his job. You know, cleaning the stones and repairing the fence, stuff like that."

"Let's go look through that shed," Jerome said. "You got a flashlight in the car?"

Lester ran back to the car for the flashlight and met them at the shed. Jerome looked toward the sound of the mower and assured himself that the old man was staying far away before he stepped into the shed and turned on the light. The forty-watt bulb hanging from the ceiling didn't do much to illuminate the dark corners of the shed.

Lee was surprised at how neat the shed was. It was large enough that the lawnmower could be driven through the door, but if all the tools and supplies hadn't been well organized, it would have been impossible to get it all inside.

Jerome took the flashlight from Lester as he moved into the corner of the building where fertilizers, herbicides and pesticides were stored. The only pesticides were ant killer and wasp spray. He picked up one of the cans of wasp spray.

"It's got nicotine in it," he reported.

"But how hard would it be to extract it?" Lee asked. "You couldn't just spray the coffee with bug killer. No one would drink it. I can smell that stuff from here."

Jerome pulled out a small notebook and wrote down the name of the wasp spray.

As they stepped back into the sunshine, Jerome looked around for Fuller and saw him sitting on the mower, staring at them.

"That man has a secret he's worried about gettin' out," Jerome said thoughtfully.

When they got back to the funeral home, Kay greeted them at the back door. They told her about their expedition and how weird Sid Fuller had acted.

"I'm going over to Alison's shop. She said I could work a half day," Lester told Lee after Jerome had left.

With the others gone, Lee piddled around the embalming room. As he worked, Kay kept popping in and out, asking questions that she already knew the answers to.

"Okay, what is it?" Lee said after the fifth time she came in, putting down the case of embalming fluid he was moving.

"What?" Kay asked.

"You keep coming in here. What's up?"

"I'm just restless. You know me. I don't like to sit around waiting for events to play out."

"So what do you want to do?" Lee asked.

"Go talk with more of Brendan's friends," she blurted.

"I'm just killing time anyway." Lee pushed the box of

embalming fluid against the wall. "Let's go."

CHAPTER EIGHT

The first place they stopped was the home of Chaz and Vickie Dixon. The house was similar to Lora Rhodes's, except that it was much cleaner and the color scheme was more subdued.

"I'm glad you came," Chaz said, meeting them at the door. He was dressed in a flannel shirt and jeans, looking like a senior model out of an L.L. Bean catalog. "I've been wanting to talk with you. Art said Brendan might have died from poison."

He escorted them into the living room and offered them seats on the couch before dropping into an overstuffed chair across from them.

"We aren't sure about the circumstances of his death. That's why we wanted to ask you a few questions, if you don't mind?" Lee said.

"So long as I can ask my own," Chaz said with a sad smile. "Brendan was a great guy. A little wild, but that was part of what made him fun to be around."

"What do you mean by wild?" Lee asked.

"Oh, nothing crazy. I guess I just meant wild compared to an old married man like myself. We'd all go out for a drink and Art, Frank and I would be ready to go home while Lyle and Brendan would just be getting started."

"You didn't mention Benny," Kay observed.

"No. Benny doesn't go out much. Frank has more health issues than Benny, but you wouldn't know it." Chaz tapped his leg. "It's the leg. He was always shy, but after his leg got busted up and he lost a couple of inches off it when they put it back together, he's been almost a recluse. Trust me, I wasn't sure he was even going to attend the memorial service."

"Is he retired?" Kay asked.

"Never worked after the Army. He managed to get full disability payments." Chaz shook his head. "Some days I think he would have been better off if the government had denied the claim. The payments just allowed him to wall himself up in that house."

"Art said Frank helps him out?" Lee said.

"Yeah, we all do, but Frank and Benny have always been close. See, Frank was with him the night Benny got hit by that jeep. I think he feels some guilt over it. Crazy how a moment in time can shape two people's lives."

"How did Brendan and Benny get along?" Lee asked.

"They were friends, I guess. Brendan liked to be near the excitement and, like I said, Benny is a bit of a downer. It takes everything Frank can do to get Benny to come to Lyle's cookouts or one of our birthday parties."

"Was there anyone who didn't get along with Brendan?" Kay asked.

Chaz shook his head vehemently. "No. He was the first guy to apologize if he thought he offended someone. The only fault he had was liking to chase the ladies, but he was always polite about that. Not like some guys. He never was a groper or the type of guy to go after another guy's girl."

They talked for a little while longer, answering Chaz's questions about Brendan's death as best they good. Finally, Chaz apologized, saying he had to drive into Gainesville to pick Vickie up from the mall.

Kay sighed as they walked over to Frank's house. "So far everyone is saying the same thing. Brendan was a great guy who never made an enemy."

"Which reiterates the question of whether he was the intended target," Lee said, knocking on Frank's door.

After repeated attempts and no answer, they were getting ready to give up when they heard a loud voice asking if he could help them.

Lee looked over at the house next door to see Frank with a pair of hedge trimmers in his hands. He walked over with Kay and explained what they were doing there.

"Benny's not in a good mood. I think Brendan's death shook him up pretty bad," Frank told them. "We can talk inside."

It seemed a little odd to be invited into Benny's house by Frank, but after what Chaz had told them, it made sense. The house was clean, and the furnishings and decorations were uninspired. Frank left Lee and Kay in the living room, then went into the back to check on Benny, but he came back alone.

"I was right, he doesn't want to talk. But I'm happy to."

Frank sat down across from them, wiping sweat from his brow. "Oh, and if you see my daughter, don't tell her I was working in the yard. She thinks I'm an invalid." He saw the looks on their faces. "I know I wasn't feeling very well on Saturday. I've got an arrhythmia that acts up. When it does, I can't hardly get around. But I wasn't going to miss the lieutenant's memorial service."

Once again, the story they got from Frank matched the ones that Art and Chaz had told them.

"What do you think?" Lee asked Kay as they walked toward Lyle and Kelly Grant's house.

"Either they've all rehearsed the same story, or Brendan really was a nice guy with no enemies. Assuming the killer got the right guy, why do good guys get murdered? I can think of at least two reasons. One, they're in someone's way. Like a guy wants a girl or a promotion, and the good guy is blocking him."

"In the movies, it's always about the good guy seeing something he shouldn't or he picked up the wrong briefcase," Lee suggested.

"And there's always the money angle. Kill the good guy for insurance or inheritance."

As they were walking up the driveway, they saw Kelly Grant come around from the back of her house. She had a pack of cigarettes in her hand and, when she saw Kay looking at it, she stuffed it quickly into the back pocket of her jeans. She smiled in response to the look on Kay's face.

"I shouldn't be smoking. Lyle doesn't like it. You're the owners of the funeral home, aren't you?" Her expression became puzzled. "What are you doing here?" She wasn't accusatory, just inquisitive.

Kay explained and Kelly invited them into the house.

"Lyle is broken up about Brendan. They were best friends," she said, taking them into the kitchen. "I think he's out in the garage." She walked to a door that separated the kitchen from the garage and knocked before opening it a crack. "Lyle, the folks from the funeral home are here."

"I'll be right there!" Lyle called back.

"Men and their hobbies," Kelly said without further explanation. "Can I get you all something to drink?"

Lee and Kay both accepted iced tea. As Kelly handed

them each a glass, the garage door opened and Lyle came in. He was wearing overalls and a confused expression.

"What can we do for you all?" he asked.

Kelly and Lyle took seats at the table with them as Lee explained they were trying to find out more information about Brendan. The couple exchanged looks.

"Brendan was my best friend. Of all the old gang, we were the ones who… were still living," Lyle said, giving Kelly another look.

"He means they went out and got drunk on Friday nights." Kelly gave him a kindly smile and put her hand on his. "Brendan was young at heart, like Lyle."

Lyle leaned over and gave her a light kiss.

"Can you think of anyone who might have had a grudge against Brendan?" Kay asked.

"Brendan? No." Lyle paused. "I mean, we had an argument with Arthur Clegg awhile back when he had a friend's car towed. But as much as I hate that guy, I can't see him killing anyone. Besides, we were the ones that were pissed at *him*. He won that round."

They asked more of the same questions and received more of the same answers.

"This was a big nothing," Kay grumbled as they walked back to where her car was parked in the street.

"It's Clegg," Lee said, pointing toward a man who was standing outside in the yard two houses down and staring at them.

Kay looked where he was pointing. "Let's go talk to him." She was moving down the street before Lee could stop her.

Arthur Clegg was at least thirty pounds overweight, with all of it centered around his waist. His hair was thin and greased back.

"You know there are rules about parking on the street,"

he said as they approached.

"We wanted to talk to you about your neighbor Brendan Rhodes," Kay told him.

"Who the hell are you?" he responded.

"We're making inquiries into his death," Kay answered, hoping he might infer that they were from the police.

"I heard he died at a funeral. That's pretty ironic. You don't need to ask me any questions, 'cause I don't know anything other than that he belonged to the group of rowdies that live on this street."

"You had a run-in with him about someone blocking your driveway, didn't you?" Kay asked.

"No run-in about it. They were having another one of their illegal block parties and a woman parked in front of my driveway. I called the cops and had her car towed. Period."

"You didn't like Brendan?"

"I couldn't care less about him or his stupid friends. Especially that one." He pointed toward Lyle's house. "How many times do I have to call the cops on his parties before he's going to learn that he can't play loud music and his friends can't park wherever they feel like it?"

"When was the last time you talked to Brendan Rhodes?" Kay asked, trying to stay on topic.

"Hey, you never showed me any identification," Clegg growled.

"We never said we were with any law enforcement agency," Kay said.

"Then get the hell out of here before I call the cops!" he shouted, his face turning an ugly color of scarlet.

Kay and Lee backed off, leaving the man fuming at the edge of his property.

"He's a nut, but since he wasn't at the memorial service, he would have needed an accomplice to murder Brendan. Can you see anyone working with that jerk?" Kay asked.

"I agree. I think he's a red herring."

They rode back to the funeral home in silence.

The next morning, the sky was cloudy and the air cold and damp as Lee and Lester drove the Cadillac hearse into Gainesville. The Garland Funeral Home was on the east side of town, taking up half a city block with the main building resembling a Greek revival mansion. The home was surrounded by a parking lot that could hold at least a hundred cars.

"Wow!" Lester said, looking at the six-car garage at the back of the building. In front of each opening sat either a hearse or a family car, all of which were as new as the hearse they were driving.

Six funeral directors who worked for the Garland operation were drinking coffee by the back door. Lee recognized half of them. Butch Jameson waved to him and walked over to the hearse.

"So you're working for the dark side?" Butch smiled.

"I wouldn't be here if I didn't need the money."

"You may as well park it. Brad, the ass, is in charge of getting us loaded up and to the church on time. Mr. Garland is already at the church with the flowers and the biers. It's going to be a hell of a funeral." Butch took a sip of his coffee and backed away from the hearse so Lee could pull up to the building.

Thirty minutes later, Lee and Lester watched as two men rolled out a trolley bearing the casket of one of the victims and headed for the Lamberton hearse.

"At least they were all adults," Lester said.

"A husband and wife, the husband's uncle and two cousins," Lee said. "They were on their way to dinner at the Brown Derby. The guy who hit them is still in critical condition."

Lee opened the back of the hearse and the two men slid the casket inside. As Lee swung the door shut, he caught sight of Brad Garland going from hearse to hearse and giving the drivers instructions. When Lester saw Brad headed their way, he hopped into the front of the hearse and out of sight.

Lee took in a deep, calming breath as Brad walked up.

"You'll be third in line driving to the church and the same when you head to the cemetery. I'll organize the pallbearers. Don't talk to anyone but me or one of my staff. Remember, this isn't one of your half-assed services."

It took all of Lee's strength not to snap back at the insult. "So I assume you want us to just wait in the hearse?"

"Exactly. My people will direct the pallbearers to your hearse and assist them in loading and unloading the coffin." Brad looked at the hearse. "Not bad. Maybe we'll keep it when we buy your funeral home."

"That won't happen," Lee said in a voice so quiet that it should have warned Brad that he was pushing Lee too far.

"Ha! After one of your mourners dropped dead? I'd guess the value of your business dropped by twenty-five percent overnight. When was the last time you had a real funeral?"

"You've been coming into the county and undercutting our business." Lee kept his eyes on the ground, afraid that if he lifted them, they would blaze into white-hot anger.

"Good business. That's all we're guilty of. It's a shame that your father didn't teach you how to run a funeral home."

The comment about his dad was the spark to the gasoline. Lee charged Brad and grabbed him by the lapels.

"Listen, you little putz, don't you dare talk about my father!"

"Get you grubby hands off me!" Brad's voice rose as he panicked and tried to pull away.

"Did you hear me? You don't talk about my father." Lee's hands were still tight on Brad's jacket.

"Yeah, why would I want to talk about… your father?"

Lee loosened his grip.

Brad knocked his hands away and backed up. He composed himself and, with a little of his mojo back, said, "If I could get another hearse in the next half hour, I'd kick your ass off our property. After this I will do everything I can to destroy you, your sister and your broken-down funeral home." He turned and stalked off before Lee could respond.

Lee looked around and noticed several of the Garland funeral directors smiling. He knew that most of them respected the old man, but despised Brad.

"You were a lot of help," Lee told Lester, who was slumped down in the passenger seat.

"Bad things would have happened if I'd had to talk to that jerk."

"Hell, I didn't handle it very well myself." Lee climbed in behind the steering wheel. "Let's get this done and go home."

CHAPTER NINE

"How'd the funeral go?" Kay asked as Lee walked by the office.

He stopped and stepped over to the door. "Do you really want to know?"

"I guess it was tough helping out the competition," she sympathized.

"I think we can look forward to them redoubling their efforts to crush us." Resigned to the conversation, Lee walked in and dropped down in a chair facing the desk. "What hope do we have of surviving?"

"Well, the good news is that we won't owe much in taxes when April fifteenth rolls around."

Lee just glared at her.

"The truth is, we've eaten through most of the money in the bank. We've got maybe three months before we start operating in the red." Kay pursed her lips and shook her head. "I don't think I can keep going if that happens. At that point, how could we ever hope to climb back out? And we still owe Chester Madison for the money he loaned us. Right now, we might be able to sell the business and pay off all of our outstanding debts. Possibly even walk away with a little for ourselves."

"I won't sell to Garland," Lee stated flatly.

"Don't cut off your nose to spite your face. If we reach that point, we'll need to take the best offer we can get," Kay reasoned.

"Garland wouldn't throw us a rope. An anchor, but not a rope. I got pissed off at that snotnose, Brad, and grabbed him. I thought for a moment I was going to punch him."

"You in jail is all we'd need."

"He said that Dad didn't know how to run the funeral home. Actually, he said Dad never taught *me* how to run the funeral home."

"He's got a point," Kay said softly.

"Dad taught me. I just wasn't a very good student." Lee sank down in the chair. "There has to be a way out of this hole." He thought of the mysterious envelope he'd found and the offer of half-price supplies. Lee considered mentioning it, but knew that Kay would never go for anything shady.

"With the Garlands undercutting our prices, I don't know what we can do. We don't have the big reserves they've got to fight a price war," Kay said.

"There has to be another way." *The envelope*, the voice in Lee's head told him.

"Maybe if their reputation took a hit." She held up her hand. "But I'm not going to stand for any underhanded tricks to do it."

"Makes you think, doesn't it," Lee said darkly.

"What?" Kay asked. She knew how badly he wanted to save the family business and his comment worried her.

"Brendan's death at one of our services isn't going to

help our reputation."

"Unfortunately true."

"Brad said as much. He pointed out that our value was going to take a hit from the scandal."

Kay raised her eyebrows. "I see where you're going, but even the Garlands aren't that… dastardly."

"Maybe not Old Man Garland, but Brad…"

"He wasn't at the memorial service. How could he have slipped poison into the thermos?"

"Old Sid Fuller acted very suspicious when Jerome was asking him questions about insecticides. I was wondering what motive Fuller might have to poison Brendan."

"You think he might be in league with Brad Garland?" Kay asked in disbelief.

"I don't know. That would certainly explain a few things. I saw Sid during the memorial service. I didn't think anything about it because he always hangs around close to the services. He told me once that he feels like the cemetery is his second home, so he wants to be a part of whatever is happening there. Hell, most of the time he knows the person being buried, or at least half the mourners."

"So it's possible?"

Lee shrugged. "I never saw him near the table with the coffee and tea."

"Brendan was walking around. Maybe he met Sid at some point and Sid was able to slip the poison into his tea."

"Sounds farfetched," Lee admitted.

The phone rang. Kay answered and talked for a minute before mouthing: *Zach.*

"Really?" she said into the receiver. "Dream Acres Road? No, I don't know where it is." She wrote down directions on a pad. "That much? Wow. Very interesting. Thanks, Zach. Dinner tomorrow. Absolutely." She hung up the phone.

"That's a big smile," Lee said, looking at her Cheshire

grin.

"Brendan had a secret. He had a house, one that the property appraiser values at $268,000 dollars."

"So the market value would be more?"

"Guaranteed."

"Where is it?"

"North side of Gainesville. A newer subdivision, according to Zach. Brendan bought the house around the time he separated from Lora."

"Think she knows about it?"

"If so, it's funny she didn't say anything."

"If he had a house, then why did he keep that apartment?" Lee wondered.

"Maybe that will be obvious when we see the house." Kay stood up.

"Now?"

Kay looked at her watch and then outside. "It would be almost dark by the time we got there. Damn it! Fine, we'll go in the morning."

"Good, I'm going over to Alison's."

"Will you be here for dinner?" Ruby's voice came from the hall outside the office.

"Do you always eavesdrop, or only on special occasions?" Kay yelled back.

Ruby stepped around the corner and into the office. "You don't have to yell. I hear what I hear. Fried chicken, mashed potatoes and green beans, with banana pudding for dessert," she said in an attempt to lure Lee into dinner.

"Sounds great. Maybe Alison and I will come over after she closes up the store."

As good as the menu sounded, Lee really wanted to get away from the funeral home for a little while. Knowing that they were probably going to have to sell it was depressing. A little voice in the back of his head was beginning to say defeatist phrases like: *Why bother?* and *It's wasted time and energy.*

"I'll keep the food warm until nine," Ruby told him. "Darkest before the dawn. Remember that."

Can she read my mind? Lee wondered. *Nah. It's probably just written all over my face.*

When he walked into the electronics store, Alison was talking to a family. Two kids in their early teens were excitedly trying to sell the idea of a VCR to their parents. Dad, slightly pudgy with a receding hairline, looked like he was on board. It was Mom, tall and skeptical, who looked unconvinced.

"We've already got a hundred titles for rent and more on the way," Alison said to Dad.

"How often are we going to want to watch the same movies? You've got a hundred and there isn't any of them I want to see," Mom argued.

"We'll be able to record shows too," the girl said, flipping her ponytail around.

"You do hate it when you miss your shows," Dad pointed out.

"I'll never figure out how to… What do you call it…?"

"Program it," the boy said. "I'll do that for you. I can, right? Set it and it will record her shows?"

"Sure can. It's easy," Alison assured them. She decided to let the three yes votes work on the nay without butting in.

Five minutes later, Mom surrendered and the discussion turned to which machine to get.

Soon they were out the door with Alison promising that she would come help set up the VCR and show them how it worked if they had any problems.

"There's another one out the door." Alison smiled.

"What?" she asked when she saw Lee's expression.

"Maybe we should hire you to sell funerals." Lee had wanted to leave his concerns down the street at the funeral home, but they seemed firmly perched on his shoulders.

"Bad?"

"Not any worse than it's been for the last year. Which is to say, yes, bad."

"I don't think I'd be any good at selling coffins." She came over and took his hand.

"Apparently I'm not either." Lee tried to smile. "I'm sorry. Self-pity is a turn off."

Alison squeezed his hand. "You can't help being depressed when you're getting the sharp end of the stick."

"It's that bastard Brad Garland." Lee went on to tell her about their confrontation before the funeral.

Some window-shoppers came in and Alison gave them a brief sales pitch while Lee tried to talk himself into a better mood.

"There has to be a way you can keep them from stealing your clients," Alison said after the customers had left.

"Kay and I have both tried to think of some way of beating Garland. The worst part is that I talked Kay into this. If she'd had her way, we would have sold the funeral home in '81 and walked away with a sizeable chunk of change. Now we'll to be lucky to get out without still being in debt."

"You'll figure something out, even if it means selling the funeral home and working for someone else." Alison was being as supportive as she could.

"I don't want to move away. Not now." He gave her a hug.

"You can work for me," she said teasingly.

"I'd be worse at selling TVs than I am at selling funerals."

The phone rang. Alison answered it and then held the phone out to Lee. "It's for you."

"For me? Who is it?"

"I don't know." She waved the receiver at him.

"Yes?" he said to the caller after taking the phone.

"Glen here. I wanted to let you know that the autopsy is done and they're going to release the body."

"How'd you know I was here?"

"Your sister told me. That's okay, I needed to talk with her too. I had a message for her from Alan."

"Alan?"

"Eckhart. The doctor you all met Sunday."

"What was the message?" Lee asked.

"For her ears only," Glen said archly.

"We'll pick the body up tomorrow."

"I guess the guy dying at the memorial service isn't going to help the funeral home," Alison said sympathetically once Lee was off the phone.

"Let's forget all that and go out to eat." He didn't want to go home right now.

"I've got to close up. Where do you want to go?"

"Anywhere as long as we can put some miles between us and this town."

Lee woke up later than usual on Wednesday, his head pounding with a hangover. He and Alison had eaten at Steak n'Shake in Gainesville before going over to the Red Lion Pub for a drink. One drink had turned into enough to make him lightheaded and a little silly. Alison had taken the keys and driven them home. Now all he wanted to do was brush his teeth and drink a gallon of water.

"About time you got up!" Kay yelled from downstairs when she heard him moving around. "I want to go look at Brendan's house."

"If you stop yelling, I'll get dressed," Lee moaned as he

stumbled into the upstairs bathroom.

Later, sitting in the kitchen and eating a bowl of banana pudding for breakfast, Lee began to feel a bit more human.

"Sugar is good for a headache," he told Kay as she gave the bowl a doubtful glance.

"You don't have a headache; you have a hangover. Y'all have fun?"

"I'm going to screw up my relationship with Alison because I can't think about anything else but losing the funeral home." Lee finished the pudding and frowned at Kay. "Happy days."

"That's a TV show, not real life. Ready?"

"Sure, we'll check out Brendan's house and then go by the morgue and pick up his body. I'll get Bertha's keys and meet you outside."

Kay stepped outside and breathed in the cool air. A front had passed through and left another perfect winter day in its wake.

"This is going to be conspicuous when we pull into his driveway," Kay said, looking at the old hearse.

"Maybe the neighbors know he's dead, so a hearse won't seem that unusual," Lee said without any conviction.

They both climbed inside and Lee turned the key in the ignition. Then they heard a *boom* loud enough to rattle the windows.

"What the hell was that?" Kay asked. "It sounded like a mortar round." She'd heard her share in Vietnam.

Lee was staring at the dashboard of the hearse, which was still running with a gentle rumbling. "Scared me. I thought it was Bertha for a minute."

He turned off the engine and they got out and looked around.

"Did you hear that?" Lester called, running out of the embalming room.

"Over there!" Ruby shouted from the landing at the top of the stairs that led to her apartment over the carport. Lee and Kay looked up and then followed her pointing finger to see a column of black smoke rising in the air.

"That looks like it could be in the cemetery. Get in," Lee told Kay.

By the time they drove the short distance to the cemetery, they could hear sirens in the distance.

"There," Kay said, pointing through the windshield as they pulled through the gates of the cemetery. The maintenance shed was gone. A smoking hole was in its place and pieces of wood and parts of tools were strewn across the nearby graves.

Lee parked as close as he could without impeding the approach of the fire engine that was pulling in behind them, then he and Kay jumped out of the hearse. They were a hundred feet from the ruins of the shed when they spotted the torn and bloody body on the ground. Lee didn't have to get any closer.

"That's Sid Fuller."

Kay ran toward the body but stopped fifteen feet away when she saw the condition of his head.

"There isn't anything we can do for him now." Kay turned and shook her head, walking back to Lee. Firemen ran past them with their hoses as two sheriff's cars pulled through the gate.

"This isn't a coincidence," Lee muttered.

CHAPTER TEN

The responding deputies questioned Lee and Kay for a few minutes, but once they made it clear that they'd been several blocks away when the explosion occurred, everyone lost interest in them. Unfortunately, none of the deputies were ones that Lee felt comfortable asking questions of and Jerome wasn't scheduled to work that morning.

"There isn't anything else we can do here," Lee told Kay.

"You're right. Let's go look at this house of Brendan's," Kay said, feeling a sense of helplessness that she'd felt hundreds of times as a nurse.

For the first several miles of the drive, the siblings were lost in their own thoughts. Then Lee broke the silence.

"Sid acted crazy when he thought Jerome suspected him."

"Blowing yourself up seems like a tough way to commit suicide," Kay observed.

"Maybe someone else didn't want him to talk."

"He could have been an accomplice or a witness."

"Is there any chance it was an accident?" Lee said to himself as much as to Kay.

"You saw the inside of the shed. What do you think?"

"Everything was neat and tidy. Not a place where accidents happen. Besides, Sid's been working there for years."

"I think it's rare for maintenance sheds to blow up, so let's take accident off the table," Kay said drily.

"Suicide seems unlikely too. Which leaves us with another murder."

"Two murders in the same cemetery in one week. I think it's safe to assume they're related." Kay glanced down at an Alachua County map that she'd dug out of the glovebox and pointed through the windshield. "The turn is coming up."

"That must be it," Lee said when he saw a driveway with an impressive sign announcing Woodland High, a gated community.

The driveway led to an elaborate entrance with stone walls and a ten-foot-high double gate sporting a large golden W and H. They both relaxed when they saw that the guard station was unoccupied.

On the other side of the gate was a large billboard showing that several of the five- and ten-acre lots were still for sale. This explained the unfinished feel of the subdivision. They passed several roads that went nowhere and cul-de-sacs waiting for home to be built.

"That's his street," Kay said as they approached the back of the development.

"These ain't cheap houses," Lee commented as he turned the hearse onto a cul-de-sac with five houses lining the pavement. All of the houses were two-story brick homes with upscale cars in the driveway.

"That's his." Kay nodded at a brick Federal-style home with a red BMW in the driveway. "Wonder whose car that is?"

"I'll park at the curb." Lee wanted to be able to make a quick getaway if things went south.

"This house is worth more than our business," Kay said as they walked up the brick path to the front door. "Can this really belong to Brendan?"

Lee walked up to the solid oak front door and pressed the button on the ornate brass doorbell. A deep, almost mournful bell ding-donged inside. They waited, but heard nothing. He pressed the doorbell again. When three more minutes had passed without a sound from inside, they stepped back down the front steps.

"Now what?" Lee asked.

Kay glanced over her shoulder at the neighborhood.

"I say we have a look around."

Lee thought about protesting, but the aftermath of the explosion had left him shaken and with a sense of urgency to find out what was happening.

"Okay, this way." He walked toward the two-car garage. "I'm beginning to think Brendan had a secret life."

"I think that goes without saying." Kay was hurrying to get around the side of the house so they'd be out of sight of the neighbors.

All the rest of the doors and windows were locked. The back yard and out-buildings were well maintained and neat, giving no clues about the owner.

"We'll get the tag number off the car in the driveway," Kay said as they came back around to the front of the house. Just then, they heard the rumble of a car engine.

"That's the BMW!" Lee yelled and broke into a trot.

They made it to the front yard just in time to see the red car back out of the driveway, spin around on the pavement and roar off down the street.

"Damn it!" Kay stomped her feet in frustration.

"I should have gotten the tag number first," Lee said.

"It was a fairly new red BMW with Alachua County tags. There can't be that many of them."

"Whoever owns the car must have been in the house or the garage."

"So why didn't they answer the doorbell?" Kay mused.

They looked back at the house one last time before getting into the hearse and heading for the morgue.

"Glen said he gave you a message from Dr. Dreamy. What was that all about?" Lee turned and smiled at her.

Kay thought about telling him it was none of his business, which it wasn't, but since she'd decided to ignore the doctor's advances, she didn't see the harm in telling Lee the truth. "It appears the Dr. Eckhart isn't very good at keeping track of important documents. He lost my number and wanted me to call him."

"And?"

"I figure that's fate telling me to let it go," she said wistfully.

"With the funeral home going under, marrying a doctor sounds like a viable backup plan," Lee joked, receiving a punch in the arm. "Hey! You used your knuckles." He rubbed the sore spot.

"I'm not going to date based on a guy's income."

"He wasn't bad looking either."

"Then *you* date him."

Kay was sounding grumpier by the minute, so Lee decided to let it drop.

Glen Doyle wasn't on duty when they got to the morgue. The woman at the desk greeted Lee with a polite smile that acknowledged their acquaintance, but nothing more than that. After a quick discussion on the phone, she informed them that an orderly would meet them at the loading dock with the body of Mr. Rhodes. They were headed back to

Lang in less than thirty minutes.

Jerome, dressed in his green uniform, was talking to Lester in the driveway when they pulled up.

"Sutton got the case," Jerome announced.

"Hell," Kay muttered.

"Tell me about it," Jerome agreed.

"So will you still be able to look into the murders?" Lee asked.

"That's the worst part. He's decided he wants me on the case."

"So that's good, then," Lee said, his tone upbeat.

"No, it's not. He just wants me working under him so he can keep an eye on me and nitpick everything I do," Jerome explained.

"And he wants to get back at us," Kay said.

"Y'all sure made an enemy of him over the Dobbs case."

"Doesn't take much to make him look bad," Kay shot back. "And I only laughed after I knew he wasn't killed by the runaway fire truck."

"He squealed like a frightened pig when he saw it coming." Lee chuckled at the memory.

Jerome held up his hands. "You know what I think of him. If it had just been Sutton, I don't know that I would have hit that truck and pushed it into the crypt."

"Regardless of what an ass he is, we can't afford to let him screw this up," Kay said in a determined voice.

"She's right. The business is already teetering on the edge. If we don't clear up these deaths, we don't stand any chance of saving the business," Lee said.

"That's fine, but you need to understand that I'm going to be under a microscope, watched by someone who'd like to see me run out of town," Jerome said. "I need my job. Especially if y'all aren't gonna be paying me."

"Did you know that Brendan Rhodes had another

house?" Kay changed the subject before Jerome could tell them that they couldn't snoop around on their own.

"Where?" Jerome asked.

Kay and Lee filled him in on what they'd discovered.

"I'll start looking for the BMW when I get to the office. I'm still pulling road duty too, so it's hit or miss on when I'll have a chance to work on it."

"I would think this would be a priority," Lee said.

"If it was a priority, then the sheriff wouldn't have handed it over to his idiot brother-in-law. When I asked Sutton, he said that no one cares about an old Army guy and some cryptkeeper who blows himself up."

"Great." Kay shook her head.

"We need to get Brendan out of the back of the hearse." Lee looked at Lester.

"I'll get the trolley," Lester said, and headed for the embalming room.

Half an hour later, Lee and Lester were busy cleaning up Brendan's body.

"You would think they could do a neater job sewing the bodies back together," Lee complained as he undid the ragged stitching where some morgue intern had closed up the "Y" incision in Brendan's chest.

"Can I finish it?" Lester asked. With the small number of funerals recently, he wanted to take every opportunity to get better at the art of embalming.

Lee stepped back and handed the curved, three-inch-long needle to Lester.

"I bet you Garland doesn't even bother cleaning up the mess that the morgue leaves," Lee said as he watched Lester meticulously sew up the incision. Lee had to remind himself to be patient as he watched Lester do a job that he could have done just as well in half the time.

I owe Lester the opportunity to practice, he reminded himself.

Besides, how long will it be before I'm *working for someone else?* Lee let his thoughts go down that dark path for a minute before shaking himself. *We aren't out of business yet.*

As Lester finished closing the chest wound from the autopsy, Lee inserted the tubes so that they could drain the blood while replacing it with embalming flood.

Lee looked hard at Brendan as the pump ran. *Where did you get that house? Why didn't anyone in your life know about it?*

Kay was working on her own tax return in the office. Like the business, she hadn't made much money, so she didn't owe any taxes. It was small comfort. She knew they couldn't go on like this.

As she was completing the form, the phone rang.

"Yes, I know I agreed to dinner," she responded to Zach Terrill's half-joking reminder.

"Six?" he asked.

"Six will be fine."

"I'll pick you up."

"Where are we going?"

"I want it to be a surprise."

"I need to know what to wear," Kay argued.

"Good point, actually. Jeans, flannel shirt, a jacket and a sturdy pair of shoes," Zach told her.

"I guess we aren't going to the Brown Derby."

"You're right," he said without elaborating.

"Okay. I'll play along."

"See you this evening," he said and hung up.

Kay thought about her relationship with Zach. It was casual to her, but how serious was he taking it? When they were together, there was an intensity to him that set off her alarm bells, but she didn't push him away. What did that mean? She needed to make up her mind. If she wasn't in it for the long run, she needed to make that clear to Zach. He was a longtime friend and she didn't want to hurt or alienate him.

Ruby had made chili for dinner. With only Lee, Ruby and Lester at the table, it would have made for a quiet meal except for the fact that Ruby and Lester talked enough for a dozen people. Lee had been lost in thought as he ate his first bowl of chili and didn't tune into the conversation until the topic of Yang's prognostic abilities came up.

"What did you say?" he asked.

"I just pointed out that Yang tried to warn us about the explosion at the cemetery," Ruby said while refilling Lester's bowl. "Do you want cheese on it?"

Lester nodded and Ruby grated a quarter pound of cheddar on top of his bowl of chili.

"How?" Lee asked, and then he remembered the firecracker. "Oh, you've got to be kidding."

"Not at all," Ruby said, reaching for his half-empty bowl. He put his hand over it to keep her from adding more chili.

"That seems like a stretch," Lee argued, though he couldn't forget some of the cat's other freakishly on-point deliveries of odds and ends over the last two years.

Ruby waggled her ladle at him as though he should know better. "You should pay more attention to him."

Lester asked if she'd ever had any other psychic pets and the two of them went off on a wild tangent that let Lee sink back into his own melancholy.

As he was rinsing out his bowl, there was a knock on the front door. Lester and Ruby were still going at it, so Lee trotted out front to answer it.

"Hi," Zach said a bit awkwardly as Lee invited him in.

"Kay! He's here!" Lee shouted up the stairs.

"Down in a minute!" Kay shouted back.

"Want a drink or something?" Lee asked.

"No. I… I've got some wine… for this evening," Zach stuttered.

"You kids," Lee joked, even though he was seven years younger than Zach and Kay. He noticed that Zach was dressed more for a hike than a night out. "Going camping?"

"Sort of… a picnic." Zach looked up the stairs, clearly hoping that Kay would appear soon.

"It's dark." Lee stated the obvious. When Zach didn't answer, he decided to let the guy off easy and not ask any more questions. Kay was more than capable of taking care of herself. Besides, Lee trusted Zach.

"I'm ready," Kay said, clumping down the stairs in her ankle boots. "I hope you weren't joking about needing sturdy shoes."

She smiled and gave Zach a light peck on the cheek as he stepped forward to greet her. His eyes had followed her all the way down the stairs, admiring the fit of her jeans and the curves that even the loose flannel shirt didn't hide.

Kay grabbed her jacket from the rack by the door. "What is this secret destination?" she asked.

"You'll find out," Zach said, holding the door for her.

Something about his attitude made her nervous. He was more assertive than his usual laidback self. Suddenly she realized that she was feeling attracted to this more determined version of Zach.

Thirty minutes later they were driving south on U.S. 441 out of Gainesville. They passed a sign for Payne's Prairie Preserve State Park, then Zach pulled off onto a dirt road.

"This is mysterious," Kay said.

When they came to a tube gate, Kay turned to Zach, who put the car in park. "What now? This doesn't look like much of a parking spot."

"I have a key." He held it up and got out of the car. "This is a friend's property."

Zach opened the gate and they drove down the narrow dirt road. The arching branches of live oak trees, illuminated by the headlights, formed a canopy over their heads.

Kay would have been concerned if she'd been on a date with anyone else. A quarter mile down what had become little more than a path, the woods opened up to reveal a bluff that overlooked the prairie.

"Their property adjoins the park," Zach told her. "Come on," he urged, climbing out of the car.

"Sure," Kay said, not sounding sure at all.

Zach went to the trunk and pulled out a picnic basket, a small cooler and something in a long case. He handed the cooler to Kay. Zach turned on a flashlight, casting a red glow around them against the moonless night.

"Can you see okay?" Zach asked.

Kay nodded. She didn't have to ask why Zach had a red filter on the flashlight. She'd learned in the Army that a red light was kindest to night vision.

They followed a short path to the bluff that overlooked the prairie.

"I guess you know all about how the prairie was formed when the lake drained over the course of a few days in 1891," Zach said.

"We came here on a field trip when I was in middle school. It fascinated me that a ferry boat used to cross the lake that wasn't there anymore."

Zach took out a telescope from the bag he'd been carrying. "You can make out the houses on the bluff on the other side. This is why I come here." He heard himself and added, "Not to look at the houses, but to look at the stars."

Kay looked up and felt a sense of wonder at the star-filled sky that stretched out above them. "I didn't know you were an astronomer."

"Hobby I picked up in college. I needed a science elective. Little did I know it would get under my skin."

"I learned most of the constellations when I was taking Latin in high school. It was an extra credit assignment," Kay admitted.

"Mrs. Durden?"

"Snappy fingers herself. Whenever she called on anyone, she'd snap her fingers." Kay snapped her own in imitation of their teacher.

"That's her. I had her for French."

"Funny, knowing the constellations meant a lot to me when I was in Vietnam. I would look up at the sky and recognize the stars. Somehow that made me feel closer to home."

"The Pleiades, The Seven Sisters, always fascinated me," Zach said, pointing up at the sky. "Here, you can look through the telescope."

They spent an hour looking at planets and different stars.

"Are you hungry?" Zach asked after a while.

"I really am." Kay sounded surprised. "I was so fascinated by the stars that I didn't notice until you mentioned food."

"My neighbor helped me pack this." Zach opened the picnic basket, took out a blanket and spread it on the ground. Next, he took out a small battery-operated lamp and set it up. "I'd have used candles, but it can get pretty breezy on the bluff."

There were cheese and ham sandwiches, potato salad, chocolate truffles and a bottle of wine.

"Wow!" Kay said as they dove into the food.

Once her hunger pangs were gone, Kay relaxed and sipped wine from her glass.

"You look thoughtful," Zach said.

"I'm relaxed, which is a very nice feeling. There hasn't been a lot of that since I moved back to the funeral home."

"Things aren't going well," Zach said. It was a statement, not a question, as she'd told him all about the problems they were having with the business.

"They're going to get worse. I haven't taken a salary in four months."

"Lee let you do that?"

"He doesn't know. The money just isn't there. Besides, my personal expenses aren't that much, so I've been able to live off of my savings."

"You shouldn't have to drain your savings."

Kay sighed. "I feel like I'm to blame. I should have insisted on selling the business when I first came down instead of pretending like I could save it. I'm a nurse, not a businesswoman."

"You're being too hard on yourself. All you wanted to do was help your brother."

"The thing is, I knew better. I never should have let him talk me into trying to save a business that had too few assets and too many deficits. Now we're on the verge of going broke." Kay took a deep breath. "I'm sorry. You put all of this together and all I brought to the picnic were my problems."

"I'll take you with all your problems." Zach leaned in and took her hand before kissing her. She allowed the kiss, but didn't let it go a step past sweet—nothing that asked for anything more. While part of her was willing, she didn't want Zach to become a complication. She had enough of those right now.

"Thank you for a beautiful evening. I should probably get home."

Zach didn't let go of her hand. "I wish you could give me some hope that our relationship can get past friends."

"We *are* more than friends. And the trouble is I don't know where it can go. I'm really not using you. There's just too much going on. I don't even know if I'm going to be staying here much longer. If we're forced to sell the funeral home, I might have to go somewhere else for a job."

"I know. I… just think we…" Zach shook his head. "I'll stop. I'm happy with any time and any type of relationship you can give me… for now."

"Thank you. That's all I'm asking. Time for me to see what's going to happen with all this mess."

Kay looked into her heart and tried to decide if she was being completely honest with Zach. She decided it was as close to the truth as she could get right then.

With both Kay and Zach lost in their own thoughts, the ride back to Lang was quiet except for the radio playing Al Stewart's "Year of the Cat."

CHAPTER ELEVEN

Lee was in the office shortly after Kay left on her date when the phone rang.

"You have Brendan's body?" Lora Rhodes asked.

Lee had left a message on her answering machine letting her know that he had picked up her ex-husband from the morgue and needed to discuss the plans for the funeral.

"When would you have time to come by and discuss the details?" he asked her now.

"I can be there in half an hour," Lora said.

Lee wasn't surprised that she was anxious to get it done. Family members usually wanted to have the details sorted as quickly as possible so they could concentrate on their grief. He could remember hearing people come by at all hours of the night when his father ran the home.

"That will be fine," he said.

When the doorbell rang, Lee opened the door to find Lora standing there, looking nervous and a little flustered.

"I've talked to some of his distant relatives. None of

them are coming down for the funeral and they didn't seem to care what type of service we have."

"Come on into the office and we can talk about the options. I know it can all seem overwhelming," Lee said gently.

Before sitting down at his desk, Lee chose several brochures from a rack on the wall.

"Do you have a budget?" he asked, knowing that almost every other funeral director would have let her look at brochures showing caskets, flower arrangements and service options *before* having the budget discussion. The clients would invariably pick high-end options, setting their sights too high for their budgets. This would almost certainly lead to the grieving family agreeing to things they couldn't afford.

Lora looked surprised to be asked. "I don't know. What does a funeral usually cost?"

"A few thousand to several thousands of dollars," Lee said honestly.

"Wow! I don't know."

"Do you think his estate can pay for it?" Lee had an ulterior motive in asking. He wanted to get an idea if Lora knew about Brendan's fancy house in Gainesville.

"Maybe. I mean he's got his car. Maybe a few possessions. He didn't take much when he moved out. Brendan wasn't a very fancy guy. Always dreaming of the big score, but never really willing to work for it. If you know what I mean," Lora said with kindness and a trace of sadness.

"I see," Lee said, disappointed that she didn't seem to know more. "Who is his heir?"

"I am. I guess. I hadn't really thought about it. I just assumed... He doesn't have any close family now that his parents and his older brother are dead. We wrote up our wills ten years ago." She looked perplexed.

"That's a question for his lawyer," Lee suggested.

"I never thought to call Santos. He's been Brendan's lawyer for years."

"Best to talk to him and make sure that Brendan hadn't made any special stipulations about his funeral in his will."

"Can we go ahead and make some of the arrangements? I really don't think he made any other plans."

Lee wanted to point out that Brendan had a house she apparently didn't know about, just to see what her reaction would be. *Don't want to let too many cats out of the bag*, he told himself.

"Of course. We can go ahead and get everything selected and then, if you'll check with his lawyer tomorrow, we'll be able to move forward. How does that sound?"

"Thank you."

They spent the next hour choosing a casket and deciding on a date, time and place.

"There's so much involved. It's like planning a wedding in three days," Lora said as she was signing the preliminary paperwork.

"Did Brendan have any other… I mean, any lady friends after you two separated?" Lee was thinking of the stealthy BMW that had driven off from Brendan's house.

"Funny you should say that. A year ago, I would have said there wasn't anyone else, but during the past year he's been… busy a lot more. After we got a divorce, he was always hanging around the house. Actually, he was around more than *before* the divorce. Of course, he'd also just retired."

"What did he say he was doing?"

"Playing golf, mostly. He did lose some weight. Ha, I guess that could be because he had a girlfriend."

"Would you have been mad if he did have a girlfriend?" Lee asked.

"No. Not at all. I've had a couple of guys that I've dated. If he had found someone, that would've been fine. Honestly, I'd been enjoying the fact he hadn't been hanging out at the house as much." Lora scrunched up her face. "That doesn't sound too good, does it? I just mean it's awkward having your ex coming and going all the time."

"I understand," Lee sympathized. He'd been watching her closely during this exchange, trying to detect any lies. All he heard was a slight hesitancy that suggested deep emotion. Did she know about a lover and was she angry about it despite her words?

When Lee walked into the kitchen at a little past eight on Thursday morning, he was surprised to see that Lester's usual seat nearest the refrigerator was empty.

"Where's Lester?" he asked, assuming that the younger man was doing some chore for Ruby. Ever since he'd moved into an apartment with a new roommate, Lester had been punctual—a considerable change from the first couple of years he'd worked for the funeral home. When Lee had questioned him about his newfound sense of time, Lester had admitted that his roommate got up at seven in the morning and would monopolize the bathroom and make a general mess. Lester found it easier to get up and out before the roommate was stirring.

"I haven't seen him this morning," Ruby said. "I called his apartment. All I got was a busy signal. I think you should go on over there and check on him."

Ruby didn't offer him a plate or suggest that he sit down, though there were pancakes on a platter near the stove that had Lee drooling.

He waved her concerns away. "Lester's probably fine. He does indulge from time to time," Lee said, miming a hit from a joint.

"He wouldn't be sleeping in when he knows I'm making pancakes." Ruby lifted her eyebrows and wagged her spatula at him. "*Especially* if he's been smoking weed."

Lee sighed and was about ready to give up and go look for Lester when Kay walked in.

"Ruby's not feeding anyone until we find Lester," he groused.

"Lester is lost?"

"I told him I was making pancakes this morning." Ruby used the spatula to point at his empty chair.

"She has a point," Kay told Lee.

"Lester has been late before," Lee pointed out.

"When I was serving pancakes?"

Lee looked from Ruby to Kay and back again.

"I can't argue with that," he admitted.

"Brendan's death and then the explosion at the cemetery could have all been aimed at us," Kay said thoughtfully. "Maybe we *should* check on him."

"That's a happy thought," Lee said, feeling his stomach grumble. He grabbed a pancake, folded it over and took a bite, then headed for the embalming room to get the keys to the family car. "Okay, we'll go check on him. I'm sure he's just recovering from a late night of hanging out."

Ten minutes later, they pulled into the driveway of Lester's garage apartment.

"There's his car." Lee pointed out the green Ford Maverick that Lester had bought for two hundred dollars and spent more time trying to fix than drive.

"Is that a good sign or a bad sign?" Kay asked.

They walked up to the door and Lee knocked.

"Sounds like someone is ransacking the place." Lee was about to knock harder when the door flew open. A frazzled Lester looked out at them.

"I don't have time, guys. Sorry, I guess I didn't call. I'm just… I don't have time." He started to close the door, but Kay stepped forward and stopped it with her foot.

"What's going on?"

"Oh yeah, I guess I didn't… Come on in. I've got to get the place cleaned up."

"Ruby was worried about you when you weren't there for pancakes," Lee chastised him.

"Pancakes." For a moment Lee had Lester's full attention, but then he shook his head. "I've got to get ready."

Kay and Lee looked at each other before following Lester inside.

"Lester, settle down and tell us what's going on," Lee ordered.

The apartment was cluttered with the standard bachelor effluvium. An ancient vacuum sat in the middle of the room, along with a trashcan.

"My mother is coming!" Lester said, his voice near-hysterical.

"I didn't even know you had… I mean have… I mean you've never mentioned your mother." Lee had never seen Lester so frantic.

"Oh, I have a mother all right," he said, shaking his head. "She is… frightening. Now, sorry, but I really have to get this place cleaned up."

"You can have the day off. That's no problem," Lee told him.

"I've got to talk to you about that too. The Rhodes funeral you booked yesterday. I've got to, like, be the lead funeral director. You know, kind of front and center." Lester's words flew out of his mouth a mile a minute as he began throwing junk in the trashcan.

"Whoa! Hold up, hoss," Lee said, stepping forward and

blocking Lester's path. "What are you talking about?"

"My mother is coming to the funeral. She's related to the ex-wife. She called me at six o'clock this morning to tell me she's flying into Gainesville at two."

Thoroughly amused, Kay said, "I get it. You need to look like a big man in front of your mother."

"You don't know her," Lester said, dodging around Lee to grab more trash. "This place has got to be clean. Like spic-and-span clean when she gets here."

"We'll talk about the funeral," Lee promised him.

Lester stopped in his tracks and looked at Lee with pleading eyes. "I've got to look... important. I know, I know, this is kinda crazy, but you don't know how she is."

Kay saw more than a hint of fear in his eyes and stepped in. "We'll make sure you look good."

Lee glanced at her with raised eyebrows.

"Look good. Not give him a promotion," she said.

"No, that's fine. All I want is to look... like someone, you know?"

"Sure, we'll arrange it so you can impress your mom," Lee relented.

"Now I got to get this cleaned up." Lester grabbed for a pile of laundry and Lee stepped aside to give him room.

"You said your mother is related to Lora Rhodes?" he asked.

"Yeah, weird, right? Mom said she's some sort of cousin. I didn't know 'cause Mom's maiden name is Wilkins and, of course, Rhodes is the cousin's married name. You know what I mean?"

"Would your mom know anything about Lora and Brendan?" Lee asked.

"How would I know?" Lester's voice was shrill and panicky. "Don't you understand? I don't have time to think. I have to have this place clean, like, really, *really* clean, before she shows up!"

"Calm down. I get it. We'll let you get back to work," Lee said.

"Have you ever seen him that way?" Kay asked when they were back in the car and heading home.

"No. He's never even mentioned his mom, let alone the fact that he's terrified of her."

"He certainly wants to impress her."

"Most kids want to look good in their mother's eyes. That seemed a little extreme."

"That was a little more than what I'd expect from a twenty-three-year-old."

"I suppose we'll find out more when we meet her," Lee said.

"We'll have to find a way to ask her questions about Brendan and Lora Rhodes."

"I was thinking the same thing. With luck, she was close to her cousin and we might learn a few family secrets."

"We can tell her it's worth her son's job. 'Cause if we don't put this murder to rest, we'll *all* be looking for new jobs," Kay said.

"It's Brad Garland that needs to be put to rest," Lee grumbled.

"Careful. In mystery stories when you say something like that, the person turns up dead."

"And your point…"

"The person who said it ends up in jail," Kay said bluntly.

"But they're usually proven innocent."

"Usually."

"Okay, okay. Can I just wish that his dad will kick his ass out of the family business and keep the family business out of *our* business?"

"That's better," Kay said as they pulled into the driveway of the funeral home.

Ruby was waiting at the kitchen door for them.

"He's fine," Lee assured her. "He's just having a nervous breakdown because his mother is coming for a visit."

"That poor boy. He's made mention of her perfectionist ways. I'm going to take off the rest of the morning and help him get ready," Ruby said, taking off her apron.

"I'm sure he can—" Kay started, but Ruby was already half out the door.

"Just put any leftovers in the refrigerator," she said over her shoulder.

Kay and Lee looked at the half dozen lukewarm pancakes sitting on a plate by the stove.

"No fresh pancakes for us," Lee said, watching Ruby head up the stairs to her apartment with her two fat cats toddling along behind her.

"Guess we know who she cares more about." Kay shook her head and went over to the stove. Looking down at the pancakes, she said, "I'm going to have some Frosted Flakes."

"I'm not proud. I'll eat the pancakes. With all the Lester drama, I forgot to ask how your date went," Lee said, putting the pancakes in the microwave.

"It was interesting," Kay said, sitting down with her cereal. "Zach is a good guy, but…"

"Yeah, I hope that's not where I'm going to end up with Alison. It would help if I knew whether we're going to be living here in six months."

"Hey, things are looking up. We have a funeral. Which would be better news if the man hadn't been murdered at one of our own memorial services," Kay said.

Lee told her all about the visit from Lora Rhodes the night before.

"For an ex-wife, she sure is a big part of his life. So how is it that she doesn't know about that house?"

"I'm not convinced she doesn't. There are plenty of

people who can lie with a straight face."

"And if she knew about the house… then what else did she know about?"

"Who was the person that drove off in the BMW?" Lee wondered.

"That house is a major clue. I'm going to do a little more snooping around and see what I can find out."

"You can't go by yourself," Lee said, knowing that Kay had a habit of taking unhealthy chances.

"I'll call Jerome. I think he has this morning off."

"Okay. As long as you don't go digging around on your own. Anyway, I need the office this morning to work on the arrangements for Brendan's funeral. I can't finalize anything until I get a call from Lora, but at least I can get the ball rolling so we have the casket and everything we need for the funeral."

Lee spent the rest of the morning placing orders over the phone and reserving the church. At noon, the phone rang.

"I talked to Mr. Santos, Brendan's lawyer," Lora told him. "He said that the only provision in his will about the funeral is a stipulation that he be buried with his uniform. Not *in* the uniform, because he's a little bigger now than when he was in the Army."

Lee thought that Lora sounded different than she had the day before. *More cautious?* he wondered.

"Of course. We talked about a military service. Do you still want to go forward with that?"

"I'll talk to Art." Lora sounded unsure. "But we can stick to everything else we discussed."

"And you're all right with the budget?"

"Oh yes," Lora said quickly, then seemed to pull back a little. "I mean, I'm sure that will be fine."

Lee thanked her for calling, then put in all the orders for the funeral. As he worked, he thought about Lora's tone on the phone. Something about it bothered him, but he couldn't put his finger on exactly what it was.

CHAPTER TWELVE

Jerome roared up to the funeral home on his motorcycle twenty minutes after Kay called him.

"We can take my car," she said.

"Oh, hell no! Not on a day like this. I had plans for a ride this morning and that's what I'm goin' to do. Ride. Here." He handed her the spare helmet he'd brought for her.

Kay was not a fan of the motorcycle, but as she looked up at the painfully blue winter sky, she shrugged and gave in.

She swung her leg over the back of the motorcycle and tightened the chin strap on her helmet. "Keep it under sixty."

Jerome flashed her a wicked grin and her stomach tightened. "I feel like flying this morning," he laughed.

Kay just had time to grab hold of his waist before the motorcycle spun in a circle and growled as it pulled onto the street.

Kay had ridden with Jerome a few times and she was always surprised how much she enjoyed the thrill of it once she was on the motorcycle. For all his bravado, Jerome was a skilled and cautious driver. Kay had once overheard Ruby tell him to be careful as he was leaving the funeral home. He'd stopped and told her that he'd seen enough accidents that he wasn't going to screw around and end up as stain on the pavement. So Kay relaxed, at least a little, and let the wind lift her spirits.

Thirty-five minutes later they pulled into the parking lot of the Gainesville Police Department. Jerome pulled up next to a couple of investigators who were leaning against their unmarked cars and talking. Kay recognized one of the men as Milton Towers. It would have been hard for her *not* to recognize him, as he weighed almost three hundred pounds and had three inches of cigar perpetually hanging out of the side of his mouth. Jerome had introduced her to him two years ago when they'd needed help with another murder.

"Jerome!" Milton greeted them with a huge smile. The other officer he'd been talking to waved and got into his car. "Man, when are they going to move you into criminal investigations?"

"You know the answer to that." Jerome stuck his hand out for a knuckle-crushing shake from Milton.

"Yeah, when hell freezes over… or as long as your sheriff is dead set on keeping that numbskull in-law of his on the payroll. Let me grab my notes from the car and we can talk about your latest problem."

Milton pulled a yellow legal pad out of his car and leaned on the hood. "I checked out the address you gave me. Zilch. There haven't been any calls for service. But here's the golden ticket. I had one of our interns dig through traffic citations going out about a mile from the house. One of them was a speeding ticket given to a woman in a red BMW with Alachua tags. Here's the lady's name."

He handed Jerome a sheet of paper listing the address for

an Annabelle Destiny on the west side of Gainesville.

"That name…" Jerome started, but he stopped when Milton held up a finger, chuckling.

"What? You don't think many parents would name their daughter Annabelle Destiny? I'd call you a cynic, but you're right. Ms. Destiny is a working girl. High-end, but a working girl just the same. She even went to the trouble of legally changing her name."

"That's a first," Jerome said.

"In my experience too. I guess we've just been dealing with the wrong class of prostitutes."

"How do you know she's a prostitute?" Kay asked.

"I found three reports with her name attached to them. In the first one, she was the victim of a beating. This was five years ago. Someone tossed her out of their vehicle near where the Oaks Mall is now. A good Samaritan stopped and called the police. I'll leave out the scandalous details that point to her being tossed out by her john. The second time, she was accused of stealing a man's wallet. The man was extremely intoxicated and the wallet was located in the hotel room they were sharing. The last one was a trespassing citation. The Howard Johnson's called the police after a disturbance in one of their rooms. The man and Miss Annabelle didn't have anything bad to say about each other, but the motel wanted them both off their property."

"Okay, that's pretty good evidence," Kay admitted.

"There hasn't been any trouble from her in the last six months, which could mean she's not been as active in the trade."

"Like she might have found a steady sugar daddy," Jerome suggested.

"That's one possibility. The other is that she's been out of town."

"Is this the address from the vehicle registration?"

Jerome asked, looking at the paper Milton had handed him.

"Yep. Who knows if it's any good." Milton picked up his pad. "That's all I've got for you."

"Thanks, Milton. We'll check this out."

"Keep me in the loop. Sounds like some of this is spilling over into our jurisdiction."

"You're always in the loop," Jerome said, putting his helmet on. Kay followed suit and climbed on the bike.

"They don't make those things big enough for me," Milton laughed as Jerome waved and drove away.

Anabelle Destiny's address matched a neat little Spanish-style duplex on a lot shaded by live oak trees dripping with moss. The BMW was parked alongside a Chevy Bronco in the shared driveway.

"Driving a BMW and living in a nice duplex. Life is being good to Ms. Destiny," Jerome said, climbing off of the motorcycle. He'd parked to the side of the BMW. "Now I wish we'd brought your car. Try and block a driveway with a motorcycle and all you end up with is a crushed motorcycle."

"Do you think she saw Lee and me at Brendan's house?" Kay asked.

"We'll know in a minute." He set his helmet on the seat and strode toward the door.

Jerome's knock was firm, but not demanding. He didn't want to put her on the defensive too early.

They heard footsteps from inside and a woman clothed in a silk dressing robe answered the door.

"Sorry, guys, I'm not buying anything and, if you're from a church, I promise you it would burst into flames if I came inside."

She started to close the door, but Kay blocked it with her foot before Jerome could react.

"We want to talk about Brendan Rhodes." Something about the way Annabelle had said "guys" had rubbed Kay the wrong way.

"Never heard of him," Annabelle said and put all her weight behind the door in an effort to close it.

With one hand, Jerome pushed it open. With the other, he pulled out his deputy's star and flashed it.

"You want to talk to us," he said firmly.

Kay felt some satisfaction at the flash of fear in Annabelle's eyes. She backed away from the door.

"May we come in?" Jerome asked.

"What are you, vampires? The door is fu... open," she said.

Jerome entered first, with Kay on his heels. Anabelle pulled her robe a little tighter around her hour-glass figure. Kay had to admit that with her long black hair and bright green eyes, she was a striking woman.

"What kind of stitch-up is this?" Annabelle's voice was bitter.

"We just want to ask you a few questions about Brendan Rhodes," Jerome explained. "Like what was your relationship with him?"

"Now I know you're joking. Use your eyes." She turned her body a little to the left and back to the right.

"So you admit you're a prostitute," Jerome said.

"I was an aspiring wife until last Saturday."

"How long had you known him?" Kay asked.

"Long enough," Annabelle said. When she saw the look on Jerome's face, she added, "Six months. I met him in Vegas."

"But you're from Gainesville?" Jerome tried to understand how they had met two thousand miles away when they both lived in the Florida college town.

Annabelle sighed heavily. "Come on back to the kitchen. I was just getting my first cup of coffee when you busted in here. I'll need some caffeine if we're going back that far."

Once they were in the kitchen, Annabelle offered them a cup which they both refused, but Kay did sit down at the table with her. Jerome took the opportunity to walk around the kitchen and look in all the corners.

"You're a snoop," Annabelle told Jerome while she took her first sip of coffee.

"That's what I'm paid for. So tell me about this meet-up in Vegas."

"Have you ever been to a big casino?" she asked, and they both shook their heads.

"They stage junkets for people that have money. I've never been clear on whether the casinos themselves are behind them, or if it's travel agents doing it with the consent of the casinos. Whatever. Sometimes they hire girls to go along. Sweeten the pot, so to speak."

"Keep the men's minds off of how much money they're losing," Jerome said with a frown.

"Look at you. A quick study. Alcohol, women, anything a guy could want as long as he's losing a bundle."

"And Brendan was on one of these junkets?" Kay asked.

"Please!" Annabelle shook her head. "He didn't have enough money. The guys they fly in are big wheels, not small cogs. Brendan was there with some veterans' tour group or something." She shrugged.

"Okay, you've explained why you were both there. Now we want the details. How did you bump into him?" Jerome asked.

"You aren't far off. I *did* kind of bump into him." Annabelle sighed again. "I got drunk. Maybe I said something to this fat pig of a millionaire that I shouldn't have. Anyway, the tour guide running the group kicked me out. I got tossed out of the group and out of my hotel room. Guess I was still a little drunk, and when I went to get in the elevator, I bumped into Brendan and we fell on top of each other. He was really sweet. A lot of guys would have copped a feel, but he just helped me to my feet."

"What happened next?" Kay felt drawn into the story.

"He took me to his room. I know how that sounds. Not that I wasn't, you know, selling it, but even an escort can be taken advantage of. Not Brendan, though. He had a room with two double beds, and he said I could sleep on the other one until I got sober. Kind of stupid of him. I could have been pulling a con and robbed him blind. Anyway, next day, I woke up and there was Brendan waiting to take me down to breakfast."

"What about your luggage?" Jerome knew that details could trip up a liar.

"Brendan went with me to the front desk. The guy running the junket had left my bags there. Only thing missing was some of my jewelry that the bit… woman I was sharing a room with probably stole. Never saw that stuff again." She took a long drink from her mug of coffee and stared out the window. "What happened to Brendan? The newspaper just said he dropped dead at the memorial service."

"He was murdered," Jerome said, watching Annabelle's face.

She opened and closed her mouth a couple of times as though she wanted to say something but couldn't come up with any words. Finally she managed, "No. He… He'd wanted me to go to the memorial service with him."

"Have you met any of his friends?" Jerome asked.

Annabelle hesitated for a second. "No. Would it surprise you to learn that most men don't take me home to meet their mothers? Or their friends." Her words were coated in bitterness. "But Brendan had fallen in love with me. It wasn't the first time, but it was the first time a man had wanted more than sex from me. He was finally ready to tell his friends about me."

"What did you want from him?" Kay asked.

"I'm not an idiot. Every day I look in the mirror and see my paycheck getting smaller. I need to get off this train before it gets to the end or the line. Brendan represented a stable life for a change. We weren't fooling each other. And you know what? We were both happy with our part of the bargain. Brendan was a nice guy, and I was a nice piece of arm candy that had learned to like him."

"How long would that have lasted?" Jerome smirked.

"I'm not stupid or an ingrate. I would have made it work for both of us."

Kay heard the sincerity in Annabelle's voice. "Where did he get his money?" she asked.

Annabelle looked at her with an odd expression on her face. "You don't know?"

"I'm asking you," Kay tossed back.

"He does truck stuff," Annabelle said hesitantly. "I mean, he used to drive a truck, but he'd retired. Though he still met up with other drivers from time to time."

Kay and Jerome looked at each other.

"Did you ever meet any of these drivers?" Jerome asked.

"I'd go with him once in a while. It was mostly at rest areas and truck stops."

"Did you know that Brendan had an apartment at Gatorwood?" Jerome asked.

"Sure," Annabelle said as though it was obvious.

"Why?"

"Oh! Oh…" Annabelle said as though she'd just gotten the punchline of a joke. "This is about his ex-wife, isn't it? Are you a detective like Jim Rockford or Joe Mannix?"

"No." Jerome stopped short of saying that he was on official business, since technically he was off duty. "Why do you think this is about Lora Rhodes?"

"Because that's why he had the apartment. So that she wouldn't know about… his…you know, money and house and all that."

"His assets?" Kay suggested.

"Yeah, exactly."

"He told you he kept the apartment so his wife would think he was broke?" Jerome asked.

"That's right."

"Were you living at Brendan's house?"

"Not exactly, but I spent a lot of time there."

"Were you thinking about getting married?" Kay asked.

Annabelle held out her hand where an engagement ring with a sizable cluster of diamonds sparkled.

"But you still kept this duplex?" Jerome observed.

"I own both halves. This was kind of my investment. Brendan didn't have anything to do with it."

"He was hiding his wealth from his ex-wife, but he wanted you to go to the memorial service with him?" Jerome couldn't hide his skepticism.

"I wasn't supposed to say much," she said quietly. "He just wanted me to meet his friends."

"Because he was going to marry you?"

Annabelle hesitated.

"Was he?" Jerome pressed.

"I… don't know," Annabelle admitted and hastily added, "He said he was."

"So why didn't you go to the memorial service?" Kay asked.

Annabelle shrugged. "I don't know. It was… confusing. I kinda got creeped out by the… you know, the graveyard thing. Also, I was able to ignore our age difference when it was just me and Brendan. You won't believe this, but we had fun. Brendan had a silly sense of humor that made him seem younger. But I thought that if I got around a bunch of his friends, I'd start seeing how much older he was than me."

"Was he disappointed that you didn't go?" Kay asked.

"He said he wasn't. He might have been relieved. I think he'd partly offered to take me 'cause I'd been accusing him of not being serious about marrying me."

"Even with the rock?" Kay nodded toward Annabelle's hand.

"Other men have bought me rings. Still, here I am."

"Can you think of anyone who might have wanted to hurt him?" Jerome asked, getting back to the purpose of their visit.

Annabelle shook her head, but then said, "He seemed, I don't know, on edge lately. I thought it was because of the ring and me pushing for a wedding."

"Nervous how?"

"He would jump when the phone rang. A couple of times he took calls and went to talk in his office."

"Did you eavesdrop on the calls?" Jerome asked.

"Not really."

"What's that mean?"

"Once I heard a man's voice, I'd hang up."

"Was it always a man?"

"Yes."

"The same man?"

"No… different men."

"Did you recognize any of their voices?"

Annabelle rolled her eyes. "How could I? I didn't know any of his friends."

After a few more questions and no useful answers, Jerome and Kay walked out of the kitchen. Annabelle followed them.

"I need a cigarette," she said, joining them on the front porch and lighting a cigarette before the front door was even closed. "I never smoke in the house. My own rule and I hate it. My plan was that, after Brendan and I got married, I'd rent out my half of the duplex. I didn't want the smell to turn off any non-smokers. Guess I don't have to worry about that anymore."

Jerome and Kay said their goodbyes and walked toward his bike.

"Where to now?" Kay asked with an eager smile.

"I know what you're thinking and we can't do that. We need to get a search warrant before we go in Brendan's house," Jerome said sternly.

"Still, it could be interesting to snoop around the place a little."

"Pointless if we find something and can't use it." Jerome looked at the duplex where Annabelle Destiny stood smoking her cigarette. "I've got an idea," he said, walking back toward Annabelle.

"Forget something?" She smiled.

"Did Brendan ever give you a key to his house?"

"Sure."

"Can we use it?"

"I thought you were a cop?"

"Yeah, I'm a deputy, but I just want your permission to go into the house and look around."

"Go ahead." She smooshed the butt of the cigarette into a flowerpot near the door. "I'll go get the key. I already got my stuff out of the house." Annabelle was inside for less than a minute. "And, no, I didn't steal anything. I may sing for my dinner, but I'm not a thief." She dropped the key into Jerome's outstretched hand.

"Thanks, I'll bring it back."

"Don't bother. That chapter of my life is over."

Once on the bike, Jerome weaved his way through the back streets to Brendan's secret house.

"Funny how empty it looks." Kay put her helmet down

on the bike, which Jerome had steered all the way up in the driveway and parked near the back door.

"All houses look empty when you know that the owner is dead," Jerome said.

He went up to the door with Kay close behind him. When he went to put the key into the lock, he stopped. "Not good," he said, pointing to a missing pane of glass near the lock.

"I'll never understand why someone would install a cottage door without a double-sided deadbolt." Jerome sighed and tried the door, which was locked. "Fancy that. They relocked it after they broke in," he said, turning the key that Annabelle had given him.

They entered the kitchen to the sound of crunching glass.

"Watch where you step and don't touch anything." Jerome dug in his pockets and managed to come up with a single latex glove. "One is better than none." He slipped it on, then flipped the nearest light switch.

"Nice!" Kay admired the expensive cabinets and appliances.

"Everything in this house looks new," Jerome commented, looking over the glasses and dinnerware in the cabinets.

"Not a lot of the usual clutter either."

"Looks like he just bought the house and had it furnished."

They wandered through the living and dining rooms. Nothing looked out of place.

"I wish that all burglars were this neat," Jerome said.

"The TV and stereo are still here," Kay said, pointing at the high-end items.

"I suspect our thief knew what he was after."

They went through the rest of the house room by room, finding nothing unusual except for two empty drawers in an office desk.

"Whatever they took was in these drawers," Jerome said.

Kay looked at them. "So someone broke into the house just to take whatever was here. Could it have been money, files, some other sort of paper?"

"People keep all kinds of stuff in their desk. Could even be a bottle of whiskey or a gun, but I'd say paperwork," Jerome agreed.

"Why?"

"'Cause I don't think Ms. Destiny would have left something valuable and portable."

"You didn't buy her 'I'm not a thief' line?" Kay asked with a raised eyebrow.

"I think it would be very easy for her to justify taking some valuables. After all, the man's dead and he'd told her he loved her. Wouldn't he want her to have something to remember him by?"

"I see your point. Two empty drawers aren't much of a clue. Do you think he was killed for whatever was in the drawers?"

"No way of knowing until we catch the murderer or the thief. All we *do* know is that someone was willing to risk a lot to get whatever was here."

Jerome dropped Kay off at the funeral home forty-five minutes later.

"I've got to get ready for work. I'm going to ask our crime-scene guys to go fingerprint Brendan's house. Whoever broke in could be our killer. Of course, he probably wore gloves, but it's worth a try."

"I'll fill Lee in on what we found. Or didn't find, I guess is more the truth." Kay gave Jerome a short wave before heading for the house.

"Did you get Lester's place cleaned up?" she asked Ruby as she passed the kitchen.

"That young man sure is worried about looking good in his mother's eyes," Ruby told her. "He's taking her out to dinner tonight."

"I'm sure he'll be fine."

Kay headed for the office. Finding it empty, she went to the embalming room where she found Lee working on Brendan's face.

"What did you find out?" Lee asked her, putting down his tray of reconstructive putty and makeup.

Kay told him about Annabelle and what they hadn't found in the house.

"Annabelle Destiny. That's a name for the record books." Lee shook his head and smiled. "So where did Brendan get his money? When I talked to Lora, I probed as much as I could. She acted like she didn't know anything about his secret life."

"Do you believe her?"

"I think that she is either ignorant about it, or she's guilty of something and is going to lie to protect herself."

"I think the next question is, who inherits the house and any money he had?"

"Lora thinks *she's* going to inherit," Lee said. "If he was talking about marrying Annabelle and Lora found out about it, that gives her a money motive. How much do you think he had?"

"That was quite a ring on Annabelle's finger."

"You said she met him in Vegas. Maybe he won the money."

"That's possible," Kay said doubtfully. "I guess it would kind of make sense. Though Annabelle mentioned that he was meeting truckers all the time."

"Those could have just been friends from when *he* drove

trucks."

"Questions on top of questions," Kay mused.

"At least we have a funeral," Lee said with a nod toward Brendan. "Shame he can't just tell us all of his secrets."

"Even if he could talk, he might not be able to tell us."

The phone rang and Kay walked over to the wall to answer it.

"Kay, this is Chester Madison. I've got a death I want you and your brother to look into."

Chester Madison owned an insurance company out of Atlanta. Kay's high school boyfriend, Rick Bruhn, had worked for the company and sold a considerable number of policies around Lang and the rest of Melon County. After Lee and Kay were instrumental in solving Rick's murder, Madison had offered them a loan to help keep their business afloat in exchange for their occasional assistance looking into local deaths that might cost his company large insurance payouts.

"Is it Brendan Rhodes?" Kay asked him now.

"Who?" Madison sounded confused. "No. It's Sid Fuller. He was killed in an explosion at the cemetery."

"Yeah, we saw it. Or at least we saw the aftermath. Why are you interested in Sid's death?"

"He had a half-million-dollar life insurance policy with us."

"Sid?" Kay gave Lee a quizzical look. "He was the maintenance man at the cemetery. Would you all really have given him a policy for that amount of money?"

"If he could pay for it. In fact, he's been paying for it for the last fourteen years. His job when he applied for the policy was as an assistant bank manager," Madison said.

"I'm going to let you talk to Lee. He knew Sid better than I did."

Lee had already walked up to stand beside Kay. "Lee

here. Sid started working at the cemetery nine years ago. I remember Dad worrying about him being a drunk."

"Rick would have checked his application when Fuller bought the policy," Madison explained.

"I'll look into it. I don't know anything about his life before he became the cemetery's sexton."

"Check on his background and find out whether this was an accident or a murder."

"Who is the beneficiary?" Lee asked.

"The original beneficiary was his wife, Roxie Fuller. But in 1975 he changed it to his daughter, Valerie Hartford."

"We'll see what we can do," Lee said.

Madison gave him a curt goodbye and hung up. Lee wasn't offended. Chester Madison was very generous to them and he never asked any questions about their still outstanding loan.

"That was interesting," Kay said. "Valerie Hartford is going to come into a chunk of change."

"Is there any possibility that his death is *not* connected to Brendan's murder? I'll talk to the board that oversees the cemetery. Sid worked for them. They'll know his background."

"I have to believe the two murders are connected," Kay said.

"I'm not sure how we can help Chester. Sid's death is almost certainly murder, which means they'll have to pay out."

"I remember talking to him when we were looking into another death, and he said that some of the policies have a… sort of morality clause where, if you were doing something illegal when you were injured or killed, then they can deny the claim. If Sid was involved in Brendan's murder, then they might not have to pay."

"I wonder what Sid's daughter is like. I'd hate it if she's a nice woman who's deserving of compensation and we find out something that screws her over," Lee said.

"Bridges to cross when you get to them," they heard Ruby say from out in the hall.

"How many times have we told you not to eavesdrop?" Kay shouted.

"You don't have to shout." Ruby appeared in the doorway.

"Guess that's right," Kay said with a frown.

"Come get your dinner. I've got pork chops, green beans and ham, mac and cheese and biscuits."

As soon as Ruby started going over the menu, Kay felt her hunger surging. She let her nose pull her toward the kitchen.

There were only three place settings on the table.

"It feels odd not having Lester here," Lee said, looking at Lester's empty seat.

"Have you figured out how you're going to make it look like he's important at the funeral?" Kay asked.

"The funeral is Saturday. I'll just let him strut around looking important. Jerome can help me with the actual work."

"He needs this," Ruby said as she cut up a pork chop for her cats. "I told you he's afraid of that woman."

"One of us should talk to his mother. I'll let *you* do that." Lee was pointing his butter knife at Kay. "I'll research Sid's background while you go meet this Valkyrie and see what information she has on her cousin, Lora Rhodes."

"Thanks." Kay was stabbing green beans while she talked. "At least if I'm talking to Mrs. Andrews, I shouldn't run into that jerk Wade Sutton. I'm not looking forward to meeting him again." Kay's prior run-ins with Sutton had left her mad enough to punch the wall. Now, whenever his name came up, all she could think of was that line from Jim

Croce's song: "…big and dumb as a man can come…"

"Maybe we'll get lucky and the case will be solved before we have to deal with him," Lee said optimistically.

Kay shook her head. "I'm not that lucky."

CHAPTER THIRTEEN

Lee was already hard at work Friday morning, making preparations for Brendan's funeral, when Lester showed up.

"Where have you been?" Lee scolded him.

"With my mother." From Lester's tone, he may as well have said he was standing in a vat of acid.

"She can't be that bad."

Lester gave him a look that made Lee rethink his comment.

"Sorry, I know parents can be hard to deal with."

"I just want to get this funeral over with so she can go home."

"Help me dress him and we'll be that much closer to being done," Lee said. Lora had dropped off a suit at nine that morning, and Brendan's uniform to be placed in the coffin.

As they maneuvered the body into the suit, Lee thought about how many funeral directors would cut the back of the deceased's shirt and jacket so they didn't have to lift and wrestle with the corpse. However, Lee carried on as his father had, dressing the body as though they were going to go for a walk down the street later that day.

"He looks good," Lester said, stepping back.

"Glad you approve."

"Hey, I helped," Lester pointed out. "Have you thought any about what I asked?"

Lee considered stringing Lester along for a while, but decided it would be cruel. "Jerome and I will do the hard work tomorrow. You can walk around and act like you're in charge."

"Thanks! I… This means a lot."

"Remember this the next time you're getting stoned on a work night."

"I'm not late very often."

"Only because you don't want to miss breakfast."

Lester smiled sheepishly. "You got me there. Okay, okay. I'll be on my best behavior for… at least a month."

Believe it when I see it, Lee thought without malice.

"The casket should be here by noon. Don't sign the invoice or let the driver leave until you're sure it hasn't been damaged."

"And if it's damaged, don't take delivery. I got it. Where're you going?"

"I want to check up on Sid's background. Did he ever tell you anything about what he did before he worked at the cemetery?"

"He mentioned a daughter a couple of times. I remember that because I couldn't imagine what she was like. He was kind of… odd. Nice enough, but… odd."

"Kay's going out too, so answer the phone if it rings."

Lester perked up at this. He liked the responsibility. "Don't worry, I got it."

Lee didn't worry *too* much. He knew that Lester was smarter than he sometimes acted.

Lee's first stop was to see Reverend Sam Beck at the First Methodist Church. Reverend Beck was one of the three board members who oversaw the upkeep of the cemetery.

"Come in," the reverend said when Lee knocked on the door of his office. "Do we have a funeral scheduled?" In his mid-seventies, Beck was still sharp, but Lee had noticed occasional moments of forgetfulness.

"No. I wanted to ask you some questions about Sid Fuller."

Beck took in a sharp breath. "It's shocking. I'm devastated that something like that could happen in our cemetery and kill poor Sid. Awful, just awful. I guess you're going to be handling the funeral?"

"I'm not sure. I just… You know Jerome, who works for me part time? He's also a deputy and I told him I'd talk to you about Sid's history." All of this was true. Lee wasn't going to lie to a minister… unless it was absolutely necessary.

"Sure, I can tell you what I know."

"You were on the board when Sid was hired?"

"I've been on the board for over twenty-five years. Sid was hired, now let me think, the year Nixon resigned. Same month. That's right. I can remember watching the news that summer. Sid wasn't our first choice. Bob Clemet was dead-set against hiring him."

"He was a lawyer, right?" Lee asked.

Beck nodded. "Mostly corporate and real estate law. Also a deacon at the Baptist church. Bob was some relation of Sid's ex-wife."

"So there were some hard feelings there?"

"Aren't there always? Sid became an awful alcoholic for a couple of years and Roxie's family felt he was… harassing her and that he shouldn't be allowed to see his daughter. You know the kind of stuff." Beck waved his hand as if dismissing the silliness of feuding families.

"Where did Sid work before you hired him?"

"He was a manager at the First Bank of Lang. Member of my church. Seemed to have everything."

"What happened?"

"Not sure. He got fired. I think that started the drinking. And, like dominos, the drinking led to the divorce. Very sad. He lived on the streets for over a year. I tried to help him. AA is what ultimately saved him. No, that's wrong, he saved himself. AA just gave him the tools."

"From bank manager to maintenance man. Kind of a strange stepdown, isn't it?" Lee asked.

"Funny that. I wish I could remember exactly the way he told it when we were interviewing him for the job. It was very moving. See, he'd spent a year getting clean, so we were willing to listen when he applied for the job. At least two of us were. Bob was angry that we even let him apply." Beck seemed lost in the past for a moment, his eyes staring out the window at the bright winter's day.

"What did he say in the interview?" Lee asked gently.

"I don't remember who asked him that very question. The point you brought up. Why did a former bank manager want to be a cemetery sexton? Sid said that when he'd been a boy, he'd mowed yards and trimmed hedges for people to make money. Did it for years until he went off to college. He told us that those years were the best ones of his life. The simple life of hands-on work was all he wanted."

"Makes some sense."

Beck nodded. "Especially if you knew his wife and the life he'd had with her. She was a climber. Very concerned with their image. I doubt I ever saw her when she wasn't dressed and made up. For years I never saw him without a three-piece suit on. That life must have been very claustrophobic for him."

"What happened to his wife?"

"Cancer. I believe your dad may have done the funeral. It was only a few years after their divorce. Now that I think about it, I think that helped Sid to dry out. He loved his daughter."

"Where is she now?"

"She's been living in New York. I left a message with her roommate that she needs to contact the sheriff's office. Apparently, Valerie has been studying abroad for the last six months."

"How old is she?"

"Let me think. Early twenties, probably. I believe she was a teenager when they got divorced."

"What do you think caused the explosion at the cemetery?" Lee asked.

"I guess it was an accident. He always kept gasoline and other flammables in that shed."

"Did Sid get into fights with anyone?"

Beck looked surprised at the question. "He was very quiet. Minded his own business. Who could he have gotten into a fight with? I don't think I ever went by the cemetery that he wasn't there. Especially lately."

"Why especially lately?"

"Oh, I don't know. When he first started the job, he was going to AA meetings a lot. There are only so many in a town Lang's size, so he would go over to Gainesville for a meeting if he needed to."

"But not recently?"

"I think he had a handle on his drinking. I even heard him talking about retirement a few months back. I don't know where we're going to find a sexton who's half as conscientious as he was. He was always looking for ways to improve things. About seven months ago, he put new locks and chains on all the crypts."

They talked for a few more minutes, then Lee left not knowing much more than he had before.

Back at the funeral home, Kay walked into the embalming room and smiled at Lester. He looked worried.

"I told Lee I'll answer the phone when you have to go out," Lester told her.

"That's what I wanted to talk to you about. I was hoping I'd get the chance to meet your mother."

"I mean… I guess… at the service." Lester was obviously nervous.

"I was thinking I could go over to your place now."

"Now? What do you want to talk to her about?"

"Brendan Rhodes."

"Not me?"

"No, not you."

"You won't say anything bad about me?" Lester looked down at the floor.

"Why would I do that?" Kay saw a vulnerability in Lester that she had never noticed before.

"I just… She would be upset." His eyes never rose to meet hers.

"You don't have to worry. I'll tell her what a great guy you are."

"That would be nice." Lester finally looked up and smiled hesitantly.

"Lester… Are you afraid of your mother?"

His eyes shot back down to the floor. "Not really *afraid* of her," he said unconvincingly.

"Was she tough on you?"

"After Dad left, she kinda expected a lot out of me. I don't… didn't live up to her expectations," Lester mumbled.

"You're a good guy. You don't have to be so hard on yourself."

"I just want to make her proud of me."

"I'll talk you up, and tomorrow at the funeral we'll make sure that you look important." Kay was surprised to find herself feeling the need to protect Lester.

"You should be able to find her at my apartment."

Kay reassured him again that she wouldn't say anything to make him look bad in the eyes of his mother, then headed over to Lester's garage apartment. When she got there, she found Lester's mother in the front yard talking animatedly with his landlord, who looked ready to punch her in the face.

"And you need to fix the light at the back door. I've made a list of all the deficiencies I've found. I'd like a written response to each and every item, or we will turn this over to the local code enforcement office." She handed him an envelope.

The middle-aged man kept his eyes averted. Not because he was ashamed or subservient, but because his eyes were burning red with anger. He was chewing on his lip as he snatched the envelope from her hand. "I will look into these," he said through gritted teeth.

"See that you do." Mrs. Andrews turned away and started back toward Lester's front door. The man shook his fist at her before turning and stomping off.

"Mrs. Andrews?" Kay hurried over to intercept her.

Lester's mother turned toward Kay, who took a long look at her. Janet Andrews was tall, with blonde hair that was styled professionally and pulled back with a hair band. She looked like she'd just stepped out of a TV show—one of those shows that thought it was very hip, but was really filled with aging actors struggling for relevance. Mrs. Andrews's eyes were dark and piercing with an intensity that felt menacing.

"May I help you?" she asked.

Kay felt herself flinch from the woman's stare. "I'm Kay Lamberton. Your son works with me at the funeral home."

"Why he wants to be a funeral director, I'll never understand. What did you say your name was?"

Kay repeated her name and stepped forward with a smile she hoped was disarming.

"Yes, well. What can I do for you?" Janet asked with only a little more civility.

"I'm working with the sheriff's office on the death of Brendan Rhodes. There are a few questions we thought you might be able to answer."

"You're working with the sheriff's office? What kind of sense does that make?" She stood there with her feet planted and a skeptical look on her face. Kay was losing hope of getting anywhere with her.

"It's complicated and, I admit, a little confusing," Kay agreed. "I'm just assisting. We've worked with them in the past. Lester said you're related to Lora Rhodes?"

"He shouldn't be running his mouth." She clamped her jaw shut and Kay figured the conversation was over before it had even started. Then slowly Janet Andrews's face relaxed and a small smile appeared. "I guess we can chat." She turned and headed into the apartment.

The place was more than clean. Kay could hardly believe that it was the same apartment she'd been in the day before.

"He'd have a nicer place if he wasn't determined to follow this silly idea of his to be a mortician, of all things. Even if he owned his own funeral home, where would he be?" She waved Kay to the couch while she took a seat across from her.

"It's Brendan Rhodes that I wanted to talk to you about."

"Most of what I know about him comes from Lora. The poor woman put up with a lot."

"Like what?"

"The man was a truck driver. What kind of life could he provide his wife?" She shook her head.

Kay was finding this woman more irritating with every word she uttered. "Before Brendan's death, had you to talked to Lora lately?"

"We always call each other in November. Our birthdays are only a week apart. I'm a little older, but we were close enough in age that we would play together at family get-togethers. Anyhow, we've stayed in contact with each other over the years. And even if we didn't meet or talk for a while, we'd always have a long phone call in November."

"What did you all talk about last November?"

"The usual. She talked about the neighborhood and Brendan. I guess I talked about Lester and his lack of ambition. Of course, we always gossip about our family."

"What did she say about Brendan?"

"Good news, for a change. At least that was my opinion, and I told her so."

"What was it?"

"He wasn't hanging around her house all the time. All for the better, if you ask me." She seemed to consider what she'd said in light of Brendan's death. "Not that I wanted anything bad to happen to him. Lora just needed a life of her own. They were divorced, after all."

"Does she have any other men in her life?"

"You should ask her." The look on Janet's face suggested that she knew something and wanted Kay to pry it out of her.

"I'm asking *you*," Kay obliged with a conspiratorial smile.

"I guess she didn't say it was a secret." Janet smiled back.

"Lora said there was a man she's been seeing and that they were getting… intimate."

"Did she say who?"

"No, and I tried to get it out of her. All she'd say was that she'd known him for years and all of a sudden they had… a… connection. Yes, that's the word she used. A connection."

"She'd known this person for years."

"That's what she said."

"Anything else?"

Janet shook her head. "She was being very sly about him. Thinking about it now, I wonder if there's something she's hiding or maybe he's hiding."

"Do you think she's still seeing him?"

"That's one of the things I want to find out. When we talked on the phone the other day, it was all about poor Brendan. I didn't dislike the man. I just thought she could do better."

"Because he was a truck driver?" Kay couldn't help pushing her buttons. To Janet's credit, she did look slightly embarrassed.

"I'm not a snob," Janet argued.

Kay thought that was exactly what she was, but she let the matter drop. "Can you think of anyone who might have wanted to hurt Brendan?"

"Honestly, no. He always seemed so… unimportant."

Kay was relieved when she was finally able to leave the woman. On the drive back to the funeral home, she thought about what it must have been like growing up with her for a mother and felt a new respect for Lester. It must have taken a lot to be raised by that harridan and still manage to grow up to be a nice guy.

Lester was taking delivery of Brendan's casket when she pulled into the driveway.

"I've got to inspect it," Lester told the driver, who looked like he was going to argue the point until he saw Kay walk up to them. The driver started to give her the up-and-down, but when Kay's eyes locked on his, he looked away.

"Do what you got to do. Just do it fast. I've got a delivery in Ocala." The driver walked back to the cab of his truck.

Kay helped Lester open the crate and look the casket over to be sure it was in good condition.

"Your mother is something else," Kay said after the truck had rumbled off down the street.

"She has high expectations," Lester said flatly.

They were passing the door to the kitchen when Ruby called out to Lester. "I've made you some hot dogs to go with the mac and cheese you missed last night."

"Lunch," he said sheepishly to Kay, then ducked into the kitchen.

Kay had always thought that his friendship with Ruby was a bit odd, but she understood it perfectly now. He'd probably been looking for a nurturing mother figure all of his life.

CHAPTER FOURTEEN

There was a hard rapping on the front door. Kay went to see who it was and instantly regretted it. Standing there in all his pigheaded glory was Detective Wade Sutton, wearing his usual ill-fitting suit and a sneer beneath his drooping mustache.

"Would you like to make arrangements for your funeral?" Kay asked innocently and watched the blood rise in Sutton's face.

"I came by to tell you and your brother to stay out of my investigations."

"I think they're the sheriff's investigations and you aren't the only person working the cases."

"I'm the lead investigator."

"Thanks for coming by and letting me know." She went to close the door, but he blocked it with his boot. "Unless you have a warrant, I'd suggest you get that flat foot of yours out of my doorway before I crush it."

They were still trying to stare each other down when Lee

came into the hallway.

"We have a guest," he observed, causing them both to look over at him.

"He was just leaving," Kay growled.

"I came here to warn you all off my cases," Sutton said peevishly.

"Don't make him stand outside. Invite him in," Lee told Kay, receiving an angry glare from her.

Reluctantly, she took her weight off the door and Sutton eased his way into the foyer.

"Why would you warn us off these cases?" Lee challenged Sutton once he was inside and the door was closed.

"They're mine."

"What happened the last time we worked on a case that was yours?"

"What?"

"You heard him," Kay said.

"I almost got killed when a fire truck tried to run me down."

"Let's be fair. The truck was trying to run a lot of people down. You just happened to be in the crowd. But beyond that, didn't the case get solved? Didn't you, as the representative of the sheriff's office, get your full share of credit?" Lee asked.

Sutton narrowed his eyes and stared at Lee and Kay as though he knew he was being tricked but couldn't figure out how.

"I guess."

"Would you mind the same thing, minus the truck, of course, happening again?"

"What?"

"The case getting solved and you getting the credit, you lummox," Kay clarified.

"Quit calling me names," he demanded.

"Then quit being a lummox," she fired back.

Sutton moved forward, chest out and an ugly snarl on his face. Lee stepped between them.

"I'm just trying to point out that we have a common goal. If we all take a deep breath and calm down, maybe we can come up with a way to work on these cases together rather than being at cross-purposes." Lee ran through this as quickly as possible in the hopes that he'd finish before blows were thrown.

"How do I know that you all aren't the murderers?" Sutton grumbled.

"How on earth could that be?" Kay said scornfully.

"You're the only connection between the two victims," Sutton argued.

"What?" Lee said, taken aback, but Kay immediately jumped on Sutton's ridiculous suggestion.

"Except for all the other ties between them. Like they both died in the same cemetery. They were both at the same funeral—albeit one was attending and the other was standing by. They both lived here in Lang. I can probably think of more." Kay wanted to poke Sutton in the chest with her finger, but she was thinking that Lee might have a point with his suggestion of a ceasefire.

Lee had shaken off his initial shock at Sutton's suggestion and nodded his head. "This is a small town. Any two people who live here long enough are going to have dozens of mutual friends and places in common. I can assure you that no one connected with our funeral home had anything to do with either death. Why would we? This is liable to sink our business if we can't come up with the actual murderer."

Sutton squinted his eyes as though trying to put the pieces of a complex jigsaw puzzle together. "Yeah, maybe," was his sophisticated and well-thought-out rebuttal.

"You wanted Jerome on the case. Didn't you think we'd be helping him?" Lee asked.

"Jerome's after my job," Sutton growled.

"Jerome wants to be in CID, but he's not stupid. You're… You have an inside track. Jerome knows that. In fact, maybe if he helps you, *you* might help him," Lee said as if this was an obvious possibility.

Sutton just looked puzzled.

This is too easy, Lee thought. *The man can be talked into anything. How high is his IQ?* "Think about it," Lee encouraged him.

They could practically see steam coming out of Sutton's ears as his eyes narrowed and he tried to make sense of what Lee had suggested. Kay, standing just out of Sutton's line of sight, was shaking her head and trying not to laugh.

"So it might work for me to let you all help on the investigation?"

"It did the last time, didn't it?" Lee asked.

"I guess."

"Didn't you get the credit for solving the case?"

"It was my case, and it got solved."

"There! With some luck, the same thing can happen with the Rhodes and Fuller cases."

"What if you screw something up?"

"We screw up and guess who gets blamed? We do! You stay clean. Wade, this is a win-win for you," Lee said encouragingly.

"I kinda see your point. You'll need to keep me informed on what you are doing," Sutton stated like a line from a movie. He'd obviously heard it from his supervisors often enough that he thought he had to say it.

"No. You don't want that," Lee said.

"I don't?" Sutton was confused.

"Plausible deniability."

"What's that?"

"If you don't know what we're doing, then you can't be held responsible for anything that we do."

Sutton took a minute or two to mull this over.

"So if you screw up, I can't be blamed." Sutton's lips turned up at the edges. "Yeah, I can see how that can work."

"No matter what happens, you win," Lee said.

"What do you get out of this?" Sutton's eyes had narrowed again as he stared at Lee. He seemed to remember that Kay was in the foyer too and turned to include her in his question.

"We'll save our business. If a killer isn't found, people will think we had something to do with both deaths, just like you did."

"Yeah, I see. You got to solve these murders or go broke. Perfect. Then you better get to work. Ha! Make sure that you let me know when you have a good suspect." Sutton turned and headed for the door. "I'll tell Jerome the same thing. I get left out at the end, there'll be hell to pay." He opened the door and left without another word.

"Talk about a deal with the devil," Kay said.

"The devil isn't that stupid."

"If you could sell funerals the way you just sold him, we'd be in the money," Kay complimented Lee.

"We better find the killer."

"Or killers."

Lee sighed. "Thanks for reminding me that we haven't even narrowed it down to one murderer. Have we gotten anywhere yet?"

"The short answer is no. We've found out about Brendan's secret life. We've learned that he was poisoned. Other than that, we're sitting on nothing."

"I want to go back and talk to his old Army buddies."

"I'd be interested to know if Art knew anything about

Brendan's house and his girlfriend," Kay agreed.

They heard Jerome come in through the kitchen and he started exchanging small talk with Ruby.

"Was that Sutton I saw drive away?" he asked when Lee and Kay joined them.

Lee gave him a blow-by-blow account of his exchange with Sutton.

"Oh boy. I wonder how that's going to play out for me. You could have given me a heads-up on your plan."

"It was a spur-of-the-moment decision. I heard Kay and Sutton arguing and thought, why not see if I could bamboozle the idiot with BS?"

"Makes me uneasy. The man's a walking time bomb of incompetence," Jerome said with a shudder.

"You were already working with him on these cases," Lee pointed out.

"And I wasn't happy about it. Every time he makes a mess, the first thing he does is look around for the closest person he can dump all the blame on. I've got a feeling that in this case it's gonna be me."

"Simplest answer to that problem is for us to solve the murders," Lee said.

"You need to look at the neighborhood," Ruby said. They all turned to look at her. "Yin was pawing at the TV screen while Mr. Rogers was singing that song at the beginning of his show. I said to myself, 'There's a clue.' They've closed off Banfield Road to put in new sewer pipes or some such."

The three of them tried to process Ruby's contribution to the discussion. The last sentence could be dismissed as her typical change of subjects in the middle of a thought, but Lee wondered about the rest of it.

"I was just saying I wanted to go back and talk to some of Brendan's friends and neighbors again," Lee said.

"But you aren't doing it because Yin suggested it," Kay said.

"You could do worse than listen to Yin," Ruby remonstrated.

"I've got the pictures from the memorial service." Jerome held up a manila envelope he'd been carrying.

"Let's see them," Kay said eagerly, instantly forgetting about Ruby and her weird cats.

Jerome pulled the photos out of the envelope and placed them on the kitchen table in a large square.

"Going across from left to right, they are in order of when they were taken."

Lee, Kay and Jerome leaned over to look at the pictures while Ruby took furtive glances over their shoulders.

"I don't know exactly what I'm looking for," Lee said.

"There is a very nice picture of Yang," Ruby said, tapping the picture of a fat tabby looking disdainfully back at the camera.

"That's a good time marker for me. I saw Lora take that picture," Lee said.

"There's the thermos on the table," Kay said, pointing to a print later in the series.

"And here, in this one you can see Sid standing off in the distance, watching." Lee tapped the next picture.

Lora had moved around while she took the pictures so that sometimes the table and people gathered around it were in the shot, and other times it was the tent and chairs of the memorial service. Other photos were pictures of individuals standing around the cemetery.

"Lora is in this picture." Kay pointed to one of Lora, Brendan, Art and several other people. It was one of the few pictures that looked posed.

"There's the table again and the thermos is gone." Jerome pointed to the fourth-to-last picture.

The next one was a group shot that included Chaz, Frank and Benny.

"That looks like it was taken from where Lora would have been standing right before she spotted Brendan on the ground," Kay said. Then she tapped the last photo in the series. It was blurry and taken at an odd angle. "What do you think this is?"

"Tilt it this way," Jerome said, turning the picture to give Kay a slightly different perspective.

"Tombstones, and it looks like she took it with the camera at her waist." Kay peered closely at the image.

"I would imagine that was taken when she saw Brendan's body. She said she was getting ready to take a picture when she saw him," Jerome said.

"She sees the body, her hand holding the camera drops to her side and she accidentally snaps a photo," Lee suggested. He leaned close to the picture and then looked back at the one that showed Sid in the distance.

"I think you can just see Sid's arm to the right of that tombstone in the distance." He was pointing to the corner of the picture of Chaz, Frank and Benny.

"Looks sort of like Chaz is looking toward Sid," Jerome observed. "Didn't they say he'd been a cook in the Army? A cook might think about using poison if he wanted to kill someone."

"Maybe they're all in on it," Lee suggested.

"So why would they kill their friend?"

"A friend who had secrets," Lee pointed out.

"Money secrets," Jerome said. "Is this going to be one of those follow-the-money murders?"

"Where exactly did Brendan's money come from and who ends up with it?" Kay asked.

"You're the businessperson. I think you should dig into that." Lee nudged her.

"Thanks. I guess I could enlist Zach's help." Kay thought about the trip to Payne's Prairie and wondered where she stood with Zach after that evening.

"And then there's Sid. It's too easy to say that Sid witnessed the murder or was a loose end that needed tying up. What if he was the killer and the others took revenge?" Lee wondered.

"Then why wouldn't they bring the evidence to the sheriff's office?" Jerome asked as he gathered up the pictures and put them back in the envelope.

"Perhaps it was some type of soldiers' code where they had to personally avenge their friend," Lee said and then snapped his fingers. "Or maybe the motive had to do with Brendan's secret life and they didn't want to expose it."

"That almost makes sense. Still, the pictures never show Sid any closer to the table than fifty yards," Kay pointed out.

Jerome handed her the envelope of photos. "I made these copies for you, but don't let anyone know you've got them. It's best if no one knows I'm sharing evidence."

"I'll put them someplace safe," she promised.

"Brendan's funeral is tomorrow," Lee stated. "We'll have a chance to see all of our suspects again."

"Except for Sid," Jerome said.

"Except for Sid," Lee admitted. "Victim and suspect. I went by the cemetery on my way home from visiting Reverend Beck. It's going to be a little awkward having the funeral with the place still smelling of the fire."

"Where's Brendan's grave?" Kay asked.

"He had three other plots near the one he donated for Danny Reynolds. Lora thought he should rest next to Reynolds, which will leave room for her on Brendan's other side."

"That ought to be fun, having the burial at the same spot where Brendan was killed while smelling the remnants of another murder." Kay shook her head.

"Lora is going to tell everyone at the church funeral that they don't need to attend the graveside service. In fact, the burial is going to be little more than a prayer by the minster and everyone tossing a handful of dirt into the grave."

"That sounds like the best plan," Kay said. "I also don't think we want to serve drinks," she added dryly.

"Good tip," Lee said.

"We all need to keep a close watch on everyone at the funeral and see if anyone is acting suspicious," Jerome reminded them.

"That will be easier to do since Lester's going to be in charge," Lee said.

"What?" Jerome looked from Lee to Kay and back again. "You're joking, right?"

"He's working on becoming a funeral director and he needs to get in the practice," Lee said with a straight face.

"You've never let me be in charge," Jerome said angrily.

"Calm down," Kay said. "Lester's mother is going to be at the funeral and… well… he needs to impress her."

"You've still never let me run the circus." Jerome didn't want to be a funeral director, but he didn't want to take orders from Lester either.

"It's important to him," Lee said.

"Lester's mother? I didn't even know anyone claimed him."

"Come on," Kay chided.

"He's going to be giving me orders?" Jerome still sounded appalled.

"Think of it more like play-acting," Lee suggested. "Everything will be laid out. Lester will just do what I usually do during the service. You know, making sure the next speaker is ready, coordinating the pallbearers. Nothing we haven't done a dozen times before."

"If *my* mother ever comes to one of our funerals, I'm going to expect to be in charge," Jerome said grudgingly.

"Absolutely," Kay promised.

"You said we should look for anything suspicious. Like what?" Lee asked.

"Someone hanging at the back of the church, or people who look like they're avoiding each other or giving each other significant looks. You know the sort of thing," Jerome said.

"I guess Sutton will be at the funeral?" Lee asked casually.

"After what happened the last time he attended one of your services, I think not."

"He didn't die," Lee said defensively.

"I'm still impressed you talked him into letting you work behind the scenes on the murders," Jerome said.

"I think even he knows that he couldn't solve a murder unless he drove up on the scene of the crime and the killer was standing there spouting off about his guilt for the whole world to hear," Lee said.

"He's not smart enough to know anything," Kay said. Even him letting them work on the case wasn't going to change her opinion.

"You have a point," Jerome agreed.

After dinner, Lester and Lee went to the embalming room and placed Brendan in the casket. Lee made a few adjustments to his makeup and placement of his hands. Since Lora had decided that there wouldn't be a viewing and the casket would remain closed during the funeral, some morticians wouldn't have worried about those small details, but that wasn't Lee's way. When he was done, he carefully placed Brendan's old Army uniform in the casket beside him.

"One more thing," Lee said, opening a cabinet drawer. He pulled out a wooden token the size of a half dollar. On one side it was printed with the name of the funeral home. On the other, it had Lee's name and the word "mortician."

"You said your dad did that too?" Lester asked as Lee tucked the token inside Brendan's coat.

"For as long as I can remember. He said that if a body had to exhumed, he wanted people to know who had embalmed the corpse."

"Like signing his work."

"Exactly. Dad ordered ones made up with my name when I graduated from mortuary school." Lee closed the casket respectfully. "Clean up and then you can head home," he told Lester.

"I wish my mother wasn't there." Lester had been nervous all evening, asking questions about different scenarios that could come up the next day while he was supposed to be in charge. Lee had tried to brush his concerns to the side.

"We'll get you through this," Lee said and gave Lester a brotherly pat on the back.

CHAPTER FIFTEEN

The next morning, Lee and Lester hurried through the omelets that Ruby made for breakfast.

"Take some of this bacon out to Yin and Yang." Ruby held out a plate with two pieces of bacon as Lee stood up from the table.

"We need to get going," he said.

"Won't take a minute. Make sure you break them into equal shares."

Exasperated, Lee took the bacon out to the cats, who were sitting in the back driveway looking eerily similar. Shaking off a mental image of the creepy twins from *The Shining*, Lee rewarded the cats for doing nothing, then brought the plate back into the kitchen and handed it to Ruby.

"I swear those two look more alike every day."

"They don't look that much alike to me. You need to spend more time with them so you can see through to their underlying personalities," Ruby told him.

"I'll do that as soon as I'm sure we aren't all going to end up on the streets," Lee said with a roll of his eyes.

Lester put his plate in the sink, rinsed it off and then turned to Lee. "I'm ready."

"Come on then."

"You didn't do a very good job sweeping up last night," Lee said as he noticed sand on the floor of the embalming room. He wasn't surprised, considering how keyed up Lester had been about his role as the lead mortician at Brendan's funeral.

Lester started to say something, but Lee told him to grab the flower arrangements out of the cooler while he rolled the trolley bearing the casket out to the hearse.

As they loaded the casket into the new Cadillac hearse, Lee could see Lester's anxiety building up again.

"How do I know what speaker is next?" Lester asked in a panic.

"Just follow the program," Lee told him.

Lester had shown up early that morning, sweaty and nervous about the funeral. At breakfast, Lee had gently gone over everything again, including a review of one of the printed programs. Lee decided that all the preparation hadn't done much to calm Lester's nerves.

"I got that. The program has the names, but how do I know the people?" Lester used one arm to wipe at the sweat beading on his forehead.

"Most of them will be the same people who were at the memorial service. If you aren't sure, you can quietly ask Lora."

"Yeah, that's a good idea." Lester nodded.

After sliding the casket securely forward into the hearse, Lee placed the two pegs in the back that would keep it in place during the drive to the church.

"You've worked a lot of funerals," Lee reminded Lester.

"Didn't you ever watch what I was doing?"

Lester nodded vigorously. "All the time. I know. But it's different when I'm doing it and… and… with you know… there."

"Your mother."

"I hate that I get this way when she's around," Lester moaned.

"We'll have your back. If I see you having problems, I'll step in and get things back on track. Just pretend like you're giving me orders. Everything will be fine, and she'll think you're the big man at the funeral." Lee closed the door and started toward the front of the hearse when a thought occurred to him. "Who does she think owns the funeral home?" he asked as he climbed into the front seat.

Lester looked out the side window.

"Lester, who does your mother think owns the funeral home?" Lee asked again.

Lester sighed. "I told her that the owners live down in Miami."

"So we just work there?"

"Yeah, kinda," Lester said in a voice so quiet that Lee could barely hear him.

"Anything else I should know?"

"I'm sorry. I just get… crazy when she's around," Lester defended himself.

"Must have been hard growing up with her," Lee sympathized.

"I spent a lot of time with babysitters and relatives, which honestly wasn't a bad thing."

They pulled into the parking lot of First Presbyterian and backed up to a side door that allowed access to the sanctuary without going up the steps at the front of the church. It wasn't as large as the Baptist or Methodist churches in town, but according to Lora, it had been Brendan's church. The pastor's secretary hadn't recognized Brendan's name when Lee had called to set up the service, but she did manage to find it in the church roster.

Lee and Lester rolled the casket through the door, down a long hallway and then out in front of the altar in the sanctuary.

"Is this where you want it?" Lee asked Lester, causing him to look up with a puzzled expression.

"What?"

"You're in charge," Lee reminded him.

"Oh yeah, looks good." Lester looked around nervously as though he expected someone to criticize his opinion.

"Come on, let's get the flowers and the rest of it set up."

Kay and Jerome joined them at the church and they soon had everything ready for the service.

"Quit pacing," Kay told Lester as they waited for the first mourners to arrive.

"And quit chewing on your fingernails," Jerome told him.

"I can't help it."

"Come here." Kay gestured for Lester to follow her. She went out the back of the sanctuary and down the hall toward the church office.

"Where are we going?" Lester asked.

"To the fountain." She pointed to a water fountain between the men's and women's bathrooms.

"Why?"

Kay pulled a small bottle out of the pocket of her slacks. "I'm going to give you half of a pill. This will calm your nerves."

"What is—" Lester started to ask, but she held up her hand to stop him.

"It's a barbiturate. It won't take much." She split the pill in half with her fingernail and handed it to him. "Take it and drink some water."

With a shaking hand, Lester took the pill from her and swallowed it. "Do you always carry those with you?" he asked.

Kay gave him an exasperated look. "Of course not. But knowing how you've been acting lately, I thought it was a good idea to bring them along. Why didn't you smoke something to calm your nerves?"

"My mother is staying with me!" he said hysterically.

"Oh yeah, I guess that *would* make it a little tough to smoke a joint." Kay smiled.

Ten minutes later, Lester was looking more relaxed as he greeted people and directed them to the pews. When his mother arrived, he gave her a peck on the cheek and a smile before escorting her to a pew near the front. After he helped her to her seat, he smiled and gave Kay a thumbs-up.

"Where's Lora?" Kay whispered to Lee.

"I haven't seen her."

"I'm surprised she's not here yet."

"That's interesting."

"I know—" Kay started.

"No. There." Lee pointed to a woman dressed in a provocative black dress that barely reached her midthigh. Annabelle Destiny had just entered the church. "Is that who I think it is?"

"Yeah, that's her." Kay's eyes were wide in amazement.

"Maybe it's a good thing Lora isn't here yet."

"Though it would be a good opportunity to see if she knew about Brendan's new friend," Kay said.

"Go talk to her."

Lester had greeted Annabelle and was directing her toward the pews. Tentatively, she took the second pew from the back.

"I'd better do it before Lora gets here," Kay said, heading for the back of the church as quickly as she could without drawing any attention.

"I had to come," Annabelle said as soon as Kay was close enough to hear her. Kay slid into the pew beside her.

"You aren't the first other woman to show up at a funeral," Kay said.

"He was divorced," Annabelle reminded her.

"You're right. And you have every right to be here. Still, it could become… awkward. It's not that uncommon for fights to break out at funerals. I just wanted to make sure that you don't intend on confronting anyone or causing a scene."

"All I want to do is say goodbye to Brendan. He was really nice to me." Tears formed in the corners of Annabelle's eyes.

"I know. We'll do our best to make it so you can do just that," Kay said and patted the woman's shoulder. She noticed that several mourners were casting furtive glances at them… mostly men.

Annabelle noticed and gave Kay a weak smile. "This is the only black dress I have."

"It's fine. Men can be assholes anywhere and anytime," Kay reassured her.

She stood up and moved to the end of the pew. Before she started back to the front of the church, Lester intercepted her.

"Where's Mrs. Rhodes?" he asked. Some of the nervousness had returned.

"I'm sure she'll be here shortly."

"When? She's the first speaker."

Kay looked at her watch. "There's still plenty of time. If she doesn't get here in ten minutes, I'll go to the church office and see if I can use the phone."

"Y'all said that I would be able to ask her about the other speakers." Lester tried to keep from whining but failed.

"Don't worry," Kay told him, though she was feeling the first twinges of doubt.

Ten minutes later, Lora still wasn't there. Kay approached the minister where he was standing discreetly at the rear of the sanctuary.

"Reverend Michaels, would it be okay if I use the phone in your office? The deceased's... ex-wife isn't here yet. Ex-wife doesn't sound very good, but..."

The elderly man put his hand on Kay's arm.

"I understand the situation. And you're right. She should be here by now." He reached under his robe and pulled out a set of keys. "It's this one," he said, handing her the ring with one of the keys pointed up.

Kay let the phone to Lora's house ring dozens of times before giving up. Then another idea crossed her mind. Hurrying back into the sanctuary, she searched through the mourners until she spotted Art Butler and his wife, Betty. They were sitting next to Lyle and Kelly Grant.

She nodded to the Grants, who gave her sad smiles as she tapped Art on the arm and asked if she could speak with him in private. As they walked toward the back of the church, she noticed a very nervous Lester pacing back and forth. A glance at her watch told her that it was time to close the doors and start the service, but she couldn't blame Lester for hesitating since the person who was supposed to help introduce the mourners and conduct the ceremonies wasn't there. *I should have given him a whole pill,* she thought.

"Have you seen Lora today?" she asked Art when they were far enough away from everyone not to be heard.

"Today?" Art looked around as though he expected to see her. "I... thought she'd be here."

"She's supposed to be. This is kind of her show." Kay was exasperated and worried at the same time, like a bride when the groom was late.

"I don't think I've seen her since Thursday," Art said. "I was painting some furniture when she was driving away. She didn't stop—just beeped her horn—and I waved."

"Was her car in her driveway this morning?"

Art pursed his lips and narrowed his eyes in thought. "I don't remember. Some days it's there and some days it isn't, so I don't really think about it. You know?"

Kay knew exactly what he meant. *What do I do now?* she wondered. Then she remembered Lester's mom. Maybe she'd know something. Kay thanked Art and escorted him back to his pew before turning to Janet Andrews, who was watching as Lester paced.

"Shouldn't you go see what your boss needs?" she asked before Kay could say a word.

"That's what I'm doing, Mrs. Andrews," Kay said with a tight smile. "We're looking for Lora Rhodes. Have you talked to her today?"

"Now that's funny you should ask. I tried calling her several times from Lester's apartment this morning and never got an answer. I left several messages on her answering machine. It's not like her. I mean…"

"Sorry to interrupt, but did she say anything the last time you saw her about the funeral or being late?"

"Sure, she talked about the funeral: about who would speak and all that. We were going to come to the funeral together, which was why I was calling her… So… I don't know." For the first time since Kay had met her, Lester's mother looked at a loss.

"We'll see if we can find her," Kay said before looking up and seeing Lee in conference with Lester.

"We have to get started," Kay heard Lee tell Lester as she approached.

"I…" Lester was a deer in the headlights.

"You have the program. I'll stand six feet back. If I see

that you need help, I'll step forward…" Lee stopped and reconsidered his plan. "Okay, no. Introduce me and I'll take on Lora's role and introduce everyone else." He turned to Kay. "Anyone know where she is?"

"No, none of them do." Kay couldn't keep the concern out of her voice.

Lee looked at her as they started walking toward the front of the sanctuary.

"Did something happen to her, or did she make a run for it?" he said softly enough that the people watching them from the pews couldn't hear their conversation.

They heard the doors shut behind them and Kay turned to see Jerome take his usual spot at the back of the church. For most of the funerals he worked, he would direct parking, which mostly involved making sure no idiot blocked the hearse or family cars. Once everyone had arrived, he would come in, close the doors and stand there to hold back anyone who might try to enter during the middle of a prayer or eulogy.

"I'm going to go talk to Jerome. Whatever has happened to Lora, it isn't good," Kay said, leaving Lee and Lester at the front and circling around to walk as inconspicuously as she could down the side of the sanctuary.

Lee started the funeral with a very short introduction where he glossed over Lora's absence by saying that she was too broken up to attend. What else could he say?

"Someone needs to go by her house and check on her," Kay said to Jerome after they'd moved into the vestibule so as not to distract from the service.

"I've got my radio out in the car." Jerome frowned. "Truth is, I'd rather go myself."

"Go. We can handle this."

"I'll be back as soon as I can." He turned and was gone.

Kay hated to let him go without her. Patience had never

been one of her stronger virtues. She eased back into the sanctuary and stood by the door.

Most of the speakers were the same ones that had spoken at the memorial service for Daniel Reynolds. The only exceptions were a few of Brendan's friends from the days when he had driven a truck for a living. They all spoke fondly of him.

The service at the church was longer than most because of the shortened graveside service. Lee stepped in whenever Lester looked like he was faltering, which happened less as they worked their way through the program. Lee couldn't help but look to the back of the church, wondering where Lora was. Why would she miss the funeral? Was she in trouble? If she was the killer, had she lost her nerve and made a run for it? Or was it possible there was a more mundane explanation for her absence?

Lee watched Kay nervously pacing at the back of the church and knew that she was as concerned as he was. Lester had just called Reverend Michaels back to the pulpit to lead the final prayer for Brendan when Jerome quietly reentered the church.

"Her car is gone. No sign of a break-in," Jerome whispered to Kay. "I put out a welfare check BOLO on her car. This isn't good."

"As soon as we're done with the service, we can try to find her. Maybe someone here has a key to the house," Kay said.

"A neighbor who can go in and check the house would be good. I don't have enough evidence of a crime to go in as a deputy. If her car was in the driveway, I might be able to justify it. I mean, she should be *here*."

"If we find someone, I want to go into the house with them. Lester's mom is a relative," Kay pointed out.

"If she has a key, or if we can get one, that would provide

me with enough cover to keep me from getting my ass chewed by the State Attorney."

Lee told the mourners that there would be a very brief ceremony at the graveside. Lester escorted the pallbearers up to the bier, where they lifted the casket and solemnly carried it down the aisle.

"Crap," Jerome said under his breath. "I haven't moved the hearse to the front of the church."

Kay watched him calmly step out of the sanctuary as she opened the doors, then he broke into a run as soon as he was outside.

The hearse was there just in time to receive the casket from the pallbearers. No one seemed to notice that Jerome was breathing hard.

CHAPTER SIXTEEN

A dozen cars followed the hearse to the graveside. Kay recognized most of the mourners as the same people who'd been present on the day that Brendan had been murdered, including Art Butler, Chaz Dixon, the Grants, Benny Hampton and Frank Hayes. Along with them were a few other friends of Brendan's. Kay also noticed that Annabelle came to the cemetery but sat in her car and watched from a distance.

"Lester is good at his job." Janet Andrews walked up beside Kay, which suited her fine since she wanted to talk to her about Lora's absence.

"You should be proud," Kay said, but before she could go on, Janet cut in with, "*You* must be proud to work for him."

Kay took a minute to choke down some of the replies that came to mind. Finally, she simply agreed, then quickly went on to tell Janet Andrews about what Jerome had discovered at Lora's house.

"That is odd." To Janet's credit, she looked concerned.

"Would you have a key to her house? Someone should go in and check to see if she left a note or any clue as to where she's gone."

"I don't. And I'm pretty sure that she always let Brendan take care of things when she went on a trip."

Kay thought that made sense since Lora and Brendan had remained close after the divorce. *So where are Brendan's keys?* she wondered.

"Did you find out anything about Lora?" Art Butler had walked up to them while everyone waited for Reverend Michaels, who was just driving through the gates of the cemetery.

Kay told him what Jerome had found.

"I don't understand that." Art shook his head, then looked off in the distance and frowned. As soon as he noticed that Kay was watching him, he looked back at her. "I'm sorry I don't have a key to her house. Brendan always looked after things when she was gone."

Kay turned to see what had captured Art's attention and was surprised to realize that it was Annabelle's car. Did he know her? Kay looked back at Art, who was now looking everywhere but toward Annabelle's car.

Reverend Michaels joined them under the tent that covered Brendan's casket. The mahogany coffin was poised on a lift above the open hole that would be his resting place for the foreseeable future.

There was a prayer, the casket was lowered and the folks who wished to came forward to toss a handful of dirt into the grave.

Kay watched all the mourners. Art looked nervous, as did Lyle and Kelly Grant. Were they all just worried about Lora, or was there something else on their minds?

"We need to talk to all these witnesses again," Kay told

Jerome, who was standing by one of the family cars. They were waiting for the mourners to leave so that they could gather up the chairs and take down the tent.

Lee walked from the gravesite toward a man standing half hidden behind a backhoe and drinking from a thermos. At the sight of the thermos, Lee felt his stomach turn. He wasn't sure he'd ever be able to look at a thermos the same way again.

"Buck. How's it going?" Lee called out to the man. Buck Watson dug most of the graves and septic tanks in the county.

Buck shook his hand. "Terrible thing about Sid being burned up like that. Can't understand it. Kept that shack neat as a pin."

"I doubt it was an accident," Lee told him.

"I figured that. Sid was an odd guy. Lot smarter than me."

Lee knew Buck well enough to know that wasn't true. Buck might not have had a college education, but his ability to lay out drain fields and his knowledge of machinery were unmatched in the county.

"You know if he had any enemies?" Lee asked.

"Sid? Ever since he got sober, he's been quiet as a church mouse. Who could he have pissed off?"

"Did you ever hear him talk about Brendan Rhodes?"

"The guy we're burying? No. But like I said, Sid didn't talk much. You know?"

"Yep. Though he was always kind to me when I was working for my dad."

Buck just nodded. "When do you want me to fill in the grave?"

"We'll go ahead and take the tent down and you can get to it as soon as we leave."

"Can do," Buck said and took another drink from the

thermos.

They got back to the funeral home by two o'clock and started to unload the chairs and tent.

"Look at those two lazy cats," Lee said when he noticed Yin and Yang sprawled out in the driveway.

"They look dead. Even I can't tell them apart when they're flopped over like that," Lester chuckled. He'd been in a maniacally happy mood since they'd seen the last of the mourners off, including his mother.

"They're breathing," Lee confirmed, agreeing that they looked like identical corpses.

He carried two of the folding chairs over to the storage shed, where a round wooden object caught his eye against the wall of the funeral home. Once he put the chairs away, he went back to investigate.

"What's that?" Kay asked, coming up beside him.

"It's one of my embalming chips." Lee was puzzled. Why was it outside?

"You do that too? I remember Dad putting those in every coffin."

Lee wasn't listening to her, but his mind was racing. "Lester!" he yelled.

"What?" Lester came hurrying over, spurred on by the urgent tone in Lee's voice.

"Think hard and don't tell me what you think I want to hear. Remember when I asked you about the floor of the embalming room this morning?"

"Yeah, you thought I hadn't swept it out last night. I didn't want to argue with you, but I know I cleaned it up before I left last night."

"You're sure?"

"What did I do wrong?"

"I think you swept out one of his embalming wooden nickels," Kay told him.

"No, that's not where this came from. I never take one out of the drawer until I'm done with the body and I'm ready to close the casket," Lee said.

"So?" Kay asked.

"Those two cats. Oh no!" Lee shouted. "Quick, quick, get the keys to Bertha!" He looked at Lester.

"They're above the visor."

Lee was already running to the hearse. Kay didn't know what was going on, but she wasn't going to let Lee run off like that. She got the passenger door open just as he started the engine.

"Where are we going?"

"Just get in!" he yelled.

Lester was standing in the driveway with a confused expression on his face as Bertha banged her rear bumper on the asphalt before Lee sped out onto the road.

"What's going on?" Kay asked.

"I could be wrong. I'm probably wrong. I hope I'm wrong," Lee chanted as he drove frantically back to the cemetery.

"You're out of your mind. Slow down." Kay braced herself as he made a hard right turn into the cemetery. "Come on, slow down!" Kay was getting worried as he sped up once he passed through the gates.

Lee slammed on the brakes as they neared Brendan's gravesite, causing Bertha to skid and lurch to a stop, but not before bumping over the curb. Lee was out before the hearse's engine stopped rumbling. Kay wondered if her brother had gone mad.

She hurried to catch up with him as he raced toward Brendan's grave, where Buck was tapping down the dirt with the bucket of the backhoe.

"No! Dig it up! Dig it up!" Lee shouted as he ran the last twenty yards.

Buck looked startled when Lee ran in front of the backhoe.

"Dig it back up! Quick!" Lee shouted as Buck idled the backhoe down so he could hear what Lee was saying.

Buck looked at Kay, who shrugged.

"What do you want me to do?"

"Dig out the dirt!" Lee was jumping up and down in frustration. "We've got to get the coffin open!"

Puzzled, Buck got back into the seat and started to remove the dirt.

"He needs to be careful or he'll damage the casket," Kay said.

"I don't give a… Don't you get it? I think Lora might be in there!"

Kay felt faint. "No. That's not possible. How could that happen?"

"I think someone got into the embalming room last night and took out Brendan's body and put Lora in its place."

"She's dead?"

"I don't know! Damn it, I don't know. How could I know?" Lee was frantic.

"What makes you think Lora is in the casket?"

"The dirt on the floor of the embalming room and the wooden token, *my* embalming token. I know it came out of the casket. How could that happen unless someone took Brendan's body out?" He hesitated. "And the cats. I kept seeing those tabby lookalikes all day. One next to the other. Then just now, they were lying like identical corpses in the driveway. They were trying to tell me that the bodies had been switched. Don't you see?"

Kay wasn't sure that she did, but she was beginning to agree that someone might have been fooling around in the embalming room. Maybe even took Brendan's body out of the coffin.

There was a solid thunk from the hole as Buck stopped digging and Lee ran over to the hole.

"Throw me that shovel," he shouted to Buck, who took down the shovel that he kept on the backhoe and tossed it over to Lee, who caught it and jumped down into the grave. "You busted the lid."

"I couldn't help it. You were acting crazy," Buck argued.

"It's okay." Lee put the end of the shovel under one edge of the crack in the lid and put all his weight down on the tool. He was grateful that Lora hadn't ordered one of the metal caskets.

"She's in here, she's in here!" Lee could see her through the hole he'd opened in the lid. He dropped down onto the lid of the casket and tried to get a good look at her. "I can't tell if she's alive."

The casket couldn't be opened in the grave, so Buck and Lee used the backhoe's bucket to get it out of the ground. Kay ran back to the hearse and roared out of the cemetery to find help.

"You realize this is the third time we've had to come to the cemetery because of one of your funerals?" asked Joe McBride, an EMT and fireman with the Lang Fire Department.

"I'm aware," Lee told him. They were watching as the ambulance crew hoisted Lora onto a stretcher. Lee felt like Job. He didn't dare ask what else could go wrong.

"At least she's alive," McBride said.

"I'm grateful for that."

"You didn't notice she was in the casket?" There was just a hint of accusation in the question.

"Whoever put her in there took Brendan Rhodes's body out," Lee explained. "I'd already closed the casket the night before, so there wasn't any reason to look inside."

"So the guy who died at your last funeral was in the casket and someone switched him out for his ex-wife. That's crazy. So where's the guy?"

"We don't know." Lee didn't want to continue recounting his recent misfortunes, so he walked off and left McBride shaking his head.

"They think she'll make it," Kay said when Lee walked up beside her.

"Small mercy."

"You saved her life," Kay reminded him.

"Who is doing this?" His frustration was palpable as he stood there clenching and unclenching his fists.

"We'll find out," Kay promised.

Jerome, still wearing his suit from the funeral, finished talking to Buck and walked over to them.

"This is some mess. Now I got to put out a BOLO for a dead body." He shook his head. "How bad off is she?"

"They won't know for sure until they get her to the hospital. There's a sizable knot on the back of her head and she hasn't regained consciousness," Kay reported.

"With luck, maybe she'll know who did this to her." Jerome was writing notes as he talked.

"That's not the way my luck has been running lately," Lee grumbled.

"What do you want me to do with the casket?" Buck called out to them.

"Our guys are done fingerprinting it," Jerome said.

"We need pictures. Our insurance should take care of replacing it," Kay said.

"I'll ask Alison. She can take the pictures. I just hope we have a body to put in the replacement coffin," Lee said.

"This is Florida. There are a *lot* of places to dump a body where it will never be found," Jerome said.

"Thanks. That makes me feel *so* much better." Lee gave Jerome a glare that would melt lead.

They explained to Buck that they wanted to get pictures, and he agreed to wait around. Once the ambulance was on its way to the hospital in Gainesville and the fire engine was pulling out of the cemetery, Lee motioned to Kay and Jerome.

"I've got something to show you two," he said with some trepidation.

"What?" Kay asked.

"Let's go back to the funeral home. It's a letter I got the other day. There's a chance it's connected to this."

When they got back to the house, Lee told them to wait in the office while he fetched the letter. Fifteen minutes later, Jerome and Kay had both read the note over at least twice.

"You say it was slipped through the mail slot?" Jerome asked.

"I thought so at the time. Now that I know someone got into the embalming room last night, I'm not so sure. All I know is that it was a foot or two from the door when I went into the embalming room Monday."

"Discount embalming supplies." Kay raised her eyebrows. "I guess we all know what that means."

"Some of that stuff that falls off a truck." Jerome shook his head. "You weren't seriously thinking of taking these people up on this, were you?"

"Of course not," Lee lied, and saw the suspicion on Kay's and Jerome's faces. "We're going broke," Lee defended himself.

"So you were going to see if we could move straight from here to a jail cell," Kay accused.

"That'd be a smooth move," Jerome said disdainfully.

"Give me a break. I didn't do it, did I? And I'm showing you the letter."

"Now," Kay said.

Jerome raised his hands to stop the bickering. "The question now is, does this have anything to do with the murders or the attempted murder?" He looked at Kay and Lee, who looked everywhere but at each other.

"I… don't know," Lee said. "I can't see how it fits into a plot to kill Lora Rhodes by putting her body in her ex-husband's coffin."

"They weren't just trying to kill Lora. Whoever did this wanted to make her disappear," Kay said.

"She's not wrong," Jerome agreed. "If someone disappears, you have to wait seven years for them to be declared dead, unless you can convince a judge that there's evidence that they are deceased before that. I haven't seen any sign that someone wanted to make it look like anything else but a disappearance."

"What kind of signs are you talking about?" Lee asked.

"Blood at a crime scene, for one. If there was enough blood in Lora's house to lead a pathologist to assume the person couldn't have survived, then that would go a long way with a judge. Or if a person was last seen on a boat and then the boat was destroyed in a storm when there wasn't much chance of the person escaping. Things like that. Now, we haven't found her car, but knowing her condition, it's obvious they didn't leave five pints of her blood in the vehicle."

"So why would someone want her to disappear?" Kay asked.

"Keeps the focus on finding her rather than finding a killer," Lee suggested.

"But if we're assuming that the same person is responsible for Brendan Rhodes's murder, then they're already the focus of an investigation," Jerome said.

"They might not have planned on his death being identified as a murder. The poison might not have been discovered, and his death might have been chalked up to natural causes," Lee said.

"I'd buy that if he had been prone to seizures or other medical conditions. A man who's in good shape for his age drops dead, then there's going to be an autopsy," Jerome stated.

"I agree. Nicotine isn't an inconspicuous poison. If you want to poison someone without it being detected, there are much better options," Kay said.

"Let's assume that Brendan's murderer *is* the person who tried to kill Lora. They wanted Brendan's murder known, but they didn't even want people to find Lora's body. What sense does that make?" Lee asked.

"Maybe they wanted Brendan's body for some reason. They wanted to steal it and needed another body to put in the coffin so it wouldn't be discovered. No, wait, that doesn't make sense. The missing body was discovered *because* they used Lora as a replacement for it. If they'd just switched the body for sandbags or something, no one would have been the wiser," Kay said.

"Maybe they were going to do that, but Lora discovered the plot." Lee was trying hard to fit all the puzzle pieces together.

"Can you fit this into the any of your scenarios?" Jerome asked, holding up the mysterious letter.

"Maybe the bad guy or guys—"

"Or gals…" Kay interjected.

"—were hoping to connect with me so they could talk me into giving them Brendan's body," Lee said.

"That makes some weird sense," Jerome agreed. "They hoped to hook you into their crooked dealings and then use that to force you to give them Brendan's body. So what's the motive and why use nicotine?"

Kay and Lee couldn't come up with a good answer.

"If Lora was disappeared because she'd uncovered a clue about the killer, then all we have to do is wait until she can talk," Lee said.

"Maybe. Depends on what she learned and when she learned it," Kay elaborated. "If she walked in on nefarious goings-on and was hit hard enough on the back of the head that she was knocked out for hours, then she probably won't remember what happened right before the attack. It's possible she won't remember anything for hours prior to being struck on the head."

"If she knew anything before that, then why didn't she tell someone?" Lee moaned.

"There's also the possibility that she played a role in Brendan's murder." Jerome was pacing now. "And the other party planned to pin suspicion on her by having her disappear."

"I like that for a motive for the body switch. Lora doesn't even have to be in on the murder for that to work," Kay said, nodding.

"True," Jerome said, looking at his watch. "I've got to get to work. As it is, I'll be spending half my shift writing up reports. It will help answer some questions if we can find Lora's car or Brendan's body. And there's this." He tapped the note Lee had received. "If it's related to the murder and attempted murder, it's the best clue we have."

"You can track down the phone number," Lee pointed out.

Jerome shook his head. "I imagine the number is for a phone drop box. People use them for ads in the paper or the back of a magazine, that sort of thing. If we're lucky, we might get a vague description of the person who came in and paid for the box."

"How do they work?" Kay asked.

"These businesses have dozens and dozens of phone numbers. When a call comes in, it gets sent to an answering machine. You just call in and retrieve your messages, the same as you would with a regular answering machine." Jerome shrugged. "But you never know, maybe we're dealing with a moron. Criminals by their very nature are stupid."

CHAPTER SEVENTEEN

As soon as Jerome left, Lee realized how long they'd already left Buck waiting at the cemetery and called Alison. She was getting ready to head out and deliver a TV, but she promised to stop and take the picture of the casket on her way back.

Exhausted and hungry, Kay and Lee wandered into the kitchen, where Ruby made them sandwiches fit for Dagwood.

"Would you please ask Yin and Yang where Brendan's body is?" Lee said tiredly as he set his half-eaten sandwich back down on the plate.

"Finish your sandwich. I'll ask them when I go up to my apartment," Ruby said seriously.

"I… never mind." Lee was going to tell her that he'd meant the comment as a joke, but he couldn't forget the moment of revelation when he'd seen the two cats flopped out in the driveway. If it hadn't been for them, would anyone have ever thought to check Brendan's grave for Lora?

"I want to go drive around and see if I can find Lora's

car," Kay stated, her jaw set in such a way that neither Ruby nor Lee felt like arguing with her.

"You shouldn't go alone," Lee said.

"He's right. I'd be glad to join you," Ruby said with a smile.

"I was thinking that Zach might go with me." Kay hadn't been thinking anything of the sort, but she wasn't going to spend hours driving around with Ruby.

"If he's not able to go, just let me know. My cousin is getting married in May."

Kay wasn't sure if that last bit was Ruby throwing out one of her usual non sequiturs, or if it was another attempt to encourage the relationship between Kay and Zach. Had Ruby purposefully suggested riding along with Kay, knowing that she would dig up an alternative? Kay didn't like to think that Ruby was that smart or that manipulative.

"I'd go with you, but I want to wait around and get the pictures from Alison as soon as possible. Getting our money back from the insurance company would be some small solace." Lee went back to eating his sandwich, trying not to think too much about the mess they were in.

Kay went into the office to call Zach.

"Sure, anything to get to ride around town with you. I'll bring snacks," he offered.

He's such a nice guy, Kay thought, but then her mind conjured up the image of Dr. Alan Eckhart. Wondering if she should be calling him instead, Kay shook her head and tried to focus. "That'd be great," she told Zach.

"I've never had a date where we went hunting for a car and a dead body," he said cheerily. "I'll be there in an hour."

While they were out, Kay figured she'd ask Zach to dig into the county records to see if he could find any clues as to where Brendan's money had come from or how much money he actually had.

"You're using him," came Ruby's voice from the other side of the office door.

Kay wanted to argue, but since she'd been thinking the same thing, she couldn't very well get mad at Ruby. Instead, she focused on Ruby's breach of etiquette. "For the umpteenth time, quit eavesdropping!"

"I thought about listening in on the extension," Ruby said bluntly.

"Why don't you come in?"

Ruby opened the door. "I didn't want to bother you."

"You just wanted to listen in on my phone conversation." Kay sighed. "I know I'm not being fair to Zach. I just…"

"He's a puppy dog and you can't help liking the fact that he's infatuated with you."

"It's been a long time since I've had a guy really hooked," Kay admitted. "It's not just that. I don't have the heart to cut him loose 'cause he does like me… too much."

"There's another possibility."

"Which is?"

"A part of you might really like him back."

"I don't know about that," Kay said, knowing that she'd had the same thought from time to time.

Ruby was walking around the room but keeping her eyes on Kay. "You aren't the type of woman that dates a man just because she likes to go out to fancy restaurants."

"I'm just feeling very indecisive lately. Maybe it's the failing funeral home. A part of me feels like I'm to blame."

"Ridiculous. The Garlands are to blame. Lee was already winning over the community, then you arrived with your business sense and all the elements were in place to make this a going concern."

"Until the Garlands muscled their way into the county. I know what the problem is, I just don't know how to fix it."

Kay's frustration was reaching a boiling point.

"Not all problems need you to fix them. Some just require you to wait for them to fix themselves."

"That sounds grand. Unfortunately, we don't have a lot of time to wait around."

"Do you really think a spoiled brat like Brad Garland is going to be able to maintain a business that requires a lot of interaction with people?" Ruby asked.

"I see your point. I don't think I've ever met anyone that likes him."

"Precisely. Sooner or later, he's going to make a mistake that will give you all the advantage."

"Better be sooner."

"Butter," Ruby said, then suddenly turned and headed for the hallway.

"What?" Even though Kay was used to Ruby's erratic behavior, it still took her by surprise.

"Need to put butter on my shopping list." Ruby's voice trailed off as she headed for the kitchen.

Lee poked his head into the office. "What was Ruby saying about butter?"

Kay shook her head. "It's nothing."

"I'm going to meet Alison. In addition to getting the casket photos, I want her to look at the photos from the memorial service."

"You think she might see something we didn't?"

"It's possible. We were all there and she wasn't, which means that her impressions of the pictures will be different than ours."

"You aren't as dumb as everyone says you are."

Lee tapped his temple. "There are a few brain cells rattling around up here." He took a deep breath. "You can go ahead and look into selling the funeral home."

Kay couldn't believe her ears. "You're giving up?"

"I'm not an idiot. I argued against selling out two years ago because I thought we had a chance of making a go of it. That's gone. I can't see how to dig ourselves out of this hole. It would be different if the Garlands would compete against us on an even playing field. In a fair fight, we'd win every time. Dad did a great job building the home's reputation. He taught me how to be a great mortician and embalmer. You've got the business sense I don't. And we have a strange but competent supporting staff."

"I wish I could say you're wrong." Kay leaned back in her chair and looked at the financial ledgers sitting on the desk. "I'll look into it, but I'm also going to keep trying to come up with a way to save the business. If not for us, then for… Dad."

"I want to keep fighting," Lee said. "I just don't know what good it can do against an enemy that has so much money in the bank. Did I mention that they have, like, twenty-five employees?"

"But do they have a pair of psychic cats?" Kay quipped.

"There is that," Lee allowed. "Would you hand me the pictures from the memorial?"

Kay unlocked the desk drawer where she'd stashed the envelope. She held it out to him, but when he tried to take it, she held onto it. "Remember what Jerome said. These are evidence. Don't show them to anyone else and remind Alison that mum's the word."

"I got it."

She let go of the envelope.

Once Lee was gone, Kay went up to her room to get ready.

For what? she wondered. *To drive around aimlessly for hours looking for a car and a body that are probably at the bottom of one of the five hundred lakes, rivers and ponds within driving distance? Oh yeah, and with a man I shouldn't be encouraging, but certainly* will *be encouraging by driving around alone with him for hours.*

She sighed as she picked out a pair of jeans and a flannel shirt to wear. *Better not make it worse by wearing clothes that would suggest this is a date*, Kay told herself.

"You might want to grab a coat. The temperature has fallen." Zach smiled at Kay when she opened the door.

She took her corduroy jacket off the hall tree and picked up a large tote from beside the door.

"What's in the bag?" Zach asked.

"Flashlights and other tools."

"You're serious about this. Okay, where do you want to start our hunt?" he asked.

"I've been thinking about it." She held up a county roadmap as they headed to his car.

"I'll drive, you navigate," Zach said, opening the passenger door for her.

"Head for Lora's house and we'll work our way out from there."

Kay looked at the map, then asked, "If you had a car and a body you needed to get rid of, how would you do it?"

"I guess I'd put the body in the trunk and drive the car into a pond or lake," he said.

Kay nodded. "That's what I thought at first. We have hundreds of lakes and ponds around here. Seems simple, but when you think about the logistics, it doesn't seem so simple. All the nearby ponds and lakes I'm familiar with have a soft, sandy bottom that slowly tapers off into the deeper parts of the water. If you just tried to drive into something like that, there's a good chance that you'd get the car stuck before it ever got into deep water."

"You've got a good point." Zach cocked his head to one side thoughtfully as he drove. "Like the scene in *Psycho* when Norman rolls the car into the swamp and for a minute it doesn't look like it's going to sink."

"Exactly. The stakes in this case would be too high to just hope that you'd be able to get the car into deep water. The killer would want to be sure the car was lost for good, or at least a very long time."

"One thing I don't understand is why the killer didn't put Brendan's ex in the car too?"

"I've been thinking about that. He wanted her to disappear, so switching the bodies kind of makes sense, but that still leaves the killer with a body to get rid of. Which would seem to defeat the purpose of making the switch. Except…" Kay let a dramatic pause play out. "…If he stuffs Lora in the car's trunk, and the car's found in five or ten years, they'll do a comparison of the body with all the missing persons they have on record. Her dental records or something else might clue them in."

"I get it. And if Lora's body is found, then the Brendan Rhodes murder investigation would be reopened."

Kay nodded. "So what does that tell us?"

"That the killer wasn't confident he could get rid of the body someplace where it would never be found."

"Right! But by placing Lora in Brendan's grave and Brendan's body in the car…"

"If the body is discovered, they would compare it to the details they have for missing men. But no one would know that Brendan's body was missing."

"What else can we deduce from this, Sherlock?"

"You're doing the thing from those books." He gave her a smile.

"I don't know what you're talking about," Kay said evasively.

"Liar. I read those… What were they? The Parker Family Mysteries, that's it! And their English Sheepdog was named Sherlock. The girl would always ask Sherlock what he thought. A reversal of Holmes asking Watson for his opinions."

"You got me." Kay laughed. "So answer the question."

"I don't know what the answer is."

"The car and the body won't be together."

Zach looked confused. "I don't get it."

"Remember, we're assuming that the original goal of the killer is to make it appear as though Lora might somehow be involved in Brendan's murder. He or she switches the body and doesn't care if the car or the body are found. The body for the reasons we've stated, and the car because if Lora was guilty and ran off, she probably would have ditched her car."

"That make sense. If the car is found with a body in it, then someone might put two and two together and figure out whose body it is."

"Especially since you'd be able to tell that the body had been autopsied and embalmed." Kay was on a roll and looked up to see that they were turning onto Lora's street.

"Where do you want me to go?"

"Just park in front of the house and I'll tell you the rest of my thoughts." Kay watched as he pulled the car up next to the black mailbox with "Rhodes" painted in neat white letters.

"Go on." He shifted into park and turned toward her, then held up his hand in the universal stop sign. "I get what you're driving at with the car and the body needing to be disposed of in separate areas. So start from there."

"You have a car and you have a body that was clearly prepared for burial. What do you do?"

"The car… I don't know… The body, I guess you bury it."

"Bury the body where?"

"Oh! The body has been embalmed, so it needs to be buried someplace where an embalmed body wouldn't raise too many questions… like a cemetery!"

"We have a bingo. My dad kept a book of notes on the different cemeteries in the county. There are thirty-four, not counting a couple of family burial grounds."

Zach whistled. "I wouldn't have thought there were that many."

"Most of them are small graveyards next to country churches."

"Right. When you start thinking about the churches, I can see it. So what do you want to do?"

"That's the body. Now where's the car?"

"Your ideas make sense so far. What do you think?"

"I've got a couple of thoughts. Going back to the idea of dumping it into a body of water, there are about a dozen places you might be able to drive it in where it would go down fast and in deep enough water that it would stay hidden for a long while."

"Not to rain on your parade, but we don't have diving gear."

"No, but even in the places I'm thinking about, you might get it into the water and have it sink, but you're going to leave tire tracks behind."

"Ahhhh, gotcha!"

"In the water is one place. But I think the killer might also have just abandoned it somewhere that it would be stolen or trashed."

"Again, I can see that. Especially if the murderer is trying to make it look like Lora ditched it."

"Another gold star for you. If I was going to disappear and wanted to put anyone chasing me off of my trail, I'd leave my car where another person might take it and drive it around for a day, a week or a month before the authorities caught up with them. By that time, any evidence in the car would be long gone."

"You would make a great criminal," Zach said admiringly.

"The way the funeral home business is going, I might have to go to the dark side."

"The most crime-ridden neighborhood in Lang is Stationtown," Zach said.

"Ten blocks that way," Kay said, pointing south.

"So we're going to drive around the worst part of town looking for a stolen car?"

"You're the one that wanted to make it a date." Kay instantly regretted using the word *date*. She hoped he didn't notice.

"I see why you needed backup. Why did you have me drive here first?"

"A couple of reasons. One, I want to get a feel for the distances. Two, I think this neighborhood, or at least the people living here, are part of the mystery." She looked around as though she expected to hear a gunshot or see a bad guy run across the road. "We better get started. Head for Stationtown and we'll drive around and see if we can find her car."

They drove the ten blocks to the community named for its proximity to the old railway depot in town. The area around the train station and the warehouses had always been a bit unsavory. Originally, the men who'd lived in the shotgun shacks and shanties worked for the railroad or in the warehouses, loading and unloading freight cars. The population was young and hardworking, and when the sun went down, they wanted to drink and chase skirts. During Prohibition, the "town" was a center for illegal alcohol and women who worked at night. Its reputation for being the place to go if you needed something that wasn't available on the north side of the tracks continued to grow until there were more criminals than victims. The sheriff's office hadn't been too concerned as long as the crime stayed inside the boundaries of Stationtown.

Even now the streets of Stationtown, some still unpaved and without streetlights, came alive at night with people looking to buy and sell all manner of illicit items.

"The city should really clean the area up," Kay said, trying to peer into the overgrown vacant lots and the shadowy driveways next to rundown shacks.

"Nobody wants that to happen," Zach said.

"Why not?"

"Most of the folks that live here are here *because* it's rundown. Anyone with a family left a long time ago. Now the good people on the other side of the tracks are afraid that, if you clean up this part of Lang, the bad elements will just move somewhere else, which could be closer to them. And, along the same lines, the sheriff's office likes to know where they can find the bad guys when they want to round up the usual suspects."

"That sounds like the type of logic I ran into in the Army."

It took them an hour, but they managed to go down every street in the neighborhood.

"That's enough of this," Kay finally said. "There are too many places to hide a car around here."

"Most stolen cars get dumped out on some country road. If it's around, the cops will pick it up."

"But how long will it take? Solving this mess is the first step to saving our business." Kay saw the look on Zach's face. "I'm not going off on that rant again. Pull into the Fast Mart. I want to look at the map."

Zach parked in a brightly lit spot near the door. They weren't that far from Stationtown and the loiterers outside the store were all drinking out of cans and bottles tucked inside paper bags.

Kay unfolded the map in her lap and studied it for a minute.

"What exactly are you looking for?" Zach asked, keeping half an eye on the middle-aged men standing around the phone booth.

"A cemetery with woods close by. I don't think our bad guy is going to take the chance of actually digging a hole in a cemetery."

"I guess I can see how, if a body that's been embalmed is found near a cemetery, everyone would assume that it was from *that* cemetery."

"Exactly."

"Why not pick an old cemetery that no one uses anymore?"

"I thought of that and marked a few. There are probably others that I don't know about."

"If you've got a couple picked out, then we should probably go." One of the scruffy-looking men had just pushed himself off the wall and was walking unsteadily toward them.

"Head to the West Lang Cemetery. It's…"

"I know where it is." Zach backed out of the parking space, trying to keep one eye on where he was going and the other on the wobbly guy who was waving his bagged bottle of beer at them.

"West Lang is one of the older cemeteries in town," Zach said once they'd parked at the cemetery.

"I think I can remember Dad burying a few people here when I was around ten," Kay said.

The air had a bite to it as the wind blew hard out of the north. Kay wrapped her coat closer around her as they walked away from the car. They each carried a flashlight.

"Wouldn't this be easier in daylight?" Zach asked.

"Don't you think whoever took Brendan's body would

have disposed of it at night?"

"Yeah," he said slowly, trying to figure out the point she was making.

"By coming at night, we have the killer's perspective on the landscape. See over there." She pointed to the lights of a house not far away. "He or she wouldn't want to be too close to that house. And over there, look how much of those woods are lit by the streetlights."

"I see your point. You wouldn't want to be too far from your car either."

"No." Kay was heading for a vacant lot that bordered the cemetery on the west side. "Let's check that out."

They found a few areas that couldn't be seen from the street because of overgrown azalea and wax myrtle bushes.

"There must have been a house on the lot at one time." Zach pointed to a concrete slab covered in moss and old leaves.

"Wonder if there's an old well. That would be a perfect place to dump the body," Kay said with a hint of excitement in her voice.

"If there *is* a well, let's try not to fall down it."

CHAPTER EIGHTEEN

After thirty minutes, they gave up and headed back to the car.

"You know the odds of us finding anything are a million to one." Zach was watching the ground, trying not to trip over a tombstone.

"I just need to be taking action. Even if it's a waste of time," Kay told him.

"And here I was hoping you were just looking for an excuse to spend the evening with me."

"I can do that anytime I want," she tossed off. After the words were out of her mouth, she realized how callous she sounded. "I didn't mean it like that."

"You did," Zach snapped.

"Maybe. I… I don't know what I want. Except right now I want to save our funeral home. For Lee, for my dad and, just possibly, for myself. I've learned over the last couple of years that I like having a home. Even if it has dead bodies downstairs and a strange woman cooking in the kitchen."

Zach unlocked her door and opened it for her. "I understand that. You have a crisis going on right now." He stopped her before she could get into the car and held onto her arms. "Answer one question. Is it possible that when the crisis is over and whatever happens happens, there's a chance that we could have a romantic relationship?"

"How can I tell you how I'm going to feel in the future? That's an unreasonable question." Kay felt her blood rise.

"I'm asking if you feel a kernel of affection for me. I don't think that's unreasonable. I'll take your answer as a no." He turned and left her standing by the open door. She got in while he climbed behind the wheel. The cold night air suddenly felt bitter.

"This was a fool's errand." Kay stared straight ahead as he started the car. "You can take me home."

Zach pulled out of the cemetery without a word. The heater did nothing to dispel the chill she felt. Kay cursed herself for dragging him out on this silly expedition. The more she thought about it, the more she realized that the only reason she'd come up with this crazy idea was so she wouldn't sit in the office and stare at the ledgers for another evening.

Kay was mindlessly watching the traffic as they drove back toward the funeral home when she saw a car that made her heart jump. "Turn around! Turn around!" she yelled.

"What?" Zach, startled, put his foot down on the brake.

"Turn around. I just saw Annabelle's BMW," Kay said excitedly.

"So? I thought we were looking for Lora's car?"

"Come on. Turn around."

Reluctantly, he made a U-turn.

"Faster."

"What am I doing?" Zach mumbled to himself while pressing down on the accelerator.

Soon they were only a hundred feet behind the car.

"It's the red BMW. Slow down."

"Why are we following her?"

"I don't know."

"Because you can't think of anything else to do," Zach sighed.

"You aren't wrong. Hey! She's turning." Kay was pointing through the windshield. "Where are we?"

"She's turning toward Lora's neighborhood." Zach squinted, trying to follow the red taillights as they drove toward Lora's street.

"Stay back. I don't want to spook her," Kay instructed.

"She could have a legitimate reason for being here."

"We'll watch and find out," Kay said with an edge to her voice. "Annabelle had as good a reason as anyone to kill Brendan."

"How's that?"

"He obviously had money. Money that no one knew he had. So where is it? Where did it come from? I'd guess she knows. Once he was dead, she could steal whatever cash he had stashed away."

"Yep, she's turning onto the dead-end road. What do you want me to do?"

"Don't turn yet. Just park over there. We can see all the way to the end of the street from there."

They pulled over and parked on the cross street, watching Annabelle's taillights as her car crept down the street before turning into a driveway.

"That's Art's house!" Kay said loud enough that Zach made a face. "How do they know each other?"

They hunkered down in the car to wait. After half an hour, Zach shifted around, reached into the back seat and pulled out a can of Pringles.

"Want some?" he offered after popping the top.

"Yes, I'm starving."

Kay's mind was racing. Was this a breakthrough or an easily explained situation?

"Maybe the old guy is just getting a little on the side?" Zach suggested.

"I'd like to know if his wife is home," Kay said, peering at the distant driveway. The only part of the house that was visible from their vantage point was the driveway and side of the garage.

"We could get closer," Zach suggested, reaching up and turning off the dome light before opening his door.

"I don't know." Kay didn't like the tone in his voice. Zach wasn't a spontaneous, take-chances kind of guy.

"Come on. I'm tired of playing games," he said and started across the street. Kay got the distinct impression that he wasn't just talking about the spying.

"Zach, come back here," Kay whispered, scooting after him.

"You want to solve this murder? We'll follow your suspect." He was already across the street and headed not onto the sidewalk, but behind the first house.

"What are you doing?" Kay hissed when she caught up with him.

"I'm going to sneak through the back yards of these houses and come up at the rear of your suspect's house," he said in an offhand way.

"You're acting crazy," she scolded him.

"I'm not going to be your puppet. If you called me up because you want my help, fine. I'm helping."

"I know I haven't been fair to you, but this is crazy."

They were behind the house on the corner and moving toward a five-foot privacy fence.

"It's my fault too," Zach admitted. "I thought that if you spent enough time with me, you'd be overwhelmed by my charming personality. I'm an idiot."

"We're stuck," Kay said when they came to the fence. "Now let's go back."

"Over there. A couple of the boards look loose." He pointed at a spot along the fence that was twenty feet closer to the house.

"No." She grabbed his arm.

He shook her loose and headed for the broken boards. Kay looked at the house. There were lights on and she could see into the kitchen. No one was in sight, so she hurried to catch up with Zach, who recklessly stomped through the bushes. Once he reached the broken boards, he pulled them aside so he could squeeze through. From the other side, he held the boards apart so Kay could get through.

The next yard had a four-foot chain-link fence. Again she grabbed his arm as he started to hoist himself over it.

"There could be a dog!" she warned.

For the first time since he'd left the car, Zach seemed to give credence to her warning. Carefully, but with enough force to make noise, he rattled the fence.

"What are you doing?" Kay asked.

"They won't hear it in the house, but any dog in the yard should come running."

"*Should*," she said drolly.

They waited, but no dogs appeared. Without any more hesitation, Zach hoisted himself up and over the fence.

"I didn't know we were going to be doing an obstacle course," Kay grumbled. Zach held out a hand and helped her over. "Who's going to help me over the fence when the cops are chasing us?" she asked.

"Your suspect's house should be next."

"Stop calling him my suspect. I just want to know what he's doing with his dead friend's girlfriend. Especially since he pretended not to know about Brendan's secret life."

While she talked, Zach was already heading toward the next obstacle, which turned out to be a privet hedge. The branches were thickly intertwined and pushing through was almost impossible. After a couple of attempts, Kay got down on her knees and managed to crawl under the thick growth.

"That's the spirit," Zach said, getting down on his knees and following her.

Once they were on the other side of the hedge, they stayed crouched down and looked toward the house. The layout was similar to the house on the corner. While the light in the kitchen wasn't on, there was enough light from the other rooms to see in.

"We'll need to get closer," Zach whispered to Kay, who grabbed his shirt. "What?"

"Stop!" Kay hissed. "If we're going to do this, let's slow down and do it right."

"Like how?"

"Like get the damn chip off your shoulder. You're mad at me. I get it. Fine. But I don't want to spend the night in jail."

Zach took a deep breath and let it out slowly before he spoke. "I'll be careful," he promised.

"Keep your face down. It's going to reflect light from the windows. They're probably in the front room, which is going to be tricky. If I remember right, they had some hedges along the front of the house. That will provide some cover."

"You've gone into full Army mode."

"Nope. This is from sneaking out of the house at night."

"I'll want to hear more about that," Zach promised, starting toward the house.

The yard was well maintained, so it was easy to cross in the dark without tripping over deadfall or stumbling in a hole. They decided to go around the same side of the house rather than split up. Out front, the azalea bushes hid them from anyone on the street while they crept along the front of the Butler house. At least it was easier to see now as light from the living room poured out onto the lawn.

"...the cops. Just keep quiet about our connection and you'll be fine. If things get dicey, I'll come forward and give them a story that will clear you." Art's voice could be heard clearly through the plate glass window.

"I'm not going to take the fall for stuff I haven't done." Annabelle's voice was softer. Kay thought she sounded scared and angry. *"You got me into this."*

"I told you to date him, not move in with him," Art said.

"Just remember what I said. I've got insurance."

"Don't threaten me."

"I'm going to protect myself because I don't know who to be afraid of."

"I'm not going to hurt you."

"What's going to happen if Lora talks?"

"I'll make sure she doesn't," Art said.

Kay felt a chill go down her spine. She reached out and gripped Zach's arm.

"How do I know you didn't put her in Brendan's coffin?"

"You don't." There was a pause, then Art said, *"All I can tell you is that I'd never hurt her."*

"I don't know... I got to go."

Kay nudged Zach. "We need to go too."

He started shuffling quickly along the side of the house. They had just gotten around the corner when they heard the front door open. A minute later, the BMW started up and roared down the street.

They retraced their steps in silence, with Kay lost in her own thoughts. Art had seemed so nice. She kicked herself for being taken in by his good ol' guy routine.

"Let's go back to the funeral home. I want to call Jerome and have him come over so we can explain what we heard, and how we heard it, to him and Lee."

Earlier, Lee had gone upstairs to change before going over to Alison's electronics shop. His feelings about her had become more complicated as the funeral home sailed further out into treacherous financial waters. He was strongly attracted to her, but there was a part of him that asked the practical questions. *What are your prospects? Can you offer her anything beyond your love? What if you have to move in a couple of months and take a job somewhere else?* All of this meant that he was both happy and depressed at the prospect of seeing her.

With the envelope of pictures in his hand, he walked up the street to the store. Alison's father had run a successful appliance repair business, but Alison's enthusiasm for the latest trends in audio and video equipment had attracted a new set of customers who were equally enthused. More than a few times, when Lee had been in the store, he hadn't understood half of the conversations going on.

Alison gave him a smile as he came in. She was explaining the different settings on a console TV to a portly man and his suspicious wife. The man would nod along with Alison's explanations while his wife frowned and pursed her lips. Alison read the room and started asking the wife about her living room décor and which of the several wooden cabinet options she was interested in. Slowly, the woman unwound and began to contemplate how the TV would look in their house.

Before too long, Alison was ringing a six-hundred-and-nineteen-dollar sale up on the cash register with the promise that the TV would be delivered the following week.

"I got a call from the *Gainesville Sun*. They wanted a copy of the picture I took of the broken casket. I told them to go pound sand," Alison said after giving Lee a hug and a kiss.

"You should have sold it to them."

"I wouldn't do that. They can write up the story, but they don't need my picture to get more people to read it." Alison held onto his hand. "What can I do to make you feel better?" she asked in a tone that suggested she already knew the answer.

"Maybe later," Lee said, squeezing her hand. "Would you take a look at these pictures and tell me if you see anything in them that could help figure out who killed Brendan?"

"I'll look, but I can't promise anything. Come on into the back. I'll look at them under the magnifying lamp."

In the repair room, Alison checked the number of the negative on the back of each print to make sure she had the pictures in order, then sat down in front of the lamp.

"Point out the victim, suspects and the thermos when we come to them," she told Lee.

Carefully, she examined each photograph. First she looked at the picture, then she scanned it slowly under the magnifying lamp.

"That's a great picture of Yang." Alison smiled and tapped the picture. Lee almost asked how she could tell which cat it was, but he didn't want to get off on a tangent. Alison let the cat picture go and focused on the rest of the photos.

"These five pictures are the most important," she stated, holding those up and putting the rest aside. She moved various pieces of radios and TVs to the side of her worktable and laid the pictures out in order.

"See the thermos in the first picture of the series? It's on the table and you can see these five people in the distance."

"That's Chaz Dixon, his wife Vickie, Benny Hampton and two guys who were with the honor guard."

"Assuming that the poison was placed in the thermos and the thermos was then handed to Brendan, I think you can eliminate those five people," Alison said.

"How?"

"Look at this next photo of the table with them standing roughly ten feet away. Of course, for a complete analysis we'd need to go to the cemetery and take measurements. Anyway, the third photo is of another group of people over by the tent, but you can just see the edge of the table where the thermos was sitting."

"It's gone."

"Right, now here's the fourth photo. It was taken from farther away and the focus is on these two people."

"That's Lyle and Kelly Grant." Lyle was holding Kelly's hand while she held something in her other hand that he couldn't quite make out.

"Behind them you can't quite see the table because they're blocking most of it, but you can see the other five people who haven't moved much from their positions in the first picture in the series."

"And we know that the thermos was moved between the first and third photos."

"Exactly. If they were talking in a group from the time the first picture was taken to the third photo, then none of them could have been the ones to put the poison in the thermos."

"That's brilliant!"

"The last picture is taken toward the tent. That's you, right?"

"Yeah, I'm with Frank Hayes, who got vertigo or something. I went over to him when I thought he looked sick. That's his daughter beside me."

"Which tells us that happened right before Brendan's destiny was set."

"Destiny. Funny you should say that." Lee went on to tell her about Annabelle Destiny, Brendan's live-in girlfriend.

"Living a secret life is never a good thing."

"Brendan's secrets led to an early grave. Not that we know where his grave is. The theft of his body is the worst part for me. When a family gives us their loved one to prepare for burial, we shouldn't lose them."

Seeing how upset he was, Alison stood up to hug him when the bell on the front door rang.

"Sorry." She excused herself and went into the front of the shop to greet her customer.

Lee took another look at the photos. Why hadn't he noticed the sequence of events with the thermos? *Because she's smarter than me*, he thought. *And I can live with that.*

Lee pushed his concerns about the future out of his mind as Alison saw the last customer out the door and locked up for the night.

"I can count the receipts at home and make the deposit in the morning. Want to walk me to my house, big boy?" she asked in a silly, sexy voice that made Lee roll his eyes and smile.

"Any time, ma'am." Lee tipped an imaginary hat and stretched his arm out toward the back door.

Two hours later, he was tucking in his shirt and kissing Alison goodnight.

"I need to be at the funeral home in case we get word about Brendan's body," he told her.

"I get it." She gave him another kiss. "There'll be other nights."

I hope, Lee thought as he pulled his coat close around him and headed out the door.

CHAPTER NINETEEN

Lee came in through the kitchen where Ruby was baking pecan pies.

"You better go on into the office. Kay and that beau of hers came rushing in here about half an hour ago," Ruby told him as she opened the oven door and pushed a wooden toothpick into one of the pies.

"What's going on?"

"Now how would I know?" She closed the oven door and looked at the clock. "They've got five more minutes."

"Before they do what?"

"The pies have five more minutes," Ruby explained.

"What about Kay and Zach? What's up? And don't give me that 'I don't know' spiel." If Kay was upset, Lee wanted a heads-up before he went in to talk to her.

"I did happen to hear her on the phone to Jerome. He's on his way. Good thing I cooked two pies."

"Forget the pies." This earned him a stern look. "Why did she call Jerome?"

"Seems that Zach and Kay overhead a conversation between Art and that woman Annabelle. Made Kay think that there might be a conspiracy between the two of them."

"Annabelle and Art?" *That's odd*, he thought.

"Pies will be ready when y'all are done playing Miss Marple or whatever," Ruby told him.

Lee went to the office to find Kay behind the desk and Zach slouched in one of the wingback chairs. They both looked up when he entered.

"So tell me," he said, sitting down in another chair.

"We should wait for…" Kay started, then they heard Jerome talking to Ruby.

"Any word on Lora?" Lee asked Jerome when he came in.

"Last I heard, she's still in critical condition. The scans showed some bleeding under the skull where she was struck. They're waiting to see what happens with that, which will determine whether they need to operate. What was so urgent that you needed me to come over now?" Jerome asked Kay.

Kay and Zach explained what they had heard while eavesdropping on Art and Annabelle.

"So Art knew," Jerome said, his eyes narrowed in concentration.

"And Annabelle lied to us," Kay pointed out. "They've been playing some type of game. Maybe Brendan found out and they had to kill him."

"This is very interesting, but why couldn't it wait until tomorrow?" Jerome asked. Like all of them, he was visibly tired.

"I… thought you could bring them in for questioning," Kay said.

"Not tonight. We can use this, but I'm not going off half-cocked. We know that they're lying now. We'll look a lot closer at both of them and try to figure out why."

"I just thought… it felt urgent," Kay said, trying to justify her response.

"When the time is right, we'll bring each of them in and question them separately. See if we can break them down," Jerome assured her.

"Let me show you what Alison was able to deduce from the photos of the memorial service."

Lee laid out the photos on the desk and then explained Alison's logic.

"This eliminates Chaz, Vickie and Benny. And I think we can strike Frank off of our suspect list too, since his daughter would have had to be involved in the murder. And, as the last picture shows, I was watching them part of the time, narrowing their window of opportunity," Lee said. "But Art is certainly not eliminated, and now we know he has a connection to someone with a motive."

"Annabelle has a *possible* motive. We don't know if she took money from Brendan or not," Jerome said carefully.

"She might *not* have a motive. Brendan was giving her a place to live and providing her with spending money. Now that he's dead, she's lost all that," Zach pointed out.

"But you heard them talking." Kay felt exasperated by Zach's reaction, or maybe it was their argument and the way he'd been acting.

"I admit it sounded very suspicious. But I agree with Jerome. We shouldn't jump to conclusions," Zach said.

"I might have been a little quick to yell fire," Kay admitted, looking at Lee and Jerome. "But when I heard those two talking, it sent a chill down my back. They're conspiring to… do something," she ended lamely.

"We're all tired. Let's get some rest and see what tomorrow brings," Lee said, feeling the weight of the day's events settle on to him again.

"Easy for you all to say. I've still got five hours of my

shift to go." Jerome's hand tapped against the butt of his gun. "Unless it's a blood-and-guts emergency, don't call me again tonight."

"I'm sorry I—" Kay started.

Jerome put his hand up. "I see where you were coming from. Like Lee said, let's see what tomorrow brings."

Jerome left with a slice of pecan pie in hand, and Lee headed for the embalming room to clean up the mess the crime-scene techs had left after they'd dusted for prints in the wake of the body snatching.

Kay walked Zach out to his car. The wind had died down, but the air was cold and their breath was clearly visible in the glow of the streetlights.

"I told you I'd look up what I can regarding Brendan's finances, so I'll do that." Zach paused and looked down at the ground. "Other than that, I think I want to give this a rest for a while. Right now, our goals just don't seem to match up."

Kay felt an odd sadness settle over her. She wondered if it was just selfishness. Did she want to keep him on the hook just so she could use him whenever she needed him? She resisted that thought. Zach was a nice man, a comfortable man, but he didn't make her heart sing. Letting him go would be good for both of them. She took his hand and brought it up to her cheek.

"I'll leave you alone as long as you want me to. I know I drive you a little crazy."

"Promise me one thing," Zach said.

"What?"

"If you're ever in real danger, you'll call me?"

"If I need you."

"That's all I ask. You're a wonderful, over-the-top madwoman who draws me in like a moth to a flame. Unfortunately, I'm afraid that if I hang around you too long,

I could end up suffering the same fate as the moth."

Zach bent down and gave her a kiss before getting into his car and driving off into the night.

Sunday morning got off to a slow start. Lee slept in until nine. When he finally made it down to the kitchen, Ruby was looking lost.

"Lester called and said that he's driving his mother to the hospital in Gainesville to see Lora Rhodes," she said, explaining her lack of direction.

"Had she heard anything about Lora's condition?" Lee asked.

"No. His mother just wants to talk to the doctors. Apparently, she's Lora's next of kin. Lora's mother died years ago from complications following an operation to remove her gallbladder."

Lee dropped down in a chair and opened the Sunday paper.

"How many pancakes do you want?" Ruby asked in a tone that told Lee that zero wasn't the right answer.

"Three will be fine."

"And bacon," Ruby told him.

"That will be great." Lee knew she was having a hard time without Lester to feed.

Below the fold on the front page of the paper was the headline that a former mayor of Lang, Jack Warner, who had held various positions in state government and run for governor twice, had died.

"This is the type of funeral we should be doing. I bet the Garlands already have it sewn up." He flipped to the back page to continue the article. "See, what did I tell you? 'Funeral to be held on Friday, flowers can be sent to the Garland Funeral Home.' A funeral like this will be high-profile. I bet there will be five hundred people there," Lee complained.

"What funeral?" Kay asked, yawning as she entered the kitchen. Lee pushed the paper over to her and tapped at the article. She looked at the name and picture. "I remember Mayor Warner. He was a nice guy. He and Dad were pretty good friends."

"My point exactly. This should have been our funeral."

"You're right," Kay said.

"How many pancakes?" Ruby made it sound more like a command than a question.

"I'm not..." Kay started, then saw Lee shake his head ever so slightly back and forth. "...going to short myself. I'll take four."

"There's bacon too," Ruby added as she finished filling up Lee's plate.

"Great!" Kay said, making an effort to sound enthusiastic. In reality, the emotional rollercoaster of the day before had left her feeling hungover.

"Ah, here we are," Lee said as he pulled out the local section of the paper. A headline read: *Woman Almost Buried Alive*. Lee scanned the article. "We're only mentioned twice and the second one refers to me as having saved the woman."

"That's good," Kay said. "Two mentions and one positive."

"Please. You know this is doom written in large neon letters."

"In that case, I guess you can look at the fact that we're already sinking as a good thing." Kay knew the joke wasn't funny, but what else could she do but laugh?

"Right now, I couldn't care less about losing the funeral home. I just want to find Brendan's body. I had nightmares about it last night. In one of them, the body showed up at a wedding. Weird."

"I had an idea last night, but we didn't get very far." Kay explained her theory about the killer getting rid of the body in or near a cemetery.

"That's not the dumbest idea I've ever heard," Lee said. "I'm game to visit some of them and have a look."

"I'm up for it. I don't think I can just sit around here thinking about the body and poor Lora. Even if she's involved somehow, I can't imagine a worse fate than to be buried alive." Kay shuddered.

"Amen," Lee said.

Soon they were heading out in Kay's car. They'd decided that it would be less conspicuous than one of the family cars.

"It's Sunday, so for right now we'll skip the ones that have churches next to them," Kay said. She took her pencil and marked two graveyards that seemed like possibilities. "The Eastside Cemetery and the Open Word Baptist Church Cemetery. Open Word is small, but who knows."

"I thought we weren't doing churchyards?"

"The Open Word church burned down two years ago, so there's just the graveyard."

"That's right. I don't think we ever buried anyone there."

"Eastside is the first one we'll come to."

"I know it pretty well. I can remember half a dozen funerals Dad had there."

The cemetery covered three acres with stones dating back a hundred years. They parked next to the gate and got out of the car.

"Do you really think there's a chance of finding the body?" Lee asked Kay.

"We won't know until we look."

They walked around the cemetery, reminding Lee of his childhood. His dad would often take him to the cemeteries when he was prepping for a funeral. Lee had spent many happy days playing among the tombstones. He could never understand people who found cemeteries creepy or depressing.

Kay and Lee split up and went along different sides of the property. There weren't any woods, but the north side bordered a vacant lot. As Lee scanned it, he couldn't see any place where a body could have been buried or concealed. Whoever owned the lot had kept it well maintained.

"Next," Lee said as they climbed back into the car.

A concrete slab was all that remained of Open Word Baptist Church. An impressive sign out front told everyone that services were being held at a vacant store in a strip mall until funds could be raised to rebuild. Despite this, the cemetery was well cared for. The stones were a mix of both professionally made and homemade. There were small sections where the graves had no tombstones at all, only outlines created with stones or shells. The cemetery was surrounded by unkempt lots on three sides.

"This looks more promising," Kay said. She left her coat in the car. The bright warm sun made up for the chill in the air.

"I'll take the west and north sides. You take the east and south," Lee said as he started through the graves.

Fifteen minutes later, he saw Kay hurrying toward him. He could tell from the excited look on her face that she'd found something.

"Come over here." She was breathing heavily from both excitement and exertion.

"What did you find?"

"I don't know. Come on." Kay waved him on as she started walking quickly back to the south side of the cemetery.

Lee smelled the odor when they were still fifty feet from the property line that separated the cemetery from an overgrown lot.

"Brendan wouldn't smell like that," Lee said, slightly offended that his sister didn't respect his embalming skills more than that. "I mean if it was summer and a few days had passed, there might be a slight odor, but nothing like that."

"I didn't want to go look in case it *is* him. I think it would be better if we discover the body together."

"You're probably right, but I'm telling you that, after all the work I did on Brendan, he wouldn't be that whiffy." Lee stepped from the cemetery's manicured lawn into the knee-high brush of the lot next door.

Following his nose and with Kay walking in his footsteps, they edged deeper into the woods. Deadfall and vines grabbed at their legs as they stepped over and around obstacles.

"There, told you." Lee pointed to a dead opossum.

"That's sad and disappointing," Kay said. Here in the shade of the woods, she shivered. "Onward and upward, as Dad used to say."

"All the time," Lee said, smiling at the memory.

They tramped back out of the woods and, when they got to the car, Kay pulled out the map.

"You know, I remember one of the Parker Family books where the killer purposefully left the bodies in different jurisdictions." Kay was studying the map.

"I don't think they would want to drive too far with the body. They didn't have a lot of time to make the switch."

"There's a cemetery just over the line not far from here. Out by the Forty-Eight Bar."

"Oh yeah. It's next to that old country church. Mount Something."

"Mount Olive Primitive Baptist."

"That's it." Lee looked at his watch. "They'll be having services."

"We'll be quiet. If anyone asks, we'll just tell them the truth," Kay said.

Kay handed him the map and started the car. Soon they pulled into the grass parking area beside a little white church. There were a couple dozen cars and trucks parked in neat rows facing the church. The church itself had been meticulously maintained and had been in continuous use since 1887, according to the historical marker out front.

"We'll just be a few minutes." Kay looked at her watch. It was just after eleven. "No one will be the wiser. The service will last for at least an hour."

They got out of the car and closed the doors as gently as possible.

The cemetery was as neat as the little church.

"Even the woods around the graveyard are neat and tidy," Lee said. The sound of a choir singing "What a Friend We Have in Jesus" could be heard coming from the church.

They walked around and read the headstones. There didn't appear to be many places that anyone could bury or hide a body without it being noticed.

"I don't see anything," Kay said. "I think I'm about done following my hunches."

"Don't be too hard on yourself. If I'd thought harder about that note I found, I might have taken some extra precautions."

"That's true." Kay looked thoughtful. "I understand being desperate, but would you really have gotten into bed with thieves?"

"I hope not, but…" Lee shrugged. "I want to save the funeral home so much that I don't know what I would have done. Of course, one of the reasons I want to save the funeral home is because I don't want to let Dad down."

"And if you saved the business by doing something illegal, you would be disgracing his memory."

"Yep. So… I don't think I would have."

"I hope you would have told me before you did anything that stupid," Kay said, slipping in behind the steering wheel of her car.

"Never. 'Cause if I have doubts about anything else, I don't for one minute doubt that you would beat my ass before letting me do something that stupid," Lee said, laughing.

"Damn straight." She smiled back and started the car.

Kay was getting ready to turn onto the country highway and head back toward Lang when Lee shouted, "Stop!"

Kay hit the brake too hard, and they both felt their seatbelts grab their waists.

"What?" she asked, ready to be royally pissed off if there wasn't a good reason for his order.

Lee ignored her and unbuckled his seat belt as he fumbled with the door. Stumbling out of the car, he jogged to the ditch.

Kay put the car in park and got out in time to see Lee jumping up and down, staring at something black in the ditch.

"He's here! He's got to be here. Bring me something to poke it."

"Poke what?" Kay was still undecided as to whether she was irritated or not. She reached inside the car and pulled out a flashlight.

Five feet from Lee, she saw what he had seen. Lying on its side was a glossy black dress shoe. She glanced around as though assuring herself that there wasn't a good reason for the shoe to be there.

"The church is full of people," she said.

"Do you really think one of them is missing a shoe?"

"Maybe some kid…" She stopped as Lee got down on his hands and knees and peered closely at the shoe.

"This is Brendan's shoe," Lee declared. "We need to call Jerome. If we can't get him, it'll have to be the sheriff's office."

"How sure are you about this?"

"One hundred percent. Period." Lee nodded his head emphatically. "I laced them in a diamond pattern and made sure that both ends of the bow were even."

"What is a diamond pattern?"

He used the flashlight to tip up the shoe.

"See, I lace the three bottom eyes first on each side and then go to the top and do the top three, forming a diamond pattern in the laces."

"You are out of your damn mind. No one cares how the dead person's shoes are laced."

"Dad did. I do."

Kay had no answer for this.

"There are some teeth marks on it too." Lee pointed to half a dozen holes in the almost-new shoe.

"So some animal moved it. Guess it's safe to say they didn't drag it the fifteen miles from our funeral home."

"I doubt it was moved more than a couple of hundred feet."

"What type of animal?"

"Do I look like Davy Crockett?" Lee glared at her. "If I had to guess, I'd say small dog, raccoon, something like that."

"Do we need to flip a coin for who stays here and who goes to find a phone?"

"It's your car. I'll wait here."

"Fair enough." Kay looked at the church and the wires running to it. "I don't think they have a phone. The building is too small to even have an office. Any chance that someone will be at the Four-Eight on a Sunday morning?"

"Doubt it."

"I'll be back as soon as I can." Kay started to get back in the car but stopped. "I need change. I cleaned out my car last week."

Lee dug in his pockets and managed to come up with five quarters, then Kay drove off and left him standing awkwardly by the ditch.

CHAPTER TWENTY

Eventually, Lee figured he didn't have to just stand there and guard the shoe. It wasn't like it was a busy street where a kid was liable to come by and grab it. Looking up and down the road, there was only one house in sight, a shotgun cottage with peeling paint and a small plume of smoke rising up from the chimney.

Lee walked through the cemetery again, trying to imagine where a person could bury a body where everything looked untouched. Another look at the neatly kept woods surrounding it didn't bring any more enlightenment. More hymns floated out of the church and Lee wondered how long it had been since he'd been in a church for any reason other than a funeral. He couldn't remember.

Every time Lee heard a car coming down the road, he looked up and waited to see if it was Kay or a sheriff's deputy. It dawned on him that the church was in Alachua County, which meant that the responding officers might be with ACSO and wouldn't know him from Adam.

At last, Kay drove back into the church parking lot and Lee met her at the ditch.

"Sorry it took so long. I had to go to the Fast Mart at the interstate to find a working pay phone. A not-very-happy Jerome is on his way."

Behind them they heard the church doors opening. Black women in hats and dresses, talking and laughing, came out with men wearing fine suits and fedoras. Several children wearing their Sunday best chased each other and played among the adults.

Lee and Kay could see a short, stout man in brilliant white robes standing at the door, nodding to his parishioners and shaking their hands. At some point, a tall man in a pinstriped suit looked their way and noticed Kay and Lee. With a quick word to the woman with him, he left the crowd and came over toward Kay's car.

"Are you having car trouble?" the man asked when he was close enough to be heard. His eyes were soft and kind.

Kay and Lee looked at each other, then Lee stepped forward with his hand outstretched. "I'm Lee Lamberton."

"Harvey Merrick." Harvey gave Lee's hand a good shake. "If you're having car trouble, we have a couple of good mechanics in the congregation."

"This is rather complicated," Lee started. "I'm the owner of the Lamberton..." Lee remembered that Kay was there. "...Actually, my sister, this is Kay." He introduced her and Harvey nodded politely at her. "We're the owners of Lamberton Funeral Home."

"Sure. Over in Lang. Y'all buried a good friend of mine five years ago." Harvey was beginning to look puzzled.

"You may have heard about some trouble that we had yesterday?" Lee said hesitantly.

"No, no, I didn't hear anything about any trouble. Sorry to hear about it, though. What kind of trouble?"

Behind Harvey, the woman he'd been talking to was making her way in their direction. Lee decided he needed to speed this up.

"To be blunt, it was a stolen body," Lee blurted.

Harvey looked incredulous. "Someone stole a body from your funeral home?"

"Yes. And… and we've been looking for it."

Harvey gave his head a little shake as though he were trying to make some kind of sense of it all. Then he said, "What can we do to help?" The rather imposing-looking woman was almost within earshot.

"That's his shoe." Lee stretched out his arm and pointed at the dress shoe resting in the ditch.

"What?" Harvey asked, shocked.

"Harvey, what's wrong?" The woman had heard his stunned question and hurried up to his side.

"It's crazy. Viola, these folks own that big funeral home in Lang. They say a body was stolen and that's the dead man's shoe."

Viola's mouth hung open in stunned silence. Then she recovered her wits and said, "I think I read something about it in the *Gainesville Sun*. A body stolen, sure enough." She looked at the shoe. "What makes you think that's his shoe?"

"I embalmed him. I recognize it… or, I should say I recognize the way it's laced," Lee told them.

"He's my brother and, believe me, he is that obsessive about the job he does," Kay added.

"If that's his shoe…" Harvey looked around as though he expected to see Brendan's body laid out on the church's lawn. "…Where's the rest of him?"

"That's what we need to find out," Kay said. "I've called a deputy who's working the case. He's on his way." Kay hoped that Jerome would show up in uniform to lend some credence to their story.

"There can't be a dead body here," Viola said, which sounded a little odd since they were standing only fifty feet from a cemetery.

"We just don't know." Lee made it sound as much like an apology as he could. "We didn't mean to impose on your Sunday."

"We'll help you in any way we can. I just don't see how," Harvey said. "I guess we could get everyone to help search the woods and all."

"I don't think that would be a good idea. We don't want to disturb any evidence. That's why we haven't even picked up the shoe," Lee explained.

"I guess you're right."

"Would anyone have seen a car around the church on Friday night or early Saturday morning?" Kay asked.

"I don't know. Friday night some of the folks get together for choir practice," Harvey said.

"That wouldn't be late enough. This would have happened after one o'clock," Lee said.

"Could we talk to them?" Kay asked. She turned to Lee and said, "The killer might have scouted the location." Turning back to Harvey, she continued, "In fact, if any of your church members have seen anybody odd hanging around the last week, the cops are going to want to know about it."

"Sure." Harvey turned to his wife. "See if you can get Manny; he never misses a practice."

Viola walked off, her high heels sinking awkwardly into the grass.

"Manny is in the choir, but he also does a bunch of the maintenance work around the church. So he's here more than anyone else." Harvey paused before asking, "Why did someone steal this man's body?"

"So they could place a woman in the casket. A woman

who was still alive," Kay said.

Harvey looked horrified at the thought. "Lord save us. Was the woman all right?"

"She's still in critical condition at the hospital," Lee said.

Viola came back with Manny following close behind. His hair was almost all grey and there were careworn furrows across his brow.

"A body, you say?" he asked Harvey.

"That's what these young people say." He nodded toward Kay and Lee.

"Have you seen anyone odd hanging around the church?" Kay asked Manny.

"It'd be odd to see *anyone* out here. We got our little community, but no store or nothin' to make anyone want to stop here. As for the church, I do the groundwork and now and again someone from out of town stops by 'cause they got kinfolk in the cemetery. But there haven't been any strangers here for months. Christmas and summer. That's when you get the occasional person stoppin' by."

Lee explained how Brendan's body had been stolen and about his discovery of the shoe. "Can you think of anyplace around here where someone might bury a body... or hide one?"

"I've never heard of such a thing." Manny shook his head. "I can't see where anyone could hide a body and one of us not notice. I keep a sharp eye out for anything out of place," he said, and both Kay and Lee believed him. He had the look of a man who takes his work seriously.

Both Harvey and Manny wanted to look at the shoe. Lee let them get close without touching it. Each was convinced that the shoe hadn't come from anyone in the community.

"Y'all are invited to have lunch with us," Viola offered. "The ladies are coming back in a little bit with the food. We don't have a refrigerator or a stove out here. They use the

Hendrickses' place."

"We set up plenty of tables and chairs out back." Harvey seconded the invitation.

Lee looked at Kay, who raised her eyebrows.

"One of us needs to stay here. You can go," Lee told Kay, who didn't wait for him to change his mind.

"She can make a plate up and bring it back to you," Viola told him.

Lee was finishing his second piece of fried chicken when Jerome pulled into the church parking area in his patrol car. He got out looking like he'd slept in his uniform.

"What's this about a shoe?"

"Over here." Lee had hoped that Jerome would be more enthusiastic. "There." Lee pointed at the shoe like a magician pulling a rabbit out of a top hat.

Jerome squatted down and studied the shoe. "You're sure this is Brendan's?"

"I always lace the shoes in a diamond pattern," Lee insisted.

Jerome frowned at the shoe. He stood up and looked around as though he expected to see Brendan's body.

"Great." He didn't make it sound that great. "I've got to get ahold of the Alachua County Sheriff's Office. We're solidly on their ground."

"We need to look for the body," Lee said and got an irritated look from Jerome.

"I'm exhausted. We had a fight at the Forty-Eight last night, then a domestic dispute that ultimately involved a knife and some wicked cuts to the man's face. Finally, to top it off, we had a nasty accident with a car full of teenagers. Now, I'm glad you found Brendan Rhodes's shoe; just don't expect me to dance for joy over it."

"I just need to find that body," Lee explained.

"I know that. I came out here, right? Now I got to let my

people know that they have to work with Alachua County's people. Neither are going to be happy about it. My people will ask me a dozen questions, all aimed at making me feel like it's my fault that they have to cooperate with another department. Alachua County will ask me a laundry list of questions with the sole purpose of making me feel like I'm coming into their county and stirring up trouble."

"We could just look for the body ourselves," Lee offered.

"Our luck, we'd find it. No, if you want to get the funeral home out of the hole, we need to do this by the book. Besides, we have a whole congregation watching us. By the way, where'd you get that plate of food?"

In an hour they had three deputies besides Jerome searching the area around the church.

"You'd think they'd have sent more than three," Lee complained to Jerome.

"Brendan Rhodes has been dead for a week. He's not exactly high priority for anyone but you," Jerome informed him.

"Thanks. I'd like to remind you that your side gig is at risk."

"I know that. I'd like to find this missing body. But no one else is that excited about it, even with Lora Rhodes in the hospital. She's still unconscious, by the way, but they've got her listed in stable condition now."

"One small piece of good news."

By five o'clock they'd searched half a mile in all directions from the church, but they still didn't find the body.

"I believe that whoever stole Brendan's body pulled into the church and thought they'd found a good place to hide it when something spooked them," Jerome said as they were getting ready to leave.

The members of the church's congregation were filtering back for their Sunday evening service by the time Lee, Kay and Jerome left with the shoe neatly bagged and labeled in the trunk of Jerome's patrol car.

CHAPTER TWENTY-ONE

If it weren't for the missing body, Monday morning would have felt almost normal. Lester was back at the breakfast table and Lee and Kay were arguing over how to get more business.

"All you found was a shoe?" Lester asked.

"The right one," Lee said.

"We need to find the body. Mom thinks it don't look good for the funeral home to lose the deceased," Lester said.

"Really?" Lee asked as if the idea had never occurred to him.

"Yeah, she says people won't trust us if we lose bodies."

Kay reached out and put a hand on Lester's arm.

"I think we all know that," she told him in a slow, calm voice. "But I don't think Lee appreciates you reminding him of the fact."

"Oh," Lester said, looking at Lee, who was grinding his teeth. "I just… She wants the funeral home to do well 'cause she thinks I'm… well, you know."

"If you found a shoe then you were on the right trail," Ruby said as she fried up a cheese omelet.

"We only have to find the other shoe and the feet that go in them," Lee grumbled.

"We're missing a clue. The trouble is, we don't know what the clue is because we haven't found it." Kay knew she was rambling, but for some reason she couldn't stop herself. "I think we're on to something with the cemeteries, but did they abandon the idea of burying him near a cemetery when they failed the first time?"

"I'd dump the body in the swamp," Lester stated. "Let the alligators eat it. Would the embalming fluid hurt the alligators?"

Lee rubbed his forehead and snapped, "I don't know. You'd be surprised to learn that at mortuary school they don't teach you about the toxic effects of embalming fluid on American alligators." He was feeling more and more angry with every silly comment and wild speculation that Lester uttered.

"I was just wondering, 'cause if embalming fluid *does* make alligators sick, you could drive around and look at all the ponds with alligators and if any gators are looking sick, you'd know that that's the pond or river where the body was dumped."

"I'm going to strangle him," Lee said to Kay.

"He's just trying to help."

"That's all." Lester sounded hurt. "I'd do anything you want to find the body. You know that."

"I know," Lee admitted. "I'm just not in the mood this morning. I thought when we found the shoe…" He got up from the table.

"Sit back down. Your omelet is next," Ruby ordered.

"I'm not hungry," Lee said over his shoulder and left the kitchen.

He stopped in the hall and tried to get ahold of his emotions. He hadn't slept well the last couple of nights and the emotional and mental strain of the last week was taking its toll on his nerves. *I have to come up with a plan*, he told himself. It had always been his way of coping. *If you have a plan then you have hope*, his dad had always said.

Lee went into the embalming room to clean the already-spotless room. He had piddled around for a few minutes when Lester came in.

"I know I'm acting stupid," Lester said by way of apology. "It's my mom being here. I always feel like I'm twelve years old when she's around."

"Don't worry about it. I'm just worried about all of us and the funeral home."

"I guess finding Brendan's body *would* help."

"It wouldn't hurt. At least we wouldn't be known as the funeral home that lost a body." Lee sat down on the stool he kept near the embalming table. "I thought we were close yesterday when we found the shoe."

"How'd you find it out there at that church?"

Lee explained Kay's logic.

"So the bad guy goes to this church planning on burying the body. He gets Brendan at least part way out of the car and then—BAM!—there's a noise or he sees someone, so he puts the body back in the car and drives off."

"I'd say that's a good guess." Lee was looking down at the floor, feeling despondent.

"We just need to figure out what he did after that," Lester said.

"Yeah, that's all."

"Come on, it isn't that hard. You've hit poor Lora on the head and put her in Brendan's coffin. Now you have to get rid of Brendan's body somewhere that it won't be found for years, and when it *is* found, the cops will think it's just a misplaced body from the cemetery."

"Yep." Lee kept his eyes on the floor.

"Now you found the perfect place. A small church out in the middle of nowhere with a nice cemetery. You get there early in the morning. You're tugging on the body, trying to get it out of the trunk so you can drag it off into the woods. That's when you see a light, maybe a car. Crap! You rush to push the body back in the trunk and while you're doing this, a shoe falls unnoticed to the ground." Lester acted out the scene as he spoke.

"We have all that figured out," Lee reminded him.

"Okay. So what do you do now?" Lester asked.

Lee continued to look at the floor without speaking.

"Come on, think. I'd want to get rid of the body fast. It freaked me out almost getting caught, so I want this done. I got to get the body out of the car so I can go home," Lester prompted.

Lee finally looked up. "You're right. You'd be done looking around. You'd want it over with. You thought it was almost over when you were interrupted."

"So…"

"You would go to the nearest alternative cemetery!" Lee stood up. "Go out to Kay's car and get the county map. It's on the dash."

Lester quickly retrieved the map and placed it on the embalming table. Lee leaned over the map and looked at all of the cemeteries Kay had marked, narrowing in on the ones closest to Mount Olive Primitive Baptist.

"Cedar Grove and Evergreen," Lee said, feeling a surge of hope. "I'm going to check them out. Want to come with me?"

Lester looked like a dog who'd been told it was going to the park and excitedly grabbed a set of keys to one of the family cars from its hook on the wall.

"Which one first?" Lester asked as they pulled out of the driveway.

"Evergreen."

As Lee drove through town and looked at all the people going about their business, he knew that they were unconcerned with his problems. Still, it seemed odd that no one appeared upset that a body had been stolen and a woman almost buried alive.

Evergreen Cemetery had seen better days. The fence was in need of repair, the grass hadn't been mowed since last fall and many of the tombstones were falling over. The cinderblock church wasn't much bigger than a single-family home and needed a new coat of paint.

"This looks promising," Lee said as he parked the car. If he'd been choosing a place to dispose of Brendan's body, he would have chosen this graveyard long before Mount Olive.

They started by walking through the tombstones. The place was so poorly tended that someone could have dug a grave in the middle of the cemetery and you wouldn't have been able to see it through the grass and overgrowth until you were within twenty feet of it.

"I don't think Dad ever buried anyone here."

"I've never been here," Lester said as he peered into a raised vault with a broken lid. "I can see the casket."

"That would be a great place to put Brendan. But it'd take a couple of people to lift up the pieces of concrete. Even then, you wouldn't be able to do it without leaving evidence."

"The moss and stuff isn't messed up," Lester agreed.

They finished with the west and north sides of the cemetery and were starting on the east side when Lee saw something that made his heart jump into his throat. In the overgrown grass were parallel lines where a car had driven along the inside of the fence.

"We need to follow those tracks," he told Lester, abandoning their search pattern.

"Why didn't we notice the tracks at the gate?"

"Even the little bit of traffic the cemetery gets was enough to wear down the grass up there," Lee figured.

They reached a spot where the chain-link fence that encircled the graveyard had been crushed when a heavy tree branch had fallen on it. From the appearance of the ground, the car had stopped and turned around there. Near the opening in the fence was a crumpled piece of paper that hadn't been there long. Lee went over and picked it up.

Lester looked over his shoulder. The paper was from a yellow legal pad and had been crudely torn.

"It's a to-do list," Lee said to himself as much as to Lester.

There were four items on the scrap of paper: duct tape, gloves, snacks, tires. The next word after "tires" started with an "r," but Lee couldn't tell anything more.

"Duct tape and gloves," Lester read out loud. "Lora's hands and feet were duct-taped."

"Come on." Lee carefully placed the paper into his pocket before stepping over the downed fence. The pine trees were close together with palmettos and other undergrowth, yet there were other areas that were relatively clear.

They followed a recently trodden path that went about forty feet past the fence.

"This has got to be it." Lee's voice was shaking from excitement as he looked at a large mound of recently disturbed earth.

"We should have brought a shovel," Lester said excitedly.

"We can't touch it. I wish I hadn't picked up the piece of paper. Come on, we've got to get Jerome out here."

They climbed back over the fence and almost ran back to

the car. Lee thought of the day before. *Should I Leave Lester here while I go searching for a phone? What are the odds that the body is going to disappear like a made-for-TV mystery movie?*

"Stay here and keep an eye on things. I'll be back as soon as I get ahold of Jerome."

"Bring me a Dr. Pepper."

An hour later, Jerome got out of his patrol car and walked over to the spot where the fence was smashed down. Lee and Lester trailed behind him. Lee had already given Jerome the scrap of paper to bag.

"You all can stay back." Jerome watched where he was placing his feet as he stepped over the fence. "Looks like you might have something!" he yelled back. "We aren't going to know until we get the crime-scene techs out here with shovels."

"Are they on the way?" Lee asked.

"I talked to Ken. He's ready, but I told him not to head this way until I called him."

"You couldn't take my word for it?" Lee asked.

"Please. You aren't exactly hitting them all out of the park lately."

"I know the body is there."

"I'm going to use my radio and call him. They'll be here in half an hour," Jerome assured Lee.

"I helped to find it," Lester said.

"That could just be someone's dead dog," Jerome said, bringing everyone back to earth.

"But what about the piece of paper?" Lee asked.

"I'm calling the techs, aren't I?" Jerome argued. "I'm just saying not to start counting your chickens yet."

Kay saw Lee and Lester get into one of the family cars and pull out of the driveway.

I'm not just going to sit around here, she told herself. Art Butler was stuck in her head. Was he in league with Annabelle Destiny? Kay was having a hard time accepting the fact that Art hadn't been honest with them.

I need to find out more about Art, she thought, then remembered Lyle and Kelly Grant. They lived right next door and Lyle had been in the Army with Art. He would know Art as well as anyone.

Kay made up her mind. She'd come up with an excuse to talk to the Grants in hopes that she could get them to give her the dope on Art Butler. She knew they had been through a lot together, but would Lyle help hide Art's duplicity? Especially when it came to the murder of another member of their circle? Kay didn't think so. She remembered that every time she'd seen them together, Lyle and Art had been cordial but not overly buddy-buddy. In fact, she thought there'd been a stiffness in the way they had interacted that suggested there was room for a wedge to be worked in between them.

She grabbed her car keys and was still debating her strategy as she went out the door. Ruby was outside feeding Yin and Yang.

"I'm going over to talk with the Grants. If I'm not back in three hours, you might want to send in the cavalry."

"You think it's wise, going to talk to suspects by yourself?"

"They aren't exactly suspects. They're more like witnesses," Kay equivocated.

Yin hissed at Yang and batted at him.

"Hey now!" Ruby scolded. "What has you all riled up?"

While Ruby was distracted, Kay took the opportunity to get away. By the time Ruby looked up, Kay was driving away.

"Did you have something to tell her?" Ruby asked Yin,

who let out a plaintive meow.

Kay gave Art's house a wary look as she passed it and pulled into the Grants' driveway, parking behind an Oldsmobile Cutlass Supreme. The couple were both old enough that she figured they wouldn't be at work.

Walking past the Cutlass, Kay wondered why it wasn't in the garage. She remembered that Lyle had been working in the garage the last time she'd visited them and figured he was one of those guys with a garage full of model trains or woodworking equipment, but no room for his car. She had just touched the doorbell when the door opened. Kelly Grant looked as surprised as Kay.

"You're the woman from the funeral parlor who came by and questioned us after the memorial," Kelly said with a slight edge to her words.

"Mrs. Grant, I wondered if I could talk with you and your husband again." Kay thought she should have been better prepared. How was she going to probe them for information on Art and Annabelle? Did they even know Annabelle?

"I guess." Kelly sounded unsure. "Lyle, the woman from the funeral home is here again." She backed away from the door so Kay could come in. "I thought we answered all your questions the other day. I guess with Brendan's body disappearing and Lora ending up in his casket, you want to ask more questions." This last came out as an accusation.

"We're as perplexed by the state of affairs as everyone else." Kay repeated the words she'd memorized as her answer to anyone who asked about the debacle.

"I bet you are." Kelly frowned. Kay was surprised by the woman's hostility. The last time they'd talked after Brendan's death, she'd seemed friendly.

"You'll have to excuse Kelly. She and Lora are good friends. She's… upset." Lyle had walked up beside his wife. She leaned into him and her expression softened. Not much, but some. Kay could understand the anger she might feel if a friend of hers had almost been killed.

"I'm sorry. My brother and I are both upset about this. That's really why I'm here. We're trying to figure out what happened." She left off the part about wanting to find whoever was responsible for the murders of Brendan and Sid Fuller and the attempted murder of Lora. Better to make it sound like more of a fact-finding mission than a man hunt.

"We're glad to help in any way we can," Lyle said.

"Of course we are," Kelly said, wiping at her eyes. "Thinking about Lora in that coffin…" She gestured for Kay to take a seat in the living room.

"I know that you all had a close-knit group of friends," Kay said, trying to open up the conversation to include Art and his wife.

"We thought we were close," Lyle said. "With everything that's happened, I'm beginning to wonder how much we know about each other."

"Everyone lived in this neighborhood, right? Including Lora and Brendan, Benny, Chaz and Vickie, Frank and Art and his wife."

"That's right," Lyle agreed.

"You all fought together in Korea and then moved here together?"

"It wasn't quite like that. Art came here first and then, well, you know how it is. You go on vacation together and everyone's talking. We bought a lot here pretty early on, but we didn't move down permanently until about ten years ago. The snow was three feet deep when we left and, after a week, we just didn't want to go back to that." Lyle shrugged.

"Art told me how you all bought the properties. You all

must think a lot of him to go in together to buy these lots. I mean, even if you liked the Florida weather, you didn't have to choose Lang or this neighborhood."

"Art can be very persuasive," Lyle said.

"He seems like a pretty nice guy." Kay was trying to give them some room to talk about what they really thought of him.

"He pulled us together when we were in Korea. I think that held over when we returned stateside." Lyle glanced at his wife. Kelly gave him a look that conveyed an unspoken message. "Don't get me wrong. Art has his rough side."

"Really?" Kay gave him more rope.

"When you're in a war zone, there are different priorities. The elements that make a man your friend, even your savior, can be very different from what you want in peacetime." Lyle and Kelly shared another look.

"I'm familiar with the hard edge you need to survive in war. I spent two tours in Vietnam."

"Art told us that when he said he'd chosen your funeral home for Lieutenant Reynolds's service. So you understand the type of actions that soldiers admire in each other when they are fighting a determined enemy."

"You mean ruthlessness?" Kay suggested.

"Exactly. A man needs to be willing to do horrible things in order to survive and to support his men. In combat, you kill the enemy without remorse. You don't always wait for captured soldiers to acknowledge their defeat. If there's the slightest chance that they might still be in the fight, you shoot. You understand?"

"I think so. A person without empathy can go far in a world where empathy can get you killed." Kay understood that it was a rare man or woman who could turn their empathy on and off. The struggles of good men and women when they returned to peacetime were a reflection of this difficulty.

"That's my point," Lyle said

"You're saying Art can be remorseless when he needs to be." Kay wanted to be sure she understood him.

"And sometimes when it isn't needed," Lyle said. Kelly reached out and took his hand.

"You saw him commit... ruthless acts?" Kay asked.

"I'm not proud of everything we did over there. There are times when the nightmares leave me shaking."

"I was under the impression that Art and Brendan got along well." Kay thought she would move the discussion to the next level.

There was a long pause so pregnant that it could have been quadruplets.

"I don't think I should say anything." Lyle shook his head.

"Lyle," Kelly said so quietly that it was almost a whisper. It was obvious to Kay that it was meant as encouragement.

"Kelly, I can't betray him."

"This isn't about him. It's about Brendan and Lora."

Kay wanted to remind them about Sid Fuller's death but didn't want to interrupt the momentum.

"Brendan and Art had their differences. Especially after Brendan left Lora."

"Art didn't like the fact that Brendan and Lora broke up?" Kay thought that was odd.

"It wasn't the breakup of the relationship that bothered him. It was Brendan moving to Gainesville. Art likes to control people," Lyle said.

"He's tried it with us," Kelly added.

"Were there arguments?"

"Not as such. Art is more... subtle. I guess you'd say he's manipulative. We learned in the Army that you didn't want to piss him off. We got to where we were constantly on guard for the signs that he was upset, or was going to be upset, with us."

"And you saw signs that he was upset with Brendan?"

"Whoa, yeah! Lots of them. The crazy thing was that Brendan was still over at his old house almost as much as he ever was."

"You and Brendan were friends. Did he ever mention any hostility between himself and Art?"

"Not much. Just a word or two here and there. He was as scared of Art as I was."

"What about Chaz and Frank?"

"They were always Art's favorites, so they weren't as worried as we were when Art was in one of his moods."

"Do you think Art could have had anything to do with Brendan's death?" Kay asked.

Lyle shrugged. "I've thought about it a lot."

"You haven't slept well since it happened." Kelly snuggled in close to him.

"Do you have anything other than your suspicions?"

Lyle gave Kelly a small nod and she sighed. "I saw him near the thermos talking to Brendan shortly before... you know."

"You're sure?" Kay was trying to remember Lora's pictures from the memorial service. Art had been in a few of them. He wasn't in any of the last images, but that didn't mean it was impossible. Brendan wasn't in any of the pictures of the table. There had been time in between the images for the murderer to step in and pick up the thermos, at which point they could have taken it to Brendan, or Brendan could have come over to the table.

"I'm sure." Kelly paused. "I'm sure it was close to the time that Brendan died."

"Did Art know Sid Fuller?"

"Who?" Lyle asked.

"The maintenance man at the cemetery. The one who was killed in an explosion."

"I don't know," Lyle said. "Maybe the guy saw Art hand the thermos to Brendan."

"That's what everyone is thinking. I mean, that Sid saw the murderer hand Brendan the thermos. We don't know that it was Art."

"If you knew someone was a murderer, you'd be able to blackmail them," Lyle said.

"That's one possibility. Or there was another connection between Brendan and the caretaker that we don't know about."

"I can promise you that Art would never stand for being blackmailed," Lyle said emphatically, and Kelly nodded her head. "I remember a corporal that saw him take some equipment from the base. The man was never seen again. Rumors were that he'd tried to hold it over Art's head to get special privileges. And the man… disappeared."

"Have you seen a red BMW parked at Art's house?" Kay asked and was taken aback when both Lyle and Kelly tensed up and stared at her.

"A BMW?" Lyle asked.

"Yes, red. Maybe a woman driving?"

The Grants looked at each other.

"What makes you ask if we've seen it over at Art's?" Lyle pushed.

"I saw one at Brendan's apartment." Kay didn't know why, but she didn't want to tell him about Annabelle visiting Art the night before.

"No." Lyle took a minute before adding, "I did see one at Brendan's funeral."

Kay had planned on asking them if they knew of anyone named Annabelle Destiny but changed her mind. The way the Grants had suddenly gone on the alert when she'd asked about the car made her decide to keep some information back. They were friends with Brendan and Lora. *They might want to avenge their friends*, Kay thought. *Or they have some evidence that they're holding back.* Either way, she didn't think she should give them more information.

"I saw it there too. I didn't know who it belonged to. I was wondering if Art might know who it belongs to," Kay lied.

She tried to think of other questions to ask, but she didn't know how to proceed without tipping her hand. "I'd better let you all get back to your… I never asked what you do for a living?" Kay looked at Lyle.

"I'm retired."

"What did you do after the Army?"

"I worked for the man, as the kids used to say. Just a nine-to-five job. Mostly pushing a pencil."

"I was a stay-at-home mom," Kelly added.

"I didn't know you had kids."

"Two. Ted lives in Tennessee and Maria is married with three children. She's in Texas now."

Kay let them walk her to the door. Kelly chatted about their kids and pointed them out in family pictures on the wall.

When Kay got home, Ruby handed her a message from Lee saying that they thought they'd found where Brendan was buried. Kay was back out the door without ever setting her keys down.

CHAPTER TWENTY-TWO

When Lee, Lester and Jerome got back to the cars, Jerome radioed in the find and requested the crime-scene van. Just as they'd settled down to wait, they heard a car speeding down the road toward the cemetery.

"She's got one heavy foot," Jerome chuckled when they saw that it was Kay. She pulled in and parked next to them.

"Is it him?" she asked as she hopped out of the car.

The others shrugged.

"We're waiting for the crime-scene guys to come dig it up. Where were you? Ruby said you went out after we left," Lee said.

"I went over and talked to Lyle and Kelly Grant," Kay said.

"You did what?" Jerome sounded somewhere between irritated and frustrated.

"I thought they might let something slip about Art and Annabelle. They live right next door."

She went on to tell them what she'd learned from the

Grants.

"Art and Annabelle," Jerome said. "Where does Mrs. Art fit into the picture? A big M for motive would be obvious if Mrs. Art wasn't home when Annabelle visited Art last night."

"I've been trying to figure that out. This is crazy, but maybe Annabelle is related to the Butlers," Kay suggested.

"What, like they're using their niece to get close to Brendan and kill him?" Lee asked incredulously.

"Maybe they planned on her marrying Brendan and then killing him, but he got wind of it and they had to speed up their plans," Lester blurted.

"I hate to admit it, but that makes as much sense as anything I've thought of," Kay muttered.

"So why Lora?" Jerome asked. "This would make more sense if Annabelle was actually *married* to Brendan. They might have wanted to kill Lora to keep her from butting in on their plans since she was close to Brendan."

"We keep throwing in the murder of Sid as an also-ran. Was he really killed because of something he saw at the funeral?" Lee wondered.

"The coroner hasn't even reached a decision on a cause of death. Sutton called him this afternoon and was told that they're waiting on the fire marshal's report, which could take weeks," Jerome said.

"What about Sid's daughter?" Lee asked.

"She called this morning. Like Reverend Beck told you, she's been studying art in Europe and hadn't heard about her father's death. She sounded pretty devastated on the phone."

"Is she coming down here?" Kay asked.

"I already suggested that she talk to you all about the funeral. She said she'd get the next flight out of New York," Jerome said.

"If the insurance is paid out, she'll get a chunk of

change." Kay remembered the call from Chester Madison and felt guilty for being so wrapped up in their own problems that they'd paid very little attention to Sid's death.

"Sounds like she has a Rock-of-Gibraltar-sized alibi," Lee said. "*If* she was in Europe."

"Are you suggesting that Sid's murder, if it was murder, is separate from Brendan's and the attempt on Lora?" Jerome raised his eyebrows.

"I admit it seems hard to see it as a coincidence," Lee said.

"Okay, I'm willing to play it out," Jerome said. "If the insurance money was the motive, and Sid's daughter and an accomplice planned to kill her father, maybe Brendan found out about it? He confronted them, so they killed him before he could mess up their plans."

The others shrugged. Before anyone could suggest an alternative, the crime-scene van pulled into the church lot and Jerome went to direct it where to park.

Ken Buchanan was the county's primary crime-scene technician. For most cases, deputies collected fingerprints and evidence on their own. It wasn't until the crime rose to the level of assault or murder that Ken was called in. In the van with him were two other civilian employees of the sheriff's office who worked with Ken when he needed help. The rest of the time they worked in dispatch.

"Where's the grave?" Ken asked. He was at the back of the van, unpacking shovels and a shifting box.

"About forty feet the other side of that gap in the fence," Jerome told him, pointing toward the fence.

"We're gonna go slow and make sure we don't lose anything as we dig." Ken had taken courses in crime-scene processing at the FBI headquarters in Quantico. In a sheriff's office run by a blowhard whose main goal was first, last and always to be reelected, Ken stood out as a ray of professional sunshine.

Lee, Lester and Kay stood by the van while Jerome and the three men crossed over the fence and disappeared into the woods beyond.

Thirty minutes later, Jerome came back.

"It's Brendan, all right."

"Thank you," Lee said with his eyes raised to the sky. "At least we won't be known as the funeral home that lost a body."

"Any clues with the body?" Kay asked.

"Nothing obvious. There's still hours of work to do before the body can be taken back to the office and get checked out properly. Whoever did this lost a shoe in the process, so we aren't talking about experts here."

"They also missed the wooden token. If that hadn't fallen out of Brendan's suit..." Lee shook his head in wonder at the luck of it all.

"Are we going to bury him?" Lester asked.

"Whenever they release the body," Lee said, looking at Jerome.

"Won't be long, maybe a day or two. Ken isn't going to want a body lying around the evidence room for long."

"Seems odd that you aren't sending it to the morgue."

"What's the point? We know how he died. There isn't anything that the doctors at the morgue can tell us that we don't already know. This is all about any incidental evidence left on the body by our casket robbers," Jerome said.

When the body was carried out of the woods, Lee could have wept at the condition of Brendan's corpse. The clothes were filthy and torn, while the makeup and hair would need to be completely redone.

"He looks like an extra from *Night of the Living Dead*," Lester said. Lee wanted to verbally slap him down for making fun of the deceased, but he had to admit that Lester was spot on.

The group around the dinner table that night was quiet as they served up and ate Ruby's spaghetti and meatballs. She heaped the food on everyone's plate regardless of what they asked for. Kay had told Ruby that she wasn't hungry and received a plate that must have weighed five pounds. On top of the spaghetti sat two pieces of Texas garlic toast.

Despite what she'd told Ruby, Kay found herself eating with surprising gusto. *The day has been long and the future is uncertain, so eat up*, she told herself.

Lester took seconds as everyone else was struggling to dig down through their first mound of pasta and meatballs.

"Excellent as always, Ms. Ruby," Lester told her with a smile. "I need to eat and run though. My mother is flying out tomorrow and she wants to go visit Lora one more time."

"Let us know how Lora is doing," Lee told him as Lester set his plate in the sink and headed out the door. He waved his hand in acknowledgement of Lee's request.

Lee turned to Kay. "So with the body back, where does that leave us?"

"With the business or the investigation?" she asked.

"Either. Both."

"You know the answer about the business. This slows the leak, but the ship is still sinking. The investigation… that's a little more complicated. My guess is that it had to have been two people moving that body around. Brendan wasn't a small guy."

"You're right. For one person to be able to do it, he would have had to drag the body most of the time. There would have been more marks on the ground, and I'd think there would have been pieces of clothing on the fence they had to get over," Lee agreed.

"I want to know where Art and Annabelle were the night the body was stolen."

"Jerome is going to talk to Sutton, even though he doesn't think they have enough information to question Art."

"That seems crazy. Art has clearly been hiding his relationship with Annabelle, and if they knew each other before Brendan's death, then Art most likely knew about Brendan's house," Kay said.

"You know that if they hit him with those questions, he'll just clam up, then lawyer up. What evidence is there that he killed Brendan or Sid or attempted to kill Lora?"

"Maybe Lora will remember who attacked her," Kay said optimistically.

"The bump was on the back of her head, so she probably didn't see her attacker. Besides, you know that with a concussion that severe the patient loses hours, maybe days, of memories."

"Whoever attacked her did it for a reason. Lora might be able to answer that question."

"Which is why Jerome has them keeping a close eye on Lora's hospital room."

"There are too many moving pieces," Kay sighed.

"That might work to our advantage. The killer or killers are having to juggle all of those little pieces and maybe, with a little bit of luck, they'll drop one."

"I dated a juggler once," Ruby said. "In Texas. He worked for a small traveling circus. Amazing hands. Anyone want more spaghetti?"

They turned down the offer and cleared their places at the dinner table. Lee and Kay couldn't wait until Lester would be able to hang around again as usual, so that Ruby could shovel a lot of the food his way while he kept her entertained.

The hands on the clock seemed to crawl on Tuesday as Lee waited for word from Ken Buchanan that he could come pick up Brendan's body. Lester spent the morning with his mother, who was scheduled to fly out of Gainesville that afternoon. For her part, Kay spent the morning making charts of the victims and suspects, and timelines of the events.

At eleven, Lester called to warn Lee that his mother wanted to come by the funeral home before she had to leave. Lester begged Lee to continue the ruse that he was the head mortician and Lee promised that everyone would play along.

"Wonderful," Kay said with a frown when she learned that Lester was coming by with his mother. Kay had the pictures of the memorial service spread out before her on the office desk.

"See anything we missed?" Lee walked to the desk and looked over her shoulder.

"I can't put my finger on it, but there's something bugging me about all this. It's like when I can't remember the name of a movie or a person's name. It's right on the tip of my tongue."

They looked at the photos from the memorial service. One photo of people around the table, which had been taken when the thermos was still present, caught Kay's eye.

"There's Art, Benny, Lyle and Kelly, which backs up the Grants' story that they were present and could have seen Art tamper with the thermos," she noted.

They looked more closely at the couples. Art was smiling with one hand on Benny's shoulder.

"Benny is making an odd face," Kay observed.

"Maybe it's Art's hand on his shoulder, or the fact that Kelly is smoking." Kelly held the cigarette out by her side in a standard smoker's pose, while her other hand looked like it was holding a pack of cigarettes.

"Where's Lyle looking?" Kay asked. Lyle had his head turned and seemed to be searching for something or someone.

"From the angle, it looks like he's looking toward the tent," Lee said. "Makes sense as that's where most of the people were still gathered."

"There's something off about this picture." Kay picked up the photo and stared at it before dropping it down on the desk with the others.

Lester and his mother showed up at noon. Kay and Lee heard Ruby invite Mrs. Andrews to stay for lunch. There was a hint of irritation and tension in Ruby's voice that caused Kay and Lee to hurry into the kitchen, where they found the two women staring at each other while Lester hung back, looking concerned.

"What are you serving?" Janet asked with her nose ever so slightly raised.

"Chicken and yellow rice."

Janet looked at the stove before walking over to it and turning on the light. As she reached for the door, everyone in the room held their breath except for Ruby.

"Don't you dare open that oven!" her voice boomed.

Lester's mother stopped with her hand on the oven door's handle. Like a gunfighter, she slowly took her hand off the handle and turned around to face Ruby.

"What did you say to me?" Her voice was hard and brittle.

"This is my kitchen. I won't have anyone looking over my shoulder."

"Your kitchen, indeed! Lester, are you going to let this… woman talk to me that way?"

"You leave Lester out of this." For a minute, Lee and

Kay thought Ruby was going to let it go with that, but instead she inhaled deeply, like a cartoon cannon getting ready to fire. "You have bullied and badgered that poor boy to the point that he's scared to death of you. I don't know how he grew up to be such a nice young man with you as his mother. I've seen him reach out with his generous heart to help all kinds of people. Here at the funeral home, he works hard and tries harder."

"He runs this home. Lester, remind her who's boss."

Lester looked like he'd been hit with fifty thousand volts of electricity and was incapable of movement.

"Lester told you he was the boss because he didn't want to disappoint you," Ruby said. "How sad is it that you're such a terrifying harridan that your own son can't be honest with you? Any mother would be proud to have a nice, kind boy who works hard and doesn't get into trouble."

"Lester is done working here!" his mother shouted. She turned to Lester, who looked on the edge of tears. "Let's go!"

"I like working here." His voice was barely audible.

"Nonsense! Come on, let's go to the airport. I'll see about getting you a ticket. You can come home and we'll discuss your future." She turned toward the door.

"I'll take you to the airport, but I'm not going home. I like it here. I like my job. You're my mother, but you don't run my life." Lester looked surprised that he'd spoken, but the words came out strong and loud.

"We'll talk about it in the car." Janet opened the door and walked out.

"I'll be back," Lester said with determination before he followed her out.

"Wow!" Lee said, looking back and forth from Ruby to Kay.

"It had to be said." Ruby shook her head. "Lester is too

good of a man to let her run him down."

"I wish I'd had the guts to say it." Kay smiled.

Finally, at three o'clock, the call came from Jerome that Brendan's body was ready to be picked up. Kay rode over to the sheriff's office with Lee. They took Bertha and parked in the back.

Lee knocked on the rear door and a second later, Jerome opened it. Lee held it open while Jerome and Ken carried out a large body bag.

"I'm coming with the trolley," Kay said, wheeling it over to them. They eased the bag up and onto the trolley.

"Did you find anything?" Lee asked Ken.

"I did my best to collect any odd fibers, seeds, pebbles and stuff. But to be honest, it's a mess. I'm not sure how much use the stuff I collected is going to be until we find a good suspect. I was able to isolate a few fibers that look like they came from a carpet, but I'll need samples to compare them to."

"He never just finds the killer's business card in the victim's pocket," Jerome joked.

"No such luck," Ken agreed. "What I've got might help to prosecute the bad guy, but it's not likely to help you find him. You'll have to do it the old-fashioned way with the little grey cells." Ken tapped his head.

"How many little grey cells do you think Sutton has at his disposal?" Jerome asked acidly.

"I'm not sure that man ever had *any* little grey cells." Ken smiled and went back inside.

Jerome turned to Kay and Lee. "I had to fill Sutton in on the progress of the investigation."

"How'd that go?" Lee asked.

"Not good. He's got the hots now for Art and Annabelle.

Wants to bring them in and grill them."

"Asking them a few questions wouldn't hurt." Kay hated the fact that she was close to being on Sutton's side of an argument.

"If we had one good piece of evidence. The closet thing we have to that is Kelly Grant telling you that she saw Art near the thermos. That's weak and it's not even an official statement. She might not be willing to sign her name to it."

"Then finding that out would be the first step," Kay said.

"I've been trying to get up with the Grants to set up an interview, but all I get is their answering machine." Jerome looked at his watch. "Maybe I'll drive over there and try to catch them at home."

"We're going out to the cemetery to see what kind of shape Brendan's grave is in. See if we can rebury him in a couple of days," Lee said.

Jerome snapped his fingers. "That wouldn't be the worst place to confront our suspects."

"At the funeral? Not that we're going to redo the funeral. I plan on just having a graveside service. It's sad that Lora can't be there."

"The doctors have her in an induced coma because of the swelling of her brain. Maybe it's a good thing she can't be there. I wouldn't want to put her through too much trauma. Everyone else, though? I'm not worried."

"You think they'll all come? I was going to call and let them know, but it's not like I was going to make a big ceremony out of it. Especially since Lora can't make it," Lee said.

"Bait them. Tell them that there will be some revelations at the service."

"That's a bold statement. Can we back that up?"

"Think about it. We know about Art. We know about Brendan's secret life. And I'm sure we can come up with a few more."

"Okay." Lee sounded unsure.

"Is Sutton going to be there?" Kay asked.

"It's the only way I'm going to be able to keep him from arresting Art and Annabelle before the service."

Kay and Lee pulled out of the sheriff's office parking lot as Jerome was headed back inside to talk to Wade Sutton.

"You mind going by the cemetery with me?" Lee asked.

"You asking me or Brendan?" Kay joked.

They pulled into the cemetery and around to Brendan's grave. After they parked, they walked up to the hole where Lora had been buried. Lee pulled back the green tarp that covered the hole.

"Buck did a good job reconstructing the grave." The backhoe had dug a much larger hole in the effort to get the casket back out of the ground.

Kay was looking around and started to walk toward the remains of the maintenance shed.

"Not much left," she observed.

"They paid Buck to haul off all the debris." Lee looked around at the cemetery. "Sid did do a great job maintaining the place." He walked over to an area that held a number of family crypts. There was a stout chain and padlock in place on the nearest crypt. "No unauthorized persons are getting into these."

"I remember coming out here during my senior year with Rick Bruhn." Kay walked down the row of crypts. "This is awful, but we got into one of the crypts and made out. He'd brought a lantern and a blanket."

"That's a little creepy." Lee laughed. "I don't know what Dad would have thought of that."

"It wasn't as bad as you would think," she said, stopping in front of a crypt with a gothic theme that included gargoyles at the corners of the roof. The family name above the door was Bauer. "This is the one. I thought I could tell someone we made out in a Bauer. Get it, bower? Bauer? That's nerd humor for you." The door now had the same kind of stout lock as the other crypts.

"Reverend Beck told me that Sid had the crypts cleaned and secured several months ago. Not many caretakers would have bothered," Lee said. "I guess it was a good idea though, seeing as strange high school students were sneaking into them."

"Seems like a lot of trouble to keep out the odd vagrant. What if the family wants to come by and visit?"

"Most of these crypts haven't seen anyone buried here in sixty years, maybe longer. Crypts have gone out of fashion."

"Did you hear that?" Kay asked, looking alert.

"What? Did you hear the ghost of Old Man Bauer?"

"No. It sounded like a child." Kay was spooked.

Then they both heard a faint, plaintive cry.

"Gads, that's creepy. I don't…" Lee stopped and chuckled, pointing behind Kay. "There's your ghost."

Kay turned to see Yang coming around the side of the crypt. Every couple of steps, the cat would stop and rub its face on the granite stones.

"Yang, you need to stay home," Kay scolded the cat, who looked at her with idle curiosity.

Kay picked up the fat cat and held it awkwardly. "You must weigh twenty pounds," she told him.

They wandered through the tombstones back to the hearse, where Kay made herself comfortable with the furry weight on her lap for the ride home.

Lee wheeled Brendan into the embalming room. Lester showed up just when Lee needed help taking off the ruined clothes.

Lee was a bit surprised that Ken hadn't kept the clothes, but since Brendan wasn't the victim in Lora's assault, his clothes weren't really relevant. It wasn't like the bad guys did much more than handle the outside of the clothes as they moved and transported Brendan from place to place.

"My mother was pretty angry." Lester shook his head as he gathered up the clothes and put them into the trash.

"I'm sorry about that," Lee said honestly. "There wasn't much I could do once Ruby got up a head of steam."

"She wasn't wrong. Trouble is, I don't know how long it will take for Mother to get over it."

"Maybe never." Lee sprayed the dirt off of Brendan. "I don't mean to be a downer, but I don't think she needs to get over it. At some point she had to learn that you are your own man. Almost all mothers have a problem with that."

"Maybe. I guess *I* need to get over it."

"That's harder said than done. Give yourself time."

They spent the rest of the day getting Brendan ready for burial. Lee was sliding the trolley into the cooler when Jerome showed up.

"I thought I'd upgrade your locks." Jerome held up a grocery bag full of hardware. "We don't want you losing Brendan again."

"That's great!"

"Here's the receipt. You can put it on my next paycheck," Jerome said, taking a stout interior lock out of the bag. "We'll do this door first since the creeps seemed to favor it."

"You saved me from sitting up the next two nights with Dad's old Winchester guarding Brendan."

"Two days." Jerome shook his head. "About that. I don't think I can hold off Sutton for two days. Can we bury him tomorrow?"

"That's fast. We need to give everybody some notice."

Lee looked doubtful.

"I'll help you call them. We can do it tonight."

"I'll need to call Buck and make sure he'll be available."

They managed to call everyone about the service and replace the locks on all the doors and downstairs windows before midnight.

"Do you have a plan for the service?" Lee asked Jerome.

"Honestly, no. I'm just going to play it by ear. If you have any ideas, feel free to share them."

"I'll sleep on it," Lee told him.

CHAPTER TWENTY-THREE

The doorbell chimed at nine the next morning. When Kay answered the door there was a petit brunette standing on the threshold and wearing a sad smile.

"I'd like to talk to someone about a funeral for my father?" she said questioningly.

"Come on in."

Kay suspected that she was Sid Fuller's daughter, but she waited for the introduction to confirm it..

"I'm Valerie Hartford. My father was killed in an explosion. I think they've got the body at the… hospital in Gainesville."

"Of course, Sid Fuller. Come with me to the office." Kay directed her to a chair in front of the desk, then sat down across from her. "I'm so sorry for your loss."

"It's crazy. My mother hated him after their divorce. From the time I was like twelve, I maybe talked to him two or three times on the phone. Then two years ago, he called me up one night and said he wanted to make it up to me."

"Make it up?"

"He was talking about his drinking and the divorce and all of that. It was nice getting to know him a little. But now he's dead." Valerie seemed confused by the swift turn of events.

"How did he try to make it up to you?"

"He was really generous. Honestly, there's no way I could have gone to Italy to study if it hadn't been for his help." She wiped at her eyes.

"He sent you money?"

"Too much, really. I tried to send some back, but he insisted. At the time I felt guilty. Now… I'm glad I took the money. I think it made him happy to give it to me."

"I don't know how to talk about this delicately, so I'm just going to tell you. There's a good possibility that your father was murdered."

"The deputy I talked to said the same thing. It's weird, right?"

"Did you tell the deputy about your father sending you money?"

"It didn't come up. The call was short. He said he'd talk to me when I got into town."

"Your father worked as a maintenance man at the cemetery where the explosion took place. How much money did he send you?"

"Altogether, close to thirty thousand dollars."

Kay's mind tried to process that. "Did he say where the money came from?"

"Just that he had it and wanted me to have the things he should have provided me with all along. I thought he had a good job. My mom called him a lot of names, but she always said he was smart. She said what pissed her off the most was how smart he was, and he just drank all his opportunities away. I knew he'd gotten sober. I just assumed that he'd gotten his professional career going again."

"He never mentioned the cemetery or anything about his job?"

"No. Mostly we talked about me. I'd ask him questions, but he'd just say it wasn't important or that he wanted to know more about *my* life."

"Did you know that he kept an insurance policy that names you as the beneficiary?"

"No." Valerie looked shocked at the idea.

"Your last name is Hartford. Are you married?"

"That's my stepfather's name."

"Did your father ever mention having any enemies?"

"Like I said, we mostly just talked about my life. He never mentioned any enemies *or* friends."

"How often did you talk to him?"

"About once a week before I went to Italy. I promised to call every month while I was studying over there. I was traveling and it wasn't always easy to get a connection."

"When was the last time you talked to him?"

"Two weeks ago. I called from Florence. He asked a million questions about Italy and what I was doing. Now I feel awful that we didn't talk more about him."

Figuring that Valerie had told her all she could, they moved on to details for the funeral. Valerie picked out the coffin, service and extras. Finally, she asked Kay if she knew any of her father's friends.

"My brother knows the members of the board that employed him, and Deputy Carter has been looking into his background and talking to his neighbors. He can help you invite people to give eulogies at the service."

It must be very odd to plan a funeral for someone you hardly knew, Kay thought as she walked Valerie out to her car.

As she opened the car door, Valerie dug into her purse and pulled out a pack of Marlboro cigarettes.

"I know I shouldn't smoke. I picked the habit up from my stepfather who smokes like two packs a day. A month in Italy where everyone over the age of ten smokes didn't help."

Kay watched her light up before getting into her rental car and driving off. *The cigarette. There's something about the cigarette*, Kay thought as she walked back toward the house.

"All that money. Where did Sid and Brendan get all that money?" Lee said after Kay came into the embalming room to repeat what Valerie had told her.

"I think this proves that there was a link between them other than the fact that they both died in the same cemetery."

"The money and the cemetery," Lee said thoughtfully.

"Maybe there's buried treasure in the cemetery," Lester said as he helped Lee put the finishing touches on Brendan. This time they had used a casket that had been on display for six months. It was close to the one that had been damaged in the first burial attempt. Kay and Lee had agreed to give the insurance money for the original casket to Lora when it came through.

"I don't think they found anything in the cemetery." Lee stepped over to the cabinet and got one of his wooden tokens to put in Brendan's suit. "I think they hid something in the cemetery." As he said the words, he could almost feel the lightbulb come on over his head.

"The crypts!" Kay said excitedly.

"Exactly."

Kay looked at her watch. "We have time to run over there before the service."

"We can go ahead and set up the tent and flowers. I'm going to call Reverend Beck and see if he's got a set of keys that would unlock the crypts."

"Do I get to go?" Lester asked plaintively.

"No, but I've got an important task for you," Lee told him. Lester looked at him like a kid being told that vegetables tasted great. "I want you to guard the casket and Brendan's body."

Lester thought about it for a minute before nodding. "I got it."

Lee picked up the phone and called Reverend Beck.

"No, Sid never gave me any keys. I never even thought about it."

"Do you have a problem with Jerome cutting off one of the locks to check out the crypts?"

"Of course not."

Lee's next call was to Jerome.

"I was almost out the door when you called," he said.

Lee explained what he and Kay wanted to do.

"I'll grab the bolt-cutters from my patrol car," Jerome promised.

Half an hour later, the three of them were standing in the cemetery. Lee had parked Bertha as close to Brendan's grave as he could get.

"We'll set up the tent and everything after we've looked in the crypts," Lee said.

"Which one should we open?" Kay asked.

"We need to open a couple," Jerome said.

"Reverend Beck said he didn't care as long as we replace the locks." Lee looked around at the two dozen crypts. "We can skip the one that had to be rebuilt," he said as he walked past the Dane family crypt. "And those three don't have the same locks," he said, pointing toward a few of the newer mausoleums. "It looks like the ones still used by the families don't have the same locks that Sid put on the other older crypts."

"So we eliminate the active crypts," Jerome said, pointing to the others with the bolt-cutters.

"I say we start with the biggest one." Kay started walking toward a large crypt. The marble was tinted green from mold. Above the double wrought-iron gates was engraved the name WEBBER.

"I remember a Pat Webber. He owned the little store out on Five Mile Road. Nice enough old guy," Lee said as he and Jerome followed Kay over to the building that was big enough to park a large pickup inside. The iron gates were chained shut with one of Sid's heavy-duty locks.

"Sid didn't go cheap on the lock, but it isn't going to be a match for my universal key." Jerome put the jaws of the bolt-cutters on the shank of the lock and, with a grunt, snapped it open.

As the lock fell off, Kay pulled on the gates, which opened smoothly.

"That's surprising." Lee looked at the hinges. "They've been oiled."

"My, my. Sid sure was a conscientious caretaker," Jerome said with a smirk. "Let's see what's inside." He pushed open the doors to the stone edifice.

The interior of the crypt was spotless. There were shelves for twelve coffins, but only seven were full. The old wooden coffins were eaten with dry rot. Two of the seven were obviously meant for children. One of the larger coffins had caved in completely and they could see the bones of an arm.

"Charming," Kay said.

"Look at the floor," Jerome said. "There isn't any dirt." He knelt down and ran his hand along the concrete. "Or even dust. This place has been cleaned out recently."

After assuring themselves that there weren't any clues as to what had been in the crypt, they left and closed the gates behind them.

"Let's check out that one." Kay pointed to the Bauer crypt.

"Home of her high-school hijinks." Lee nudged Jerome.

"I admit I've been in the crypt in the past," Kay said with a mischievous smile.

The Bauer crypt was half the size of the Webber mausoleum. Jerome cut the shank on the padlock, and they swung the gate open and went through the inner door. Light came in through stained-glass windows at the front and back of the crypt. Inside were six shelves for coffins, with only two occupied.

"These are old lead coffins," Lee said, admiring the workmanship. The brass plaques identified the occupants as Andrew Bauer and his wife, Helga.

The span of open floorspace was as clean as the Webber crypt.

"It sure wasn't this clean when I was in high school." Kay shook her head.

"Whoever was working with Sid had plenty of time to clear them out," Jerome said.

"Think there's any point in looking through the rest of them?" Lee asked.

"Why would they leave anything in the others when they went to so much trouble to clean these out?" Jerome said.

As they were leaving, Kay bent down and picked up a small piece of cellophane. "Look." She held it out to the others.

"Looks like a wrapper off a cigarette pack," Lee said.

"People are pigs," Jerome muttered.

"I thought you cops were the—" Lee started until Jerome acted like he was going to punch him.

"Don't go there," Jerome laughed.

Kay put the trash in her pocket.

"Let's set up the tent, chairs and flowers and get back to the funeral home," Lee said.

"I want to look at something," Kay mumbled to herself as they entered the house forty-five minutes later.

"We need to leave in an hour," Lee told her. She walked toward the office, lost in thought.

Lee and Lester loaded the casket bearing Brendan's body into the new hearse.

"With luck, you'll make it to your final resting place this time," Lee said as he closed the rear door of the hearse.

He turned to see Kay crossing the street and coming toward them. She was carrying the envelope with the pictures from the memorial service.

"Where's she been?" Lee wondered out loud.

"I'll be ready in fifteen minutes." Kay sounded excited as she waved the envelope at them and headed for the back door.

When they pulled into the cemetery again, there were already a couple of cars parked by the curb near the gravesite.

Lee saw Jerome and Wade Sutton sitting in Jerome's patrol car. Jerome was talking, but Lee couldn't hear what he was saying. Sutton looked angry, but then he always looked angry.

Art and Betty Butler were already sitting under the tent. On the other side of the aisle were Frank Hayes and his daughter Jenny, Chaz and Vickie Dixon and Benny Hampton.

"We'll wait until a couple more able-bodied men get here to act as pall bearers," Lee told Lester.

Kay was standing at the end of the tent, looking excited or anxious, Lee couldn't decide which. He walked over to her. "What's up?"

"I think I've got an idea about what's going on."

"Share," he urged.

"Not yet. I want to see how our special guest appearance goes," she said, looking toward the entrance to the cemetery.

The special guest star was to be Annabelle Destiny. Jerome had tracked her down and, without telling her that they knew she'd met with Art, gave her a time to show up at the cemetery. After a discussion, Kay, Lee and Jerome had decided that, for maximum impact, she should arrive about half an hour into the service.

Two more cars drove through the entrance. The first car belonged to Lyle and Kelly Grant and behind them was Sid Fuller's daughter, Valerie. Kay had invited her since they believed that her father had been murdered by the same people who had killed Brendan and attacked Lora. Reverend Michaels arrived a few minutes later.

Lee asked Lyle Grant, Jerome, Wade Sutton and Art Butler to help him and Lester carry the casket to the gravesite. Reverend Michaels followed them into the tent and watched as they placed the casket on the lowering device. Lee always wondered why the person who came up with the device hadn't named it something a little less on-the-nose.

"I'd like to thank everyone for coming here to inter Brendan Rhodes," Lee began the service. "We all know about the circumstances that have brought us back here. I'd like to point out that Detective Sutton and Deputy Carter have joined us to talk to everyone after we've paid our respects to Mr. Rhodes. Now I'm going to turn it over to Reverend Michaels, who will lead us in a prayer for Brendan's soul and for Lora, who is still in a coma."

Lee stepped into the background so that he could watch the people sitting around the grave. Everyone bowed their heads and appeared to pray. *Which of them is faking it?* Lee wondered.

At one point, as the reverend talked about the solemn

necessity of saying goodbye to those we love, Jerome made his way over to Lee. In a whisper, Jerome warned him that Sutton was on the warpath.

"He's convinced that Art and Annabelle are in this together. The only thing he's not positive about is whether Art's wife is involved," Jerome whispered while keeping an eye on Sutton.

"I'm less sure by the minute," Lee said.

"Brendan had a safe deposit box in Gainesville. One large enough for a small fortune. The tellers say he visited it a couple of times a month. We have it staked out."

"And Sid was sending money to his daughter. Drugs?"

"No hint of that, but we'll get dogs out here to sniff around the crypts if we're still in the dark after this little get-together."

"Kay's got something up her sleeve," Lee whispered to Jerome. "Before we left the funeral home, she disappeared for the better part of an hour with the pictures from the memorial service. Now she's being all secret squirrel about it."

CHAPTER TWENTY-FOUR

As Reverend Michaels was finishing up his service and about to conduct the last prayer, a red BMW turned into the cemetery and came roaring down the road to where the other cars were parked. The reverend stumbled as everyone turned to look at the newcomer, but he managed to get their attention back long enough for a short prayer.

Finished, he stepped away from the lectern and Lee came forward, motioning for everyone to stay in their seats. They did as instructed, but everyone was staring at Annabelle as she got out of the car and walked toward the gathering.

Kay stood up and moved to the casket as Annabelle approached the tent.

"I believe that some of you already know Ms. Annabelle Destiny." As Kay talked, her eyes were pinned on Art and Betty, who were both looking very uncomfortable.

When Kay looked over at Lyle and Kelly Grant, she saw them scrutinizing Annabelle. Lyle looked like he wanted to jump up and confront her, unlike the Butlers, who looked like they wanted to crawl under their seats.

"Hi everyone," Annabelle said in a soft, somewhat embarrassed voice.

"Annabelle, why don't you tell everyone why you're here?" Kay said.

"Brendan and I were in love."

Wade Sutton stood up and Jerome hurried over to his side. When Jerome put a hand on Sutton's arm to stop him from speaking, the detective gave him a cold look and shook him off.

"We need to get down to business here," Sutton's voice boomed, causing everyone to focus on him. He pointed his finger at Art. "You know this woman?"

Art tried to avoid everyone's eyes.

"Do you?" Sutton repeated.

Art kept his mouth shut and looked down at the ground.

"What about you?" He pointed at Annabelle. "Do you know that guy?" The pointing finger went from Annabelle to Art.

"I know her," Art said, and Sutton smiled.

"What is your relationship to her?"

"She's my niece," Art said, looking Sutton straight in the eyes.

Lee could barely contain his shock. He'd been joking when he'd made that suggestion about their relationship.

With visible effort, Sutton rethought his accusations and said, "So you admit that you were in cahoots with her."

Art's left eye was twitching. "I don't know what you mean by cahoots. We were trying to help Brendan." Art stopped and looked around at everyone sitting there. "I found out he was spending a bunch of money. Brendan didn't have much beyond his pension, so I got to wondering where the money was coming from. When I asked him about it, he just laughed me off. I tried spying on him, but that didn't get me anywhere. Then I got a crazy idea." His wife made a sound somewhere between a snort and a chuckle. He looked at Betty but went on. "Annabelle wanted to be an actress from a young age. I remember my brother taking us to see some of her plays when she was in high school. Her mother's been pushing me for years to help her out because she'd… gotten into some… trouble. I could kill two birds with one stone, so to speak. Find out what Brendan was up to and give Annabelle some better life choices, as her mother likes to say."

"She's a prostitute!" Sutton said.

At that, Art leaped to his feet. Both Frank and Benny stood up and grabbed for Art, whose fists were balled up and ready for action. Both men had to hang on for all they were worth. Lee hurried over and got between Art and the detective, noticing that Jerome hadn't even tried to intervene.

"Brendan and I fell in love," Annabelle blurted, which caused everyone to turn and look at her.

"Where did the money come from?" Kay stepped in and asked her.

"I never found out."

"That's hard to believe," Sutton growled. "And I don't believe this whole uncle-niece thing." He waved his fingers at Art and Annabelle.

"Are you a moron? Why would I lie about that?" Art asked.

"I believe them!" Kay said loud enough to assume centerstage.

"Of course you would," Sutton said dismissively.

"I think I know where the money was coming from," Kay told them. She reached into her pocket and pulled out the cellophane wrapper she'd picked up in the crypt. "Would you like to tell us where you got cigarettes without tax stamps?" Kay asked, looking straight at Kelly Grant.

Kelly's jaw worked up and down, but no sound came out. Slowly, she turned her head to look at her husband, who was frowning at Kay.

"Why are you asking my wife?"

"Because I saw her with an illegal pack of cigarettes the day we talked to you after Brendan's death. She tried to hide it and pretended that she was hiding it from you. But there's a picture of her smoking beside you at the memorial service. And if you magnify the picture as I did, you can see that Kelly is holding the same or another pack of untaxed cigarettes." Kay pulled the photograph out of her pocket and tapped it. "You can see the pack doesn't have a stamp across the top."

Now everyone was looking at Kelly.

"I don't know where I got that pack. Someone must have given it to me."

"The next time I came and talked to you and your husband, you tried to throw Art under the bus by telling me you saw him tamper with the thermos."

"Why you…" Art turned and growled at Kelly and Lyle. "Smuggling sounds like you. I suspected you were involved in the black market in Korea and Japan."

"What was your job before you retired?" Kay asked.

Lyle looked like he wanted to run.

"I'll tell you." Chaz stood up. "He ran a dispatching center for a big trucking company out of North Carolina."

"North Carolina would be a great place to grab cigarettes. I guess you still know a lot of truckers."

"Like poor Brendan," Frank said. "He always did look up to you."

"He was an idiot. Flashing money around." Lyle's hands clenched into fists and he stared straight at Annabelle. "Then he met you. Got all soft. Talking about how he didn't care about the money anymore."

"But that wasn't the last straw, was it?" Kay pressed Lyle.

"Lieutenant Reynolds dying got him all sentimental, worried about his soul and talking about how he needed to do the right thing," Lyle spat. "Weak is all he was. He said he was going to confess. Told me he could do it where I wouldn't be implicated. Telling me was bad enough. I might have been able to persuade him. Trouble was, we have partners. Big partners. He shot off his mouth to them, and they told me I had to take care of him."

"Why nicotine poisoning?" Kay asked.

"They wanted to send a message. Do it in a so way that all of the guys would know that Brendan got it because he was going to betray the organization."

"Sid didn't like you killing Brendan," Lee said, catching up to the narrative.

"I gave him good money for storing the stuff here in the cemetery. He was a putz. He got what he deserved," Lyle snarled.

"I wish you'd died in Korea," Art raged at Lyle.

Everyone could hear the sound of Sid's daughter sobbing as the men argued.

"Cigarettes weren't your only game," Jerome said. He reached into his jacket pocket and pulled out the scrap of paper Lee had found when Brendan's body was discovered, and the note that had been slipped through the door at the funeral home. "The handwriting on these two notes is the same. You all dealt in stolen goods."

"The organization has drivers all over. If you want something, we can arrange for it to fall off of a truck. After Brendan was dealt with, Sid started worrying about what the two junior detectives here might do. So I decided to test the waters. See if I could get you—" He looked at Lee. "—on board by selling you deeply discounted merchandise. I was going to help you out with your competition problem."

"So this guy—" Sutton stuck his finger out at Art again. "—isn't guilty?"

"I told you to stop sticking your finger in my face." Art grabbed Sutton's arm and twisted it around, causing Sutton to lose his balance. Sutton reached out with his free hand and grabbed wildly to keep from falling. His hand latched onto a fistful of Jerome's coat. All three men fell on top of the casket, which creaked ominously.

Everyone was focused on Art and the struggling lawmen as they awkwardly managed to untangle themselves. When everyone looked back at Lyle, he and Kelly were racing across the lawn toward their car.

"Son of a bitch!" Jerome scrambled after them, followed by Lee and Kay. Bringing up the rear was Wade Sutton, clumping along like an overweight bear.

When the Grants got to their car, Lyle reached for the door handle and pulled. Nothing happened. He tried again, then screamed with rage and began trying to get his key into the door's lock. Kelly was on the passenger side, yelling in frustration while she looked around wildly.

Jerome slammed into Lyle and took him to the ground. Kelly turned and started to run, then realized there weren't any options left and just stopped and dropped to the ground. Sutton went around the car and slapped handcuffs on her.

"We need some backup, 'cause I'm taking Butler in too for assaulting an officer!" Sutton yelled to Jerome, who was struggling to get Lyle under control.

"The sheriff's going to be happy to have these crimes solved. Probably better not to muddy the waters with some old coot who has friends in the neighborhood," Jerome argued. He didn't want Art to get into trouble for doing something that he wished he had done. The only thing that would have made it better was if Art had managed to get in a punch or two.

"We'll see," Sutton said, hoisting Kelly up off the ground.

He did call for backup, but only so they could take the Grants to the jail in separate cars. Putting husband and wife bad guys in the back of a car together was never a good idea. Either they would help each other escape or, more likely, try to kill each other.

"I can't believe it. That was officially the largest funeral I've ever conducted," Lee said three days later, still walking on air.

"Thank Jerome," Kay reminded him. "He realized what was probably going on when he searched the Grants' house and saw Brad Garland's name and number on a message pad."

"And then it just happened to get leaked to the *Gainesville Sun* on the same day that they served the search warrants."

"And the rest is history. Jack Warner's family wasn't going to have their patriarch's final public appearance marred by scandal. You did a great job stepping in and taking over," Kay complimented him.

"The arrangements had already been made," Lee admitted. "And I was able to use the lower-tier Garland employees. Old Man Garland was also very gracious and professional, all things considered."

"I think he was embarrassed by his son's actions. Brad bought stolen caskets and embalming supplies so he could undercut us and drive us out of business."

"With Garland's getting a black eye out of all this, we should pick up enough business to get back on our feet."

"Don't count your chickens, but yes, the future looks brighter," Kay agreed.

Lee pulled the hearse into the hospital lot and parked in

one of the spaces by the morgue entrance reserved for pickups.

"You can't park here," Kay admonished.

"Of course I can. Where else am I going to park Bertha? She's too long for regular parking spaces," Lee argued.

"You have a minor point."

They rode up to the fourth floor and, after a quick stop at the nurses' station, found Lora Rhodes's room. Art and Betty Butler were just leaving.

"Thank you," Art said, giving both Lee and Kay hearty handshakes that left them flexing their hands afterwards.

"How are you?" Lee asked Lora, who was sitting up in bed and looking like she'd been dragged behind a car for a block. But the smile she wore suggested that she was improving.

"Alive, thanks to you," she said.

"Thanks to two fat tabbies." Lee explained about his sudden revelation that had led to their rushing to the cemetery to save her.

"I guess I owe them a can of tuna."

"Has Jerome been by to question you?" Lee asked.

"Him and that neanderthal. I wasn't able to tell them very much. I don't remember anything about the attack."

"Do you know why they attacked you?" Kay asked.

"Yes. I found out from Brendan's lawyer about his other house. I don't think he knew that Brendan hadn't told me. He just casually mentioned it. Stupid me, I thought I'd play detective, so I went to the house and broke in. I found Brendan's papers in a locked drawer of his desk. I remember looking at them and... that's all. Deputy Carter told me that Lyle admitted he'd come to the house and was going to get the papers, but discovered me there and knew he had to get rid of me."

"Apparently it was Kelly's idea to make you disappear by

putting you in Brendan's coffin," Lee said.

"I'm not surprised. She's hated me ever since I dropped a cake she baked fifteen years ago."

"Brad Garland confessed that he helped them with the plan. His way of getting back at us. He figured it was a win-win situation. If Lora was buried and Brendan's body remained undiscovered, that was fine. If Lora was discovered or Brendan's body was found, then there would be a big scandal with us at the center and his plans for ruining us would be advanced," Kay explained.

"It's so sad. Brendan grew up poor and there was always a little part of him that craved… security, or maybe a special life, something more than he could easily reach. But I don't understand what the Grants were doing with the money."

"When the deputies searched the house, they found a small fortune in rare coins and stamps in three humidity-controlled safes in the garage," Kay told her.

"I heard you were sneaking around the hospital," came a rich, deep male baritone from the hallway.

They all turned to see Dr. Alan Eckhart standing in the doorway. He came in and introduced himself to Lora.

"I didn't mean to interrupt. I just wanted to apologize to Kay for losing her number." He was smiling and watching for Kay's reaction, which was to blush.

"Give it to him again or I'll give him mine," Lora said with a laugh.

"I suggest we skip the number exchange this time and just make a date for dinner. Say Saturday? I'll pick you up at seven?"

"I…" Kay noticed Lora and Lee looking at her expectantly. "What the hell. Sure."

Kay and Lee return in:

Search for Death
A Mortician Murder Mystery–Book 4

ACKNOWLEDGMENTS

The idea for this series owes a lot to my wife's own upbringing. When I first met my future father-in-law, he was the only funeral director in a small, North Florida town in the 1980s. My wife has vivid memories of playing hide-and-seek in the casket room, being driven to school in a hearse and being fascinated by the mysteries of the embalming room. I hope these memories add a little realism to this series about a challenging and often misunderstood profession.

Cover Design by Melody Barber
www.aurorapublicity.com

ABOUT THE AUTHOR

A. E. Howe lives and writes on a farm in the wilds of North Florida with his wife, horses and more cats than he can count. He received a degree in English Education from the University of Georgia and is a produced screenwriter and playwright. His first published book was *Broken State*. The Larry Macklin Mysteries is his first series and he released a second series, the Baron Blasko Mysteries, in summer 2018. The first book in the Macklin series, *November's Past*, was awarded two silver medals in the 2017 President's Book Awards, presented by the Florida Authors & Publishers Association; the ninth book, *July's Trials*, was awarded two silver medals in 2018. Howe is a member of the Mystery Writers of America, and was co-host of the "Guns of Hollywood" podcast for four years on the Firearms Radio Network. When not writing, Howe enjoys riding, competitive shooting and working on the farm.

www.ingramcontent.com/pod-product-compliance
Lightning Source LLC
Chambersburg PA
CBHW061530210726
48287CB00006B/1908